Nowhere to Run

The Prophets of Yahweh Series

Book 1

To Monica

From Bonny

2019

Jensina Wilson

My Granddaughter

ISBN: 1976395135
ISBN-13: 978-1976395130

Printed by CreateSpace

Written for
Mr. S. Collins

ACKNOWLEDGMENTS

Thank you to my editor, for all of his advice, insight, and superior work.

Special thanks to my family, for their support, encouragement, and inadvertent inspiration; and thank you to those special people that are such slow readers they may never reach the end of this book.

Deserving of mention is Ms. Anna, for her bolstering enthusiasm.

And of course, thank you to my readers.

BIBLICAL REFERENCES

Jonah ben Amittai:
Jonah 1-4
2 Kings 14:25
Matthew 12:39-41...

Amittai:
2 Kings 14:25
Jonah 1:1

Amos:
Amos 1-9

Amaziah the priest of Bethel:
Amos 7:10, 12, 14

Emperor Ashur-Dan III:
c. 770 B.C.

King Jeroboam son of Jehoash:
c. 780 B.C.
2 Kings 14:23,27
Hosea 1:1
Amos 1:1

* * *

Gath Hepher, Israel:
2 Kings 14:25
Joshua 19:13

Joppa, Israel:
Jonah 1:3
Joshua 19:16
2 Chronicles 2:16...

Samaria, Israel:
1 Kings 13, 16, 18, 20-22
2 Kings 1-3, 5-7, 10, 13-15, 17-18, 21, 23
2 Chronicles 18, 22, 25, 28...

Hebron, Judah:
Genesis 13, 23, 35, 37
Exodus 6:18
Numbers 3:19,27...

Jerusalem, Judah:
Joshua 10, 12, 15, 18
Judges 1, 19
1 Samuel 17:54...

Tekoa, Judah:
2 Samuel 14:1-2, 4, 9
1 Chronicles 2, 4
2 Chronicles 11, 20...

Dumah, Assyria:
Located in southern Assyria

Nineveh, Assyria:
Jonah 1, 3, 4
2 Kings 19:36

* * *

Abba:
Hebrew for Father
Mark 14:36
Romans 8:15
Galatians 4:6

PROLOGUE

The sea raged with startling ferocity, making a ruin of the *Midnight Runner's* sails before any of the sailors could think to furl them. Captain Chenaniah gripped the tiller with quivering hands, pushing with all his strength to move his craft into a position where the waves would break on its bow. His crew dashed about with vigor born of desperation, throwing as much cargo overboard as they could, working to lighten the craft. The *Midnight Runner's* stern lifted clear of the waves as something rammed into her.

Chenaniah released the tiller in sudden panic. Had they hit a rock? Staring hard at the water, he tried to see what they had struck. He spotted a dark shape beneath the surface of the wild waters. The shape moved around the ship before diminishing and eventually disappearing. The sight left the captain shaken. He had heard of monsters of the deep, great leviathans that prowled the waters. Few ships ever returned from encounters with such creatures, and those that did were forever scarred by the experience. A heartbeat passed as Chenaniah stood gazing into the depths, his mind drifting for a moment to calmer days of blue skies smiling down on his milky white sails.

A wave rose high to port, and Chenaniah rushed to the tiller, trying to steer the ship to face the incoming water. The torrent smashed into the ship with bruising force and the men grabbed hold of anything that would keep them from being swept away. Chenaniah lost his grip on the tiller as he was knocked right off his feet. For a terrible moment, he felt nothing but the water, hard and violent and hurling him about on his submerged deck. Visions of soft grass and gently sweeping hills filled his mind. He longed for land, for familiar trees and solid houses, landlocked cities, and endless valleys; but no. The sea was his life, and this was the end of it. Suddenly he could breathe again as frigid and harsh air stung his lungs. He opened his eyes and gazed about.

His men lay groaning on the deck, some bleeding and others unconscious from being thrown about and slammed against the ship's decking. Chenaniah felt the deck tilt beneath him. Forcing his sore body to move, he stood, his eyes widening in horror. A third of the *Midnight Runner* was clear of the water, and a monstrous wave pushed the craft downward. The crew scrambled to secure themselves as boxes, ropes, and other items slid across the deck and slammed into the starboard side.

On a sudden inspiration, the captain opened his mouth and shouted with all his strength, "Great goddess Leucothea! Have mercy on us!" The rising waters drowned out his plea. His men, upon hearing their captain, began calling out to their gods as well. None of them, in all their lives, had ever encountered such a storm. The *Midnight Runner* listed at a sixty-degree angle, and Chenaniah clung desperately to what remained of the rigging as the wave rose steadily higher. Time seemed to stand still as the crew wailed pitifully, all their earlier bravado gone. Chenaniah felt panic well up within his chest. It took him a moment to realize he was holding his breath, and likely, so was everyone else on board.

Forcing himself to take a breath, he called a final encouragement out to the crew that had stood by him for so many years. "Take a deep breath and hold on tight!" Then he drew a second breath as the ship hovered straight up and down for a moment before crashing down into the turbulent sea.

Chapter One
Thirty years earlier — c. 788 B.C.
Gath Hepher, Israel

Jonah sat bolt upright in bed. Sweat poured down his back and soaked his rough tunic. As he drew loud, gasping breaths to calm himself, his thin shoulders trembled with fear. His sister, Zillah, crept over to him from her mat on the other side of the room. Gathering him into her arms, she stroked his back gently. Her dark tresses fell over him like a protective cloak.

"There now, Jonah, it's all right," she soothed. In the silence, he remembered the dream. It was unlike him to have nightmares, but this one he understood. Ever since Mama had died, memories of her created feelings of hopelessness and fear. Jonah began to sob.

"Shh." Zillah nestled him close.

"Mama...I want Mama."

Zillah's hand stilled on his back, and she stiffened. With halted movements, she gently laid him down on his thin mat and pulled a tattered blanket over him. "Mama isn't here," she told him softly, "But I am. I will sing for you until you fall asleep." She sat down and began in a quiet soothing voice to sing. *"I will sing of the Lord's great love forever; with my mouth I will make your faithfulness known through all generations. I will declare that your love stands firm forever, that you have established your faithfulness in heaven itself..."*

1

Jonah curled into a frail ball to ward off the night chill. He closed his eyes, letting the words of his mother's favorite Psalm wash over him like a gentle wave. As Zillah's voice grew softer and softer with weariness, he felt himself relax and was soon fast asleep.

The breakfast table was uncommonly quiet the following morning. Jonah's father, Amittai, sat at his accustomed seat looking uncomfortable as Zillah divvied out their meager meal. Caleb, Amittai's eldest, gazed at the small portion despondently.

Seeking to lift the mood, Amittai broke the silence. "My daughter, I am very grateful that you're willing to feed us all. If I or Caleb were forced to make anything resembling a meal, I fear we would all starve."

Caleb laughed appreciatively, but Zillah only managed a thin smile.

"Abba is right you know," Caleb told her. "Your cooking is nearly as good as Mama's was." He grinned good-naturedly, but when he saw the grim expressions on the others' faces, his smile vanished.

Jonah was sorry that the mood had to be so dismal. His brother was great fun and was always the most optimistic and cheerful of them all. If only Mama could come home one bright morning and make the whole family happy again. It was what he wished for with all his twelve-year old strength, but it was not to be. No one could bring his mother back to the land of the living. She was gone, forever.

"All done," Jonah mumbled. He rose from the table to escape the oppressive atmosphere, but his sister stopped him.

"Jonah, you've hardly eaten anything. It's hard enough to put meat on your bones when you eat full portions." Despite her accusing tone, her eyes shone with understanding. In a lighter tone, she added, "Mama would want you to eat it all, Jonah."

"And if you don't, then I will," Caleb gently teased.

Zillah turned to fully face him, hands on hips. "I know. You eat enough for all of us, Caleb."

Jonah sat back down and smiled. His brother was lean and muscular and, unlike Jonah, had little difficulty eating everything, seemingly to grow taller by the hour. At the age of seventeen, Caleb stood a full head taller than Abba with a few years more to grow. Looking at him now, however, Jonah saw his shoulders slumped in weariness, and the lines of worry and the shadows of lost sleep on his face had aged his face beyond his years.

Life in Gath Hepher was difficult to say the least. The land was incompliant, and the sky remained dry and cloudless. The wells yielded little in the way of water, and even that tasted brackish. The small, scattered flocks of sheep staggered about in exhaustion and malnourishment as they plodded about on the rocky hillsides.

Abba often said it was all because of King Jeroboam's disobedience toward Yahweh. Abba often spoke of Yahweh. Caleb also seemed to have inherited this passion and had helped Jonah grow in his own young faith. Zillah, on the other hand, refused to have anything to do with God or religion. She insisted that she had no time for such things, but Abba pushed back and usually managed to persuade Zillah to join in evening prayers, or to be faithful to the rituals written in the Torah. When Jonah thought of Yahweh, it always brought him pain. Mama had loved Yahweh; she had loved His laws, explaining that by keeping them she would be seen as obedient and pure in His eyes. Again, he longed for Mama to return, he longed to see her beautiful dark eyes and hear her joyful voice, a voice that his sister once carried, before Mama had left them. Turning his eyes upward, Jonah gazed at Zillah a while, watching her working with the same diligence as she always had. They were very much alike in appearance, his mother and sister. In fact, Zillah would likely look exactly like Mama when she was older. The thought comforted him, though he found his own dark eyes, a trait of the family, filling with tears.

His thoughts finished, Jonah rose from the table and went out back with his father to gather firewood. Abruptly he turned, "Abba, why did Yahweh take Mama?"

Amittai's hands stilled, his body bent over a small pile of wood. "Why do you ask such questions, son? I do not know the mind of the Lord." Seeing the look of dissatisfaction in Jonah's dark eyes, he continued, "I can, however, do my best to explain something to you."

He set down his work and knelt before his son. His tousled gray-streaked hair shifted as he did so, and the weathered lines of his once handsome face seemed to increase in number. "Whatever Yahweh does has purpose, Jonah. Never doubt that. It may take you and I the rest of our lives to see it, but Yahweh has purpose in..." He paused, unable to speak the name. "He has a purpose in your mother's passing. And besides," he added, standing and placing a gentle hand on Jonah's head,

"She is in a better place now. A place without pain or sorrow—a place of happiness—and she would want us to be happy as well." His tone indicated that the conversation was at an end.

Every day was the same to Jonah. Each morning, he rose and attended to his chores, gathered wood, fed their milk cow and donkeys, and tossed grain to the chickens. Later in the day, he would eat the morning meal before heading out to the field to work beside his father and brother. The field was a full mile walk from their home, an inconvenience they could not afford to complain about. A wealthy farmer owned the land, one who could afford to dig deep wells and irrigate his fields. By the time they returned home at the end of the day, Abba and Caleb were sunburnt to an unpleasant red hue and their tunics were soaked through with sweat. Jonah merely tanned and he seemed to get darker each summer.

The day before the Sabbath each week, they would receive some grain, potatoes, and occasionally leeks or cabbage. The portions were divvied out to the workers according to their social status. Families with blood ties to important nobles or well-known merchants received larger portions than those who were common peasants. Amittai had no connections whatsoever. His family had always been shepherds or farmers, barely able to make ends meet.

Zillah began gathering their stock of water skins and tied them together. "Jonah, when you are finished eating, you and Caleb need to go to the spring down in Nazareth. Bring the donkeys and load them with these water skins."

Jonah happily wolfed down his remaining bread and dried dates, thrilled to be going on an adventure with his brother. The sun beat down as Caleb loaded the skins onto Lentil and Melons' backs. It was no coincidence that the donkeys had been named after food. Abba had been in the market one day, staggering about in search of a compassionate vender who would give him a good deal. He had stumbled upon a sign, which had read, "Two donkeys for the taking. A melon and bag of lentils will be given to whoever takes these two donkeys. I have no more need for them." Abba had been so desperate that he had gladly accepted the donkeys, and now they were part of the family. They were used to haul water from the closest water source in Nazareth. Mama had objected to having two extra mouths to feed when they had first arrived at home, but she, like the rest of the family, had come to see the usefulness of having a pack animal as well as a guard animal around.

They set off as the sun started its farewell course into the evening sky. The scent of evening filled the air, a crispness that made Jonah feel light and carefree. Now was the best time to travel in Gath Hepher. When the sun's heat was dying away, the night's cool would be welcomed. Caleb walked briskly ahead with Lentil in tow while Jonah tromped along behind him, tugging at Melon's lead with all his strength. It was a three-mile walk down to Nazareth, and the pair gladly took a bit of rest by the spring when they arrived. The small oasis was a common watering hole for passing travelers, but today, no one was in sight. Jonah began unloading his skins and ambled over to the spring.

"Jonah, look!" his brother cried suddenly.

Wheeling smartly, Jonah saw Caleb reach up into a tree and pluck a small date hanging from an overloaded branch. With a squeal of delight, Jonah joined him. They ate their fill before breaking off a bough and carrying it over to Melon who stared at the swaying branch with mistrust. Once she realized that the fruit was edible, however, it was all Jonah could do to keep the hungry creature from devouring the entire thing. Filling the water skins, they talked of idle things: the weather, field-work, and the antics of Zillah's latest attempt at scaling fish that Abba had bought in the market.

"Did you see the look on her face when she saw the eyes?" Caleb asked, his eyes twinkling merrily.

"Yes, and when Abba told her that she had to take off *all* the scales?" Jonah fell over and began rolling about laughing uproariously.

Abruptly, Caleb planted a hand over his mouth to stifle his giggles. Leaning in close, he whispered, "Take the water skins and load them quickly. It looks like we're going to have unwelcome company."

Jonah spotted a small band of rough looking men as he hid behind a massive dead jujube tree. He held the mules tightly by the leads and fed them dates one at a time to keep them quiet. Typically, passersby were of no concern in Israel, but the telltale tinkle of chains made anyone from those parts freeze in dread. The men were Arab slave traders, passing through on their way south, to Egypt most likely. The thought made Jonah shudder. He remembered the story in the Torah of Joseph being sold to Midianite slave traders. The Arab slave traders were not afraid to help themselves to any peasants they found whenever they got the chance. Jonah watched as the men set up camp nearby. Meanwhile, Caleb crept over and crouched down beside him. Dusk had settled over the small oasis, and it was getting harder to see.

"When it's dark, we have to leave," Caleb said.

Nodding his understanding, Jonah curled up into a ball to await nightfall. He rested his head on a small rise in the earth and dozed.

A sudden pop and snap resounded in the quiet stillness. The donkeys had given up their futile attempts to spit out the date pits and had switched to simply chomping on all parts of the dates. Jonah bolted upright, momentarily forgetting to keep his head down. Then, remembering, he abruptly ducked his head and whispered, "What—"

Angry shouts cut him off. He was unable to understand, though he could hear the sounds clearly. Caleb seized Jonah by the hand and took off toward home. Jonah knew they would never make it. As short and easy as the walk was, running at breakneck speed would never work. Even worse, there was nowhere to hide except behind trees, and of those, there were few large enough. He risked a nervous glance over his shoulder, and saw the men mounting their camels. Others were on foot and gaining on them quickly.

Forcing himself to look ahead, Jonah released his vice-like grip on Caleb's hand, knowing he could run faster that way. They dashed across rock-strewn, hard-packed sand, broken only by small clumps of grass here and there. The clumps were just tall enough to cause Jonah to falter any time he stumbled into one in the waning light.

A soft crack of thunder sounded from behind them. A moment later, Jonah realized the sound was whips cracking as the pounding of pursuing feet filled his ears. Caleb began running faster now, urging Jonah to do the same. It seemed an age since they had begun their flight, and he was certain they must be nearly home, but when they passed a shrunken acacia, he groaned aloud. The acacia showed that they had only run a third of the way. He stumbled suddenly and fell hard against the rough ground.

Caleb halted, spun around, dashed back, and pulled Jonah to his feet. "You're doing great, Jonah," he panted. "I would carry you on my shoulders, but then if I stumble, we'll both go down." Jonah managed a thin smile as they began running again. His breath was coming hard now, each inhalation an audible gasp.

"We're almost there," Caleb lied. He glanced over at Jonah, then his eyes widened, "Jonah, look out!"

A man on camelback had come up beside Jonah swinging a lasso over his head. Caleb grabbed a rock as he ran by it and hurled it at the man. Caleb was generally bad at throwing or catching anything, something Abba hoped he would grow out of. That day, however, he was fortunate. The man toppled off his camel, and Caleb made a grab for the reigns. He missed them by a hairsbreadth and got a hard kick in the shin for his efforts.

"Keep going!" Caleb shouted at Jonah, who had paused a few yards away. The thunder of the camels was louder now as the slavers closed the gap. "Don't stop! I'm right behind you."

Jonah turned and sprinted away, but he knew that Caleb would not be behind him. Abba had been kicked in the shin once, and had been unable to walk for several days. Jonah cleared these thoughts from his mind and focused on one goal. He had to get home and tell Abba to gather some men to rescue Caleb. After a few minutes, he passed another marker. He was two-thirds of the way back, but another of the slavers followed hard behind on camelback. Jonah swerved away and felt something brush his arm—a lasso.

Pressing on faster, Jonah dodged around rocks and bushes always watching the swinging rope and preparing to dodge away from it. Suddenly a second lasso spun through the air. Two men on camels circled around him, trying to get a good throw. The first man urged his camel into a gallop and passed Jonah on the right. As Jonah turned left, the second man appeared on that side of him as well. They slowed their pace to match his and squeezed in closer, spinning the lassos skillfully. Whoosh. A lasso swung toward his head. Jonah ducked, and the other one hit him in the back. His muscles ached from the constant dodging, and exhaustion caused him to stumble over one of the cursed clumps of grass. Jonah tumbled forward and saw blur of brown in front of him. The rope settled easily around his torso and arms, and with a tug from the rider, it tightened around him.

Sunrise found Zillah standing, hands on hips in front of the house. It wasn't unlike her two brothers to go running off on some adventure, but they had always been back in time for their supper. After at least a half hour of arguing, she had finally managed to persuade Abba to leave for the fields. Better to have him out of her hair. He was worried as a mother hen; it was his way. Abba should know by now that his sons were thrill seekers, always getting into trouble. "They're probably sitting around the spring stuffing themselves with dates. There might have been a line to get water. They likely had good reason to stay overnight," she had reassured him. But now, hours later, she wasn't so sure.

She turned to go inside and start the morning meal when a figure appeared on the horizon. She let out a sigh of relief, thinking it to be one of her brothers, but when the figure came closer, she saw it was an older man about Abba's age. He looked like a merchant, finely dressed with a rolling gait and smooth gestures. She watched him stop every person outside and say something to them before moving on. At this point, Zillah wished she had let her father stay home. As the man raced closer and closer, she heard him shouting something. It sounded like a warning. A few moments later, he was close enough for her to hear his words, and they sent her scrambling inside to shut and bolt the door.

"Arab slave traders! Arab slave traders! Everyone stay inside!" The man ran by her house yelling at the top of his voice. Zillah pushed some furniture up against the front door before running out the back one. She bolted across the yard, heading for the fields. Even men were not safe when Arab slave traders were in the area. She had to stop intermittently but her adrenaline allowed her to hurry on, stumbling haphazardly as she ran. Abba, oblivious to the danger, was bent over a pile of grain, tying the stalks into bundles. When he saw Zillah racing toward him, he dropped the bundle he was working on and ran to meet her.

"Zillah, what—"

"It's Arab slave traders!" She bent over, placing her hands on her knees as she panted. "Quickly, Abba, we must get home!" She grabbed his hand, but he stood firm, deep in thought.

"Are you sure they're Arabs?" His voice was tight and worried.

"Yes, Abba, a messenger came through town shouting a warning. Come, we must hurry." She tugged hard and managed to pull him a few steps before he planted his feet again.

"Zillah, are Caleb and Jonah back yet?" he asked.

"Why no, they haven't been back since...oh no." She dropped to her knees in horror. "You don't think...?"

"I cannot be sure." He fell silent for a moment. Then, gathering his composure, he lifted her to her feet and they started running home.

Jonah staggered along with the caravan, tears streaming down his face. Heavy chains clamped firmly around his arms and legs, intensifying the struggle to walk. The sun stood like a torch in the sky, baking all beneath it like a furnace. Jonah's mind felt muddled and hazy as he tried to concentrate on each weary movement. His feet throbbed as the scraped skin tore and bled, and when he tried to swallow, he found there was no moisture in his mouth. Every breath he took stank of sweat and blood, adding to the unbearably hot, dry air. To his left, stood waves of drooping grain, waiting for harvest. He vaguely heard small rodents scurrying about, harvest mice clambering up the stalks to nibble on the kernels while foxes prowled in search of prey. To his right there was nothing but parched land—an endless sea of brown dotted with flecks of dull green. The crack of a whip sent bolts of pain along his back.

"Addaru, addaru," one of the men bellowed as more whips cracked down.

"Hey you, boy," one of the slaves called over to Jonah, "he's telling you to move your hide a little faster so he can bake a little slower." Nervous laughter rippled through the group until another slave trader brought a whip down squarely on the talkative boy's shoulder, and he cried out.

"Quiet, you fools," another slave hissed, "unless you all want to be dead by morning." Jonah glanced over at the dejected boy who had called out to him, and knew the warning to be valid.

Near the rear of the caravan, Caleb limped along, unaware that his brother was also a captive. His mind swam with worries both for himself and for his family. His leg felt as if someone had stuck a knife in his shin. He had tried conversing with those around him to lift the settled depression, but it was no use. Just moments ago, he had seen a young boy whipped for speaking too loudly and knew enough to keep his own mouth shut. Murmurs and timid whispers passed through the caravan as they neared a small town. Most likely, the slavers were looking for an easy capture or two as they paraded down the center street. It wasn't until Caleb lifted his head to gaze around that he moaned aloud. Most slave traders headed south to sell their captives, but they had headed north instead. And his gentle hometown of Gath Hepher was in grave danger.

As the caravan plodded slowly past the hushed town, eyes peered out from windows and ears listened through securely locked doors. Zillah and Amittai crouched in their home, gazing anxiously at the oncoming caravan. The ominous clinking of chains seemed like thunder in the still air. The caravan drivers knew they were being watched, but most seemed unconcerned. A sudden shout pierced the air, and a large group of men armed to the teeth with axes, sickles, clubs, and daggers emerged from the houses to block the road. The caravan came to a rumbling halt and all eyes watched the confrontation tensely.

The witnesses held their breath in apprehension, so did the slaves, and the mob of men. Even the chickens out in the yard ceased their endless clucking as if fearful that a single sound would bring the sun down on their heads. Only the slavers remained calm. Then, there was the whisper of fabric. The cloaked Arab slave traders threw off their covers, revealing their true identities.

Assyrians.

In all her worst nightmares, Zillah never could have imagined such a thing. Assyrians on Israelite soil—impossible. But the black hair, ebony eyes, dark complexion, and muscular soldiers' stance was unmistakable. Suddenly she gave a gasp of realization. Zillah had heard rumors that Assyria was weakening, though the current king was preparing to build a new capital and even new temples. They would need slaves for this, and they likely thought Israel and other small surrounding nations would be easy prey with their little towns and thin walled cities. And of course, every caravan would have to be small, but well-armed with the best soldiers. They would have had to enter as Arabs or else they would have been turned back at the border.

Her father must have been thinking the same thing, because he said, "Assyrian soldiers should not be within Israelite borders. The only reason they are not dead is because they were disguised as Arabs. What cowardly deceit." His voice carried a note of disbelief and disgust. Zillah, however, conceded the brilliancy of the plan. The king in Samaria would not be able to control these small guerrilla forces crossing his borders to steal away men, women, and children. She shuddered involuntarily and turned her attention back to the standoff. There was another soft swishing sound, and she saw the Assyrians draw carefully concealed swords. They moved as one, positioning men around the caravan with a thick wall of men at the front. The rest were spaced evenly on the sides and behind the train of slaves.

Suddenly, Amittai stood and shouted, "Jonah!"

Zillah didn't have time to comprehend. Before she could react, he pushed aside the furniture blocking the door and unbolted it. By the time she jerked to her feet, her father was outside and drawing the dagger he kept tucked in his belt.

"No, Abba!" she called to him, but it was too late.

She saw the glint of metal as one of the Assyrians felled her father. Before she could go to him, a shout rang out from the mob of townsmen, and in an instant, pandemonium broke out. Men fell on both sides, and at first, it was hard to tell what the outcome would be. Before long though, the Assyrians' devoted training and careful organization came into play. The front row of soldiers deflected the haphazard attacks of the angry men while a second row slung rocks into the melee. Blood ran in the streets as the outnumbered Assyrians fought off the townsmen with deadly efficiency. Zillah stood frozen with shock in the doorway as she watched the scene play out before her through a thin veil.

Other families were leaning out of windows to watch. The Assyrians were ruthless, especially since the men of Gath Hepher had chosen to fight them, arousing their ire as well as their infamous bloodlust. As a majority of their soldiers finished the off the local men, the remaining soldiers poured into every house, dragging out the occupants and adding them to the slave train. Any that resisted were killed. Zillah saw the Assyrians break down her neighbor's door and drag out the kind gentleman and his wife. She watched them being dragged toward the caravan, and it was then that she saw him.

"Jonah!" She rushed out into the street and raced toward her brother, ignoring the slashing of blades and angry shouts around her. Her only thought was to free him and Caleb and escape from this massacre. She never made it to his side.

The train, now much larger, continued on its way to Assyria, leaving behind broken hearts, and streets running with blood.

Days ran together in an endless blur as Jonah and Caleb marched along with the others toward an unknown future. Tales of horrors ahead were passed around the caravan by the most terrified and imaginative. Caleb heard of his father and sisters' tragic end and that Jonah was a captive. He needed to find his brother. Since they were not chained together, Caleb managed to inch his way toward Jonah even under the scrutiny of the guards. Thankfully, he could keep up with the caravan despite the pain in his leg, and after four days of slow progress, he made it to his brother's side.

Being together made things easier, but each day was still brutal as whips cracked and the slavers shouted irate threats in the ugly Assyrian language. The Assyrians. Jonah hated them with every bone in his small body. They had killed his family, and they were carrying him and his brother and countless others into slavery. It was infuriating that Yahweh would simply abandon them to this wasteland of grief and despair. Yahweh, the God of his father, Amittai. Yahweh, the God of his mother. Both were gone forever. Yahweh had been powerless to help them.

Day and night Caleb continued to pray for deliverance, for strength, courage, and the ability to love his enemies. Jonah did not understand why his brother would waste his time on a God that was never present, incapable, and useless. At first, Jonah prayed too, pouring out his heart, pleading with all his soul to be away from this terrible caravan, and to roll back time. Back to when his mother was alive before the terrible fever came. Before the Assyrians. Before the loss of his home, his family, his life. Time, however, would not be turned. And the heavens were silent as stone.

"Jonah. Jonah." Caleb shook him awake. "I need you to come with me."

Jonah, puzzled, sat up and stared at his brother. "What do you need?" He rubbed the sleep from his weary eyes. Dark shadows hung under them, giving him the appearance of a beggar that never slept, which was not far from the truth. It was difficult to rest on the hard ground and impossible to relax while waiting for the command to get up and start another weary day of walking. The last prisoner to wake got a cruel beating.

"Come with me, but be quiet." Caleb helped him up and they crept around a tent, out of sight of the guards. Then, keeping camels, trees, or tents between them and prying eyes, they made their way to the edge of the camp. It was a simple thing to do, creep away, but with shackled feet it was not possible to go very far by daybreak, and those that had tried, sorely regretted it. Once away from camp, Jonah breathed in the clean air of the free world. Others were there too, tall and brawny men like Caleb. They were clustered close behind a group of acacias. Seeing Caleb, they beckoned him closer.

"We were just discussing the best way to prevent the guards from noticing the activity when we start work," one of the men told Caleb, casting a curious glance at Jonah.

"This is my younger brother, he is quick and may serve us well," Caleb explained. "Have you found a solution?"

Another man, his shimmering gold hair easily visible despite the darkness, answered, "How about we each stand near a guard, and when a signal is given, we will give those devils a good knock for all the beatings they've given us?" There was an unmistakable gaiety in his tone that made Jonah uneasy. And he was relieved when several others objected. The conversation itself was absurd. Escape from the Assyrians? Impossible. Still, for the next hour, they brainstormed ideas. Jonah recognized that only the longing to escape kept these men willing to discuss the plan, for in spite of all their disagreements, they managed to settle on a solid strategy. Aaron ben Joshua was called to condense the plan and explain it so that none could misunderstand.

"Alright, my brothers," he said, leaning in and lowering his voice, "Here is what we will do."

Chapter Two

"Addaru! Addaru!" The familiar command was barked at them as whips cracked, causing birds to scatter from the palms and flee in all directions. Every animal, human, and piece of nature seemed to shy away at the sound of that cracking whip and from the sight of the Assyrians' dark, cold eyes. How long had it been since those whips had become commonplace in his life? Jonah could not recall. Days, maybe months? Time was lost in the desolate wasteland. He could not wait for night to come. Indeed, the day so far was the longest day of his life that he could remember. Every step seemed an effort. Every inch the sun moved across the brilliant sky felt like years.

A few hours before nightfall, murmuring and whispering started up within the caravan. A knot of dread formed in Jonah's stomach. That only happened when a town could be seen by the slaves in front. If that town remained quiet, the caravan would pass through without any incident. However, should any rise up against the slave traders at the injustice of what was being done, then there would be a battle—much like the one in his own hometown of Gath Hepher.

As it inevitably would, the rumors reached back to Jonah and Caleb like the licking flames of fire.

"Did you hear?" A boy of about fifteen nudged Jonah with his elbow. "We have been in Assyrian territory for days now." He met Jonah's gaze and his deep green eyes burned with fire. He gestured with a chained hand to the slave caravan, before chatting on like a narrator, his voice brimmed with mock cheer. "Welcome to Dumah, the city where slave caravans are dispatched. Since these slavers are such brilliant clods, we are headed north by way of south so that more of the journey can be in Assyrian territory. It's a half way point, of sorts. You see, Dumah is about sixty days hike southwest of Israel. But to get to the heart of Assyria—the land that requires our expert building skills—" his voice dripped bitter sarcasm "—that part of the world is another few months march northwest, more or less. So we are half way there, and we have reached a sort of rest stop where no resting will likely be permitted." He cut off with the precision of a well-trained guide. The grin that broke through his solemn face made the sun shine brighter, though more gently, and if his sienna hair had been any lighter, it would glow. His jubilant arrogance, and audacious sarcasm made Jonah smile.

"Don't be so cheery." Caleb nudged him from the other side. "This change will spoil everything." He was careful not to use the word "plan," for they were still unsure of how much Hebrew the Assyrians understood.

"It will have to wait then." The boy sighed heavily and they fell into silence.

The mud-brick castle stood outlined by the setting sun as the caravan entered Dumah. Sights, smells, and sounds long since forgotten, bustled around the weary travelers. Merchants of every kind hawked their wares, mothers beckoned their children, and goats and pigs ran hither and thither causing pedestrians to stumble and dodge in the street. Near the center of the city lay a temple to Ishtar. The goddess's priests hurried about the courtyard, preparing for an evening sacrifice, their white robes swishing rhythmically with their even strides.

"Pagans through and through, but the Lord's children all the same." Caleb sighed.

"Lord's children or not, they deserve His wrath and judgment," Jonah grumbled bitterly.

Caleb angled a curious look at him. "Such an opinion you have, my little brother." He smiled. "But we cannot judge them simply by deeds or what they deserve. 'He does not treat us as our sins deserve or repay us according to our iniquities.' Remember from King David's psalms?"

Jonah remembered. In defense, he retorted, "The Torah also says to 'show no pity: life for life'."

With a sigh, Caleb fell into silence, which ended their discussion. Jonah, however, found it more difficult to let go of all the things the Assyrians had done, not to mention a reputation for war, cruelty, and ruthlessness that was known in every land and by every people.

The caravansary was packed full of chained slaves, traders, and a whole lot of Assyrians. A chain was passed through the arms of the prisoners so that they could not be stolen or lost in the winding streets. Jonah felt the need to sit down as another length of metal was laid heavily on him. The shackles on his feet, arms, and now the chain passed through them made even standing a great effort.

"Go ahead, have a seat," advised the boy that had conversed with Jonah on the trip. "That way, if they beat you for it, I'll know not to do the same." The challenge was unnecessary. The caravan drivers barked out an order that meant they should sit down. Many sighed with relief as they sank to the ground, but Caleb seemed unable to settle down and rest.

Seeing this, the boy remarked, "I told you we would be unable to rest didn't I?"

Once again, Jonah smiled. "You have a way with words that could make even the dourest slave driver cheery." He paused to let the compliment settle. "I do not think we were properly acquainted. You were too busy giving me an orientation of Assyria if I recall correctly. I am Jonah ben Amittai; this is my older brother Caleb. I would greet you properly," he held up his shackled wrists ruefully, "but I am rather unable."

"It is an honor to meet you, Jonah ben Amittai." The boy gave a formal nod, "Caleb. I am Anan ben Jonathan."

"Do you know what happened to your father?" Jonah asked.

"No, I don't. Jonathan is actually my adoptive father. My birth parents died several days after I was born. I do not know how. I was raised by Jonathan who came by in time to save me from starvation. Jonathan gave me his name when I became thirteen." Anan shook his head sadly. "He was away on business when these nice fellows came along. With all the destruction the Assyrians caused in my town, it won't take him long to put two and two together."

Silence settled over the caravan as the orange sphere sank vividly into a purple sky trimmed with scarlet. The dull bricks turned a gentle pink hue as darkness fell. A blanket of brilliant stars shone overhead as the weary travelers met under the cover of darkness.

The plan was discussed with caution since they were in a more confined space and would be more easily overheard.

"What happens after we escape?" Caleb asked the group.

"I suppose we'll go back the way we came," Aaron replied simply.

"Yes, but how will we survive without food and water?"

"We won't. We will need to steal some of both I suppose." Aaron took in the nodding heads of agreement. "If we all contribute what we remember about the journey down to Dumah, we can plot our trip back. There are enough of us that we should be able to form a rough map, one that focuses on landmarks and approximate locations of wells, towns and such." Jonah watched his brother with pride as Caleb joined the hour-long discussion. When they were satisfied with the mental map they had created, Aaron laid out the adjusted plans as clearly as the night before. They were ready.

As before, the day passed slowly. The camels were repacked with supplies and the drivers enjoyed themselves, drinking and celebrating their arrival in Assyrian territory. All there was left to do was head east, cross the Euphrates, and then follow the Tigris north to Assyria.

The caravan set off at midday, just after the height of the blazing sun. The prisoners walked quickly, eager to put as much distance between the caravan and Dumah as possible before nightfall. If the drivers took note of this, they likely thought it was because of a day's rest in the city. Once again, the brilliant orb began to sink until only the very top could be seen on the horizon. Dusk settled, and the crickets chirruped as the desert larks sang their evening song. Once the stars began to appear in the darkening sky, camp was set up. Tents were pitched, and the slaves were made to gather firewood. The night had finally come.

Jonah twirled a stick that was carefully fitted into a hole in another piece of wood. His hands ached with the effort of spinning it back and forth, but he was soon rewarded with smoke, and after a moment, a promising ember. He added some dead grass and blew on it gently until tiny flames licked at the twigs and leaves he had piled up. Then taking some larger sticks, he built a neat tepee and watched it catch in the dry air.

"Well done, Jonah." Caleb was watching him while pitching a tent for one of the drivers. He crept a little closer and added, "It will serve us well that you can make a fire when we are gone." The corner of his mouth tipped in a smile before he turned and continued with his work.

The nightly rations of food and water were passed out, and slaves and slavers alike settled down to rest. Jonah tossed and turned on the hard ground, unable to sleep. He could hear the restless movements of many others as their minds churned with excitement and worry. Tonight, they would escape, and with luck, they would soon be free to go home. Home. Jonah did not even know where his home was anymore. He would never go back to Gath Hepher, not with his family gone. No, he and Caleb would travel to another city in Israel. They could be merchants or farmers and live in peace—in safety. He closed his eyes and sleep claimed him.

"Jonah, it is time." In an instant, Jonah was on his feet. Caleb placed a gentle hand on his shoulder. "Easy, or even the camels will feel your energy." They grouped with the others a short ways from camp.

"Is everyone ready?" Aaron asked. They nodded unanimously. "May Yahweh have mercy on us all."

Jesse, son of Gershon, crept stealthily around the camp. His held his chains tightly so they would not clank. He had watched, as instructed, the movements of the guards and knew which one was in possession of the keys. He untied a small pouch from his belt and gently lifted the guard's tent flap and peered inside. The man was fast asleep, snoring like a pig.

Jesse peered into the gloom to make sure the guards on shift were on the other side of the camp, then he slipped inside and lowered the flap behind him. He took deep breaths, one after the other, trying to calm his breath and pulse. Taking the open bag, he placed it under the man's nose and listened as the raucous breathing eased into a shallow rhythm. The herb potion had done its work. Jesse carefully lifted the keys from the man's belt and unlocked his own shackles. He then locked them on the guard's wrists and ankles. How ironic, he mused, unable to hold back the smile that swept across his freckled face. Jesse slipped out as silently as he had entered and sped off with the keys in hand.

Caleb was relieved when the metal bonds fell off, and he felt light as air. Jonah too paced in circles, enjoying the sensation of free limbs.

Aaron, Caleb, and another man called Ishvi jogged silently over to where on duty guards were leaning up against some palm trees. Each of the Hebrews was armed with a bag of herbs collected along their journey, and they completed their task with efficiency. The soldiers soon fell into a deep slumber, were hastily shackled, and dragged out of sight.

All the prisoners, save a few that stayed in the camp to prevent suspicion, gathered behind the tents of the drugged guards, gratefully rubbing chaffed wrists and ankles. Each received a tiny bag of the sleeping herbs, and they fanned out around the camp, closing in on the occupied tents. Aaron stood near the central campfire watching carefully, his lengthy frame creating a seemingly endless shadow in the moonlight. Before long, every tent except for three had a man or woman out in front with one hand raised. It was time. Aaron double-checked everyone's position before lifting his right arm high. A collective breath was held until he jerked his arm down, and the contents of the bags of herbs were tossed over the sleeping soldiers. Everyone raced out of the tents and stumbled toward the central campfire—almost everyone. Aaron counted heads and found two to be missing.

"Where are Caleb and Jesse?" he asked anxiously. No one seemed to know.

"Aaron!" Someone shouted of a sudden, "Assyrians!"

Three soldiers, roused by the stomping of feet and low murmurs, emerged from the shadows pushing Caleb and Jesse before them. "Anyone moves, they die," declared one of the soldiers in rough Hebrew, holding a dagger close to Jesse. To the group's astonished faces, he said, "Yes, fools, I speak Hebrew. Now everyone on ground."

As Aaron and the others slowly got on their knees, there was a sudden flurry of movement. Ishvi hurled a rock at the guard holding Jesse, and as the man ducked, Caleb grabbed the knife from his hands. The three soldiers drew their deadly swords in a fury and advanced on the group of escapees.

"Imkhas! Strike!"

Suddenly Assyrian soldiers swarmed over the campsite.

"Where did these dogs come from?" Aaron asked, enraged.

"We knew you plot something," the guard mocked. "So we sent men to wait until you regroup, and now..." He laughed mirthlessly. "Now we have you trapped. Any bright idea in empty heads?"

He had been joking, but Aaron responded anyway. "Everyone run toward the trees!" The group bolted in the direction of the acacias. Aaron called out behind them, "Head north and don't stop!"

Feet pounded the earth until the very ground seemed to shake. It was only then that Jonah realized just how many prisoners there were in the slave train—at least a couple hundred. It was just like that terrifying day so long ago. He was running for his life, with pursuers close behind and his brother at his side.

"Keep going, Jonah, we'll make it! You'll see!"

Jonah believed him, for he had no choice. The Assyrians were close behind them, and a few had been recaptured, but still, the escapees managed to outpace even the well-trained soldiers. Abba had once told Jonah that those who run for their lives have more motivation than those that pursue them, and it was true. Three quarters of the group had managed to get away, and they scrambled frantically over rocks and small hills to put distance between themselves and the slavers. The Assyrians, having recovered a few slaves and needing to secure them back at the campsite, had halted their pursuit and turned back. It was likely, however, that they would send out soldiers later to find the remainder.

The group sat down in the lee of a hill as the sun began to rise and its heat beat down though it was still early. About thirty water skins had found their way into the hands of the escapees, and a few were passed around.

"We should keep moving," Aaron announced, rising slowly and stretching lanky limbs. "They will be searching for us soon, now that they can see better." He scanned the crowd, as if to see if there was any resistance to his recommendation. "A leader should be chosen to keep the peace. This leader must be chosen well so that there will be little malcontent."

Ishvi rose to his feet. "I would have none other than yourself for our leader. After all, you have brought us this far."

Jesse also stood. "I agree wholeheartedly with Ishvi. Are there any against Aaron ben Joshua being our rightful leader?" No one moved. "Then all is well. The vote is unanimous; we want you to be our leader." He turned and gave a formal nod to Aaron.

"So be it." Aaron announced flatly, but gratitude and pleasure were clearly written on his face. "Alright, let's put some space between ourselves and that ruthless bunch."

The journey ever northward progressed without incident, much to everyone's relief. No soldiers came streaming over the rocky hills, no robbers attacked the meager food and water they carried with them, and the weather was uncommonly fair. That night, Jonah laid his head down in contentment and stared up at the brilliant night sky. He heard his brother humming softly beside him along with the quiet whispers of other children his age unwilling to rest. A gentle night breeze brushed his face, and the sweet summer air lulled him to sleep.

Light, brighter than the sun, brighter than any natural thing shone in Jonah's eyes. He shot to his feet before staggering backward in terror and covering his eyes.

"Jonah." The power of the voice knocked him over, and he curled into a feeble ball. "Jonah, do not be afraid." He opened his left eye cautiously. A man stood before him, the hood of a white cloak covered his face, but the radiance of it was too much to look upon anyway. The great light was behind the man, and Jonah turned away for fear he would go blind. He shut his eyes tightly as the world around him swirled dizzily. "Adonai has seen your ordeal," the man told him, his voice firm yet gentle. "Be strong, for He is with you." The light dimmed, and Jonah heard his name spoken again. He opened his eyes.

"Jonah?" Caleb bent over him worriedly. "Jonah, are you alright?" Jonah nodded slowly. The light was gone, and so was the angel. "You were whimpering, and I thought you were hurt or something. Are you sure you're okay?"

"I'm sure." But his voice sounded small and hollow. "Just a bad dream."

"Alright." Caleb looked doubtful, but he lay back down and kept his silence. When Zillah had been very little, she had been plagued with nightmares, but she had soon outgrown those. It was uncommon for Jonah or Caleb to have a bad dream, but with all that had happened over the past months, Caleb probably understood. Besides, Jonah was

still young, though he felt very old inside. He was thirteen now, his
birthday having taken place sometime during their endless march
toward Dumah. Caleb had given him his own ration of food and water
to celebrate Jonah becoming a man, but the cheer was false. Caleb was
the rock that Jonah clung to, the very reason he sought to go on each
day as the rocky desert passed slowly beneath his bare and blistered feet.
If he should lose his brother too...

"Caleb?" Jonah turned to his brother, pushing hard at the
unwanted thought.

"Yes?" Caleb's voice was drowsy.

"Where shall we go?"

"Go?"

"Where are we going to call home now?"

"Well, I suppose we will go back to Gath Hepher and—" At the
horrified expression on Jonah's face Caleb broke off.

"I never want to go back there," Jonah stammered.

"I see." Caleb rested his head back on his hands and closed his
eyes, thinking. "Would it be alright if we went back? Just to...in case
they are still alive?"

"You were going to say 'to bury them' weren't you?" Jonah
asked accusingly.

Caleb carried on in a voice that feigned nonchalance, avoiding
having to answer. "You would not want to march off to some other city
if they were still alive and well in Gath Hepher would you?"

"No." Jonah slumped in defeat. "But I don't want to go."

"And if they are not there, we will go and live someplace else. Just
you and me."

"And Anan?"

"If he wants to. Though he'll likely check for his father first."

"Well, alright then." Jonah lay back down and closed his eyes.

"What did you dream about?"

He gave a start. "I dreamt that you talked and talked until my ears
fell off!"

"That is very funny coming from you." Caleb laughed lightly, but he
had not missed Jonah's attempt to avoid the subject. "What did you
really dream about, little brother?"

"Nothing." Jonah turned away from his brother and closed his eyes,
silently pleading with him to be quiet. Caleb obeyed and rolled over.

Minutes passed in silence, and soon his breathing became steady and even with sleep. Nonetheless, Jonah knew his brother would not let the subject rest, but there was no easy way to explain his dream, even if he had been willing. Jonah nestled close to his brother and drew the serene night air close about him like a cloak. He soon fell asleep with thoughts of his father, mother, and sister swirling in his mind.

Chapter Three

A dreary dawn met the travelers as Caleb nudged Jonah into wakefulness.

"Good morning, sleepy head. I thought you would snooze the day away." The only reply was a mumbled groan. "Foggy out isn't it? Oh well. A light mist never hurt anyone, unless you are made of sugar." He prodded Jonah teasingly. "But you seem human enough to me."

"I will be more angry dog than human soon, Caleb. Let me sleep," came the muffled reply.

Two entire months had passed since their miraculous escape from the slavers. The new group of travelers had moved through the desert, using their carefully prepared plan as a guide, before stopping at a well-watered oasis. Here they had stayed for four blissful days, an agreeable contrast to moving every morning. According to their collective memory, they were just east of the capital of Judah, Jerusalem. Now old companions parted ways to return to their respective homes in hopes that a new life could be begun.

Nonetheless, everyone knew that whatever lives they had left behind would never be again. Happy days of sunshine and friends were dreams from a lifetime ago. Most of the towns from which the group had been stolen were burned to the ground, the inhabitants long gone. Like Caleb, many wanted to return for a short time to collect what memories that were left before leaving to start anew. Jonah was weary to the bone from walking endlessly, and the rest had been bittersweet.

Ishvi, Aaron, and the other men he and the rest had looked up to were now parting ways. Many had once been carpenters, potters, farmers, shepherds, or scribes. Others, like Jonah, had barely been able to make a living before losing their homes, and faced an uncertain future at best. The familiar fury at the injustice of his situation consumed Jonah until he could think of little else. He was so depressed and listless that nothing could pain him further, of this he felt certain.

Later that day, the group split into three. One headed north toward Israel, another headed east to Jerusalem, and the third dispersed altogether in all directions to find distant relatives or friends. Caleb, Jonah, and Anan were in this third group.

The sun beat down with ferocity, increasing the need for water, of which there was little. Anan spent the day humming tunes and ditties to cheer his companions.

"I am glad you decided to come along, Anan," Jonah informed him as evening closed in around them.

"I am unsure if I agree," complained Anapa, an Egyptian merchant and the only other traveler accompanying them north. "It is good that my warehouse in Hebron is only a few days away, otherwise I might head south just to keep away from this...this talkative person."

Anan glared at him with wounded dignity. "Talkative person? Talkative person you say! Why I'll show you talkative! I will be going on and on until dawn tomorrow and nothing but an arrow through my skull will keep me from talking on until you set foot in your dusty warehouse." He put a twist on those last two words, mocking Anapa's acute accent.

"Dusty warehouse?" Anapa retorted, enraged. Then he caught himself. Realizing that he was repeating the very same babbling speech as Anan. "You are a serpent of a clown," he muttered under his breath.

"S-o you s-ay," Anan replied. They fell about laughing heartily, the sound surrounded them in the thick, dusty air until the very breeze barely seemed to contain its mirth. Even the stony-faced Anapa managed a thin smile.

A few short days later, Anan waved vigorously to the retreating figure of Anapa. "Farewell, my dusty old friend. So sorry this journey must end. Glad I was to see you smile. Goodbye, you merchant for a little while."

"So long, babbling monkey, with your disposition so annoying." Anapa's crisp voice floated back to them over the cool breeze of dawn.

The day was pleasant, for the time being, until the sun rose to its height and baked them like bricks in an oven.

"He needs a lesson in rhyming, Anan." Jonah giggled.

"That may be, but I'll bet he could sell water to the ocean, whereas I do not even know how to haggle."

"You would not need to." Caleb said solemnly. "As soon as you opened your mouth, the merchant would sell his entire booth to you for a shekel just to get away." The brothers grinned at Anan's indulgent smile, touched with a bit of injured ego.

"My good friend, you wound me with your lashing tongue."

"Then remind me to speak at great length to any Assyrians we meet." They fell silent, sobered by the mention of the Assyrians until Anan started giggling.

"What's so funny?" Jonah asked incredulously.

"Nothing." Anan turned away and stared at the horizon, a line of brown or green depending on which crops the farmers chose. Despite a gallant effort, he soon found himself sputtering once again for no apparent reason.

"You are a clown!" Jonah cried at the sight of Anan clutching his stomach in helpless mirth.

Caleb put his hand on his brother's shoulder. "What a sorry sight that is. He will either die of laughter or be forever cured by it." He attempted a stern and disapproving face, but it was little use. Laughter, like yawning, was contagious, and soon the trio were stumbling along laughing uproariously for no apparent reason at all.

It was the middle of the afternoon when the small square of blackened land became visible. A few dead date palms stood forlornly beside the faint path of a road.

"Look at what they did," Caleb moaned, covering his face with labor-hardened hands. The burnt crops and blackened trunks were a sorry sight against the background of a sapphire sky. A flock of red-rumped swallows fluttered noisily above them before landing in one of the date palms.

"A little ways away from home aren't they?" Anan commented, attempting lightness. Red-rumped swallows frequented the wetlands. However, due to the uncommonly dry weather, their natural habitats had dried up, leaving only cracked dirt to show were marsh had once been. The birds had been forced to move into a world of unfamiliarity, an ironic mimicry, Jonah thought, watching the little birds swoop to catch insects as the sky was alive with them. Gath Hepher was a pitiful scene, a lonely ruin on a lonely rise. Most of the houses were empty, their occupants long gone. Despite the change, Jonah felt a twist of familiarity upon seeing his home after more than four months. The travelers stood uncomfortably where the central street began and glanced around at the few townspeople attempting to return Gath Hepher to its original state.

"I guess we should check the house first," Caleb said, though it came out as a question.

"Alright." Jonah led the way down the street, toward the very heart of the town.

The door was difficult to open, as it always had been, and it creaked on poorly made, un-oiled hinges. Jonah's eyes widened when he saw the great black spots on the walls where fire had touched them. Undoubtedly, their home, like the surrounding fields, had been set ablaze not long after the battle ended. The one room house still held a faint smell of smoke. Despite this, much of the interior was as it had been when they had left. The cushions surrounded the small hearth, and a pot of water was set to boil within. Four seats surrounded the table, and dishes were laid out for the evening meal. The breeze drifted in through the windows, one on the south side, the other on the north, placed to prevent overheating from too much sunshine. The sleeping mats were rolled up and neatly stacked in a corner, and the chickens clucked noisily in the yard. In a daze, Jonah crossed the room and stepped out the back door. Waves of memory enveloped him as he relived the familiar action. He opened the shallow grain bin and found a small amount still inside. Tossing a small handful to the waiting birds, he watched them devour the kernels with great enthusiasm.

"It took me all day to round these up. They fled in all directions along with a couple dozen others when the onslaught began."

Jonah whirled at the voice and ran full force into the strong embrace of his father.

"Abba!" Caleb threw his arms around Amittai and gripped him fiercely. All three fought tears while Anan stood unnoticed in the doorway. He turned as if to head inside, then addressed them uneasily, "I guess, I'll just, uh..."

"Anan, meet my father Amittai." Jonah beckoned to his friend. "Abba, this is Anan ben Jonathan. He has traveled with us all the way from Dumah." Amittai stood reeling in shock for a moment at the mention of the Assyrian city nearly eight hundred miles away. After a heartbeat, however, he cleared his throat and mumbled a polite greeting to Anan.

Jonah was too elated to notice his father's bemusement. His father was alive and surely his sister was too! What a blessing it was that they both made it through the raid. He ran around to the other side of the house, calling back over his shoulder, "Anan, you should meet my sister Zillah. I know you'll like her a lot. She practically raised me since Mama died and...Zillah?" He had completed a full circuit around the house without seeing his sister. "Zillah?" He called, running down the small slope toward the fields.

"Jonah, come here please." Amittai's voice barely carried to where the small figure stood staring at the empty plots of land. Yet the odd quaver in his father's voice was unmistakable, and it made Jonah's heart drop like a stone in his chest.

He trudged back up the rise and stood before his father, bracing himself for anything. It made little difference.

"Zillah, isn't here, son." He took a deep breath. "She's dead. The Assyrians killed her, Jonah."

"I hate them!" The sudden shriek startled the group. Jonah stood with balled fists, shaking with unrestrained rage. He glanced up and suddenly noticed a massive scar across both of Abba's arms and a gash on his forehead. "I hate them! I hate them!" Jonah turned and fled toward the fields, running, not seeing, hearing, or feeling anything but his pent-up anger and grief. He ran past burnt houses, trees, and fields alike, blinded by tears.

"He wants to leave." Caleb leaned close to his father, his voice filled with concern. "And I understand. With all the memories, it cannot be easy for him. It isn't easy for any of us."

"Alright, we will go somewhere else, but where? Caleb, we have no family or friends elsewhere."

"I know where you could go." Anan's voice drifted between them. Caleb turned. "Your hometown?"

"Yes, it's near Tekoa. Jonathan might be there, and you could all live with us. He is a merchant, much like Anapa, and he is doing well enough in foreign trade to house all of you until you can find work."

"We could never ask such a thing of your father," Amittai cut in.

"You could repay him."

"Yes, we could, Abba." Caleb leaned back in satisfaction. "It is a good plan, better than the alternative of wandering around Israel in search of a place to stay."

"But it would be charity." Amittai shook his head. "And there is nothing to suggest Anan's father would be willing to loan us shelter and food."

"Abba," Caleb said, his voice faintly accusing, "don't be so proud."

"And my father would be delighted to help you all," Anan added. "Jonah and Caleb have been like brothers to me, encouraging me during those lonely days of traveling."

"It was more the other way around. We would have been dull and listless as chained mice if we had not had your good cheer and rather lengthy bouts of babbling."

"There is nothing dull and listless about mice," Anan corrected. "I find the creatures fascinating."

"I have every right to be proud," Amittai said, returning to the previous subject. "My two young sons have traveled fifteen hundred miles and returned home grown men."

"I sure hope not," Caleb muttered. "If it only takes four months to make Jonah a man, imagine when he is my age. He'll be ancient!" They laughed gaily, but each cast a concerned eye at the sullen form huddled in the corner.

More solemnly, Amittai said, "I know I'll regret this, but will you tell me about your journey?"

Caleb leaned farther back, resulting in his chair sliding backward with an earsplitting screech. Scooting it rather unceremoniously forward, he sighed heavily before delving into the story. "Jonah and I were captured near the well in Nazareth, Abba. We met Anan just before we reached Dumah. Each day felt like a thousand years. We would start the day as soon as the sun came up, and we would each be given a ration of food and water, then we would begin to march." The story came easily, flowing smoothly out like a rivulet of water. Caleb talked late into the night about the long days of traveling, the miseries and fears the captives had faced, the cities and towns they passed through, and their escape near Dumah, ending with their journey back to Israel.

When Caleb finished, Amittai rested his elbows on the table and his head in his hands, deep in thought. In the end, he said nothing and only embraced Caleb, squeezed Anan's shoulder affectionately, and unrolled his sleeping mat. He laid it beside Jonah's in the corner and stretched out on it, watching the small figure clutching his sister's blanket, staring at nothing. Soon Caleb and Anan's low murmurs died away, and they blew out the lamps. Caleb rolled out his mat beside his father's.

Anan glanced at the remaining mat before whispering, "I fear that sleeping outside has ruined me. There is nothing that can compare to sleeping under the stars." There was a touch of his familiar humor in the statement. Caleb nodded agreement and rose to his feet. Side by side, the pair crept out the back door into the still, dark night.

Chapter Four

"Come, boy, fetch some water—lively now." The pinched face of the physician turned accusingly toward Jonah, his voice high and squirrelly. "The cleanest you can find."

Jonah ran to grab a jug and brought it to the man.

"Very good, very good." The physician took a cloth and, soaking it with the water, laid it over the feverish brow.

Jonah stumbled about the room in a panic. This couldn't be happening...it couldn't. But it was.

"Come, boy, cease your pacing. You will only make things worse." The clear blue eyes watched Jonah with sympathy. "Those other two shouldn't have left you here on your own, child. It is never kind to leave one so young on their own."

Jonah stopped obediently and went to kneel by the mat. His father lay pale as death. His chest barely moving.

"His fever, though not severe, is at its height. If it breaks, he will recover." The man glanced at Jonah's doubtful expression. "His fever cannot get worse." The words were little consolation, and they left Jonah feeling hollow.

A burst of laughter broke the stillness, and Caleb entered the house, Anan at his heels. As soon as they were through the door though, the laughter stopped. So palpable was Jonah's grief at Amittai's ill health that the newcomers also fell under the gloomy spell and crossed the floor in sullen silence.

"We went down to the old town storehouse to see what crops had been saved for the famine." Caleb extended a plump bag of grain. "The Assyrians were so bent on taking more slaves that they didn't notice our weathered storehouse and with the decrease in the population, there is plenty for all." Jonah took the bag and emptied it into the grain bin by the hearth.

"How did you get in the storehouse, Caleb?"

"It is open to anyone, though monitored until Gath Hepher gets back on its feet." The town storehouses were usually closed to all but the poorest who had no work. Widows and orphans were permitted to take a small share without being pressured to pay in any way. Later, however, if they were fortunate enough to find work, they were expected to give a small portion of their crops to the storehouse managers who calculated the amount saved up and how much could be given and how much should be saved for emergencies. Jonah crouched over the small stone mortar and poured a handful of grain into it. Recalling his sister's movements, he ground the grain with the pestle, crushing the kernels with steady, rhythmic movements.

"Don't get too used to housework, Jonah. Jonathan has a servant who takes care of those sort of things." Anan's voice boomed loudly in the small room, louder still because of the deathly silence; but Jonah didn't seem to hear. The others chose to let him be, assuming he needed a task to preform.

Jonah continued grinding until he was rewarded with fine, light flour. He gently dipped his finger in the center of the pile to create a well. Lifting the smallest jug of water he could find, he poured a little into the well and set down the jug. Jonah then blended the flour with the water until he had dough. Taking a breadboard, he set the ball down and began to knead. Luckily for the lump of dough, he was small, and though he pressed and rolled with all his strength, he did little harm to the mixture. Then he divided the dough into four and pressed the four balls into flat loaves a little bigger than his hand. He carried the board over to the fire and laid the loaves on the smooth stones placed at the edge of the flames. He watched the searing rocks cook the dough until four flat wafers appeared. Picking them up gingerly, he half dropped them onto the board then sucked his nearly burned fingers. All eyes watched him as he passed out loaves to Caleb and Anan. There was a momentary hesitation in his steps before he squared his shoulders and brought a loaf to his father.

"Very good," the physician said when he saw the bread. "Your father needs something to eat." A hand reached up to gently take the loaf from Jonah.

"Thank you, son." The voice was barely audible, and it rattled like wind through branches.

"Of course, Abba," he said, his voice breaking as well.

Caleb mumbled the blessing and silence fell over them again as fingers broke the bread, and they began to eat. The physician drew a small loaf from his own bag and ate it before returning his attention back to Amittai. Three pairs of eyes watched worriedly as the physician went about his work. He replaced the wet cloths and administered herbs, all the while having to nudge Jonah out of his way as the child worried over his abba.

"Would it be best if we stayed here, or gave you room to work?" Caleb asked, casting a pointed glance at Jonah.

"It makes little difference. And I doubt you could get the child to leave even if I needed him to."

The man was right, Caleb knew. Ever since Amittai had fallen ill the previous day, Jonah hadn't left the house. Caleb also knew how critical it was that Abba survive and recover from his fever. Because if he did not, Caleb would lose Jonah as well.

Two weeks passed and still there was no change in Amittai's condition. Fall had arrived and, with it, cooler weather. Life settled into a constant yet uneasy rhythm.

"Caleb. Caleb, wake up." Anan knelt in the grass beside his friend, shaking him gently. The pair had grown close during the month since their arrival in Gath Hepher, partly because they were nearly the same age, and with Amittai sick and Jonah unreachable, they were the only other people in the house—aside from the physician who came weekly. He was in high demand after the trauma of the Assyrian raid. And because of it, he charged very little which was rare among physicians. He spent most of his time traveling from village to village, spending a small amount of time at each patient's home. Presently, Caleb rolled over, making a soft sound of inquiry.

"It's Jonah; you need to get up, Caleb." Anan nearly fell backward as Caleb rolled to his feet.

"What is it, Anan? What's wrong?" Caleb came fully awake, glancing about nervously into the darkness of the night.

"He's gone."

"Gone?"

"Gone, Caleb. Jonah is gone."

Chapter Five

The night lay still and silent. Nearly impenetrable blackness shrouded the land. Jonah rested by the road, crouching beneath an enclosure of foliage. Branches brushed his tattered tunic, and his skin was rough with dust. Farther down the road, he could see the capital of his nation, Samaria, surrounded by sloping hills. It was a glimmer of peace that seemed out of place. If he strained his eyes, he could make out the occasional twinkle of a lit room near the walls or the campfire of a traveler just outside them. He was also a traveler, both weary and sore from walking for three days. In another few, he would reach his destination, Tekoa, the new home Anan had offered.

At first, he had felt guilty about his decision to leave early, before his father was healed. But Caleb had once told him, "If you feel a call to faith, Jonah, you have God's permission to test it." And Jonah had decided to do just that. He would trust his dream, that vivid, seemingly impossible, vision. If God had truly decided to speak to him, then God would have to prove that He was trustworthy and heal Abba.

Jonah rose and continued stumbling down the road. Potholes and rocks impeded his steps, and he had nearly twisted his ankle a score of times. If he reached the city tonight, he could sleep beside some kind stranger's fire. A gust of wind made him shiver and hug his arms around himself. His sister would have advised against walking up to a stranger and speaking to him, but Jonah was not afraid of most people anymore.

The first traveler he saw was a drunk looking Moabite with a shaggy beard and strange clothing. Using prudence, Jonah veered away from the man and searched the horizon for another twinkling fire. He spotted one to his right and, upon nearing it, saw a Judean warming his hands over the flames.

"Shalom." Jonah stepped into the firelight. Lifting his hand in greeting.

"Shalom, young boy." Jonah blinked a moment in the firelight, well aware that he must indeed look younger than his thirteen years. He was a man, the same as every thirteen-year-old male, but in a way he was glad the Judean thought him young. Perhaps he would be especially kind. The Judean's gentle brown eyes met his with cautious curiosity. Stretching out his lanky frame, the Judean asked, "What brings you to my campfire?"

"I am traveling to Tekoa."

"Tekoa?" He raised his eyebrows. "From where?"

"Gath Hepher."

"That must be a good forty miles from here. What sort of incentive would a boy like you have to travel alone all that way?"

"I am running."

The man gave a start, looking Jonah up and down as if suddenly wary. "What for? Who from?"

"The Assyrians came through my town." From the understanding in the man's eyes, Jonah knew he didn't need to say any more. "May I?" He gestured to the fire.

"Please, the night is chilly." The man settled back, the rocky soil crunching beneath him.

Jonah settled himself down, a pang of guilt entering his mind as he examined his strange surroundings. Surely Anan and Caleb would know where he had gone and why he had needed to go.

The man was talking again, his voice low and smooth. "I live just outside of Tekoa. The Assyrians came through my town as well." He gazed past Jonah's shoulder, his Adam's apple moving as he swallowed a lump that appeared to be grief. "I adopted a boy, a young child long ago. He grew up to be much like me. I gave him my name when he was thirteen. I was away on business...I'm a merchant, you see." He trailed off, looking down into the flames. "The land is burnt and blackened, boy; the whole town was shaken by the Assyrians. And even though they have recovered, you still wouldn't want to go there. Is there nowhere else you can live? No one else to care for you?"

"No," Jonah lied.

"You may call me Jonathan." He snorted disdainfully. "Means Yahweh has given. What a name, and in this time, it is so out of place."

"Call me Jonah," Jonah muttered in a soft voice. Pain, sorrow, and grief, things he had tried to be rid of were slowly creeping back in.

Jonathan put his hands behind his head and closed his eyes, his body limp with fatigue. "I have three other sons, you know. They are all grown and one lives in Jerusalem, and the other two are in Anathoth. I hardly see them...once a year maybe. I just returned from visiting my third son. I checked in on him to make sure he was all right. My youngest is the one who is gone. He is the one I told you was adopted. I determined to love him as my own when I found him. So, I named him Anan, fourth born child. In truth, he might just be my favorite son, though I'd never admit it to him—if he were alive." Jonathan passed a hand over his face, grief marking his friendly features.

Jonah was about to make a response of sympathy when something clicked in his mind. Anan, fourth born child...Jonathan, adopted a boy...he lives in Tekoa. He had been so distracted by his own thoughts that he had not seen it before. "Your son's name is Anan?" he asked, disbelievingly.

"Was." The reply was soft.

"He is alive."

Jonathan raised himself onto one elbow, watching Jonah coolly. "Don't try to cheer a broken man, child. It is a pointless battle."

"It is true. I traveled with him. We were both prisoners of the Assyrians. He is at my home in Gath Hepher!" Jonah was now on his feet, pacing excitedly.

"Anan, alive?"

"Yes!"

"Take me to him." Jonathan rolled into a sitting position, gathering his meager belongings, and stuffing them into a bag.

"He is likely on his way to Tekoa. We might miss him if we traveled to my home. It would be best to wait at your home." Jonah watched as his new friend digested the information.

Jonathan shook his head firmly. "I know Anan; he will follow the road. It will be hard for us to miss him."

"But what if he arrives in Tekoa before we do? He might think you're dead or gone."

"Or he will think I am away and will return soon."

Jonah sighed, unable to change the merchant's mind. He allowed himself to relax with the realization that he could still test Yahweh. If he and Jonathan did not cross paths with Anan on their way to Gath Hepher and instead found Amittai still lying sick with fever, all would be different, yet all would be the same.

A hand shook his shoulder and brought Jonah into wakefulness. Jonathan knelt over him, eagerness in his eyes. Dawn had arrived, the fire was out, and the scattered camp of the previous night was neatly put away. The morning was pleasant, a rosy pink hue melting into the world around them. The sky above was a mixture of purples, pinks, oranges, and at the very top stretched a majestic deep blue. The great city walls towering nearby were dusted in color, giving the drab stones a pleasant flush of orange. Even the birds seemed to think the morning beautiful, and their cheerful song matched the setting. Jonathan passed over half a loaf of bread which Jonah took gratefully. He had hardly begun to eat when the merchant began pacing around him, a goatskin bag slung over one shoulder.

"I suppose I can eat and walk." Jonah rose, still chewing, and followed Jonathan north, toward Gath Hepher. It was like keeping up with a migrating bird. Jonathan half walked, half ran down the road. Energy and exuberance dominated his every step and motion. He talked continuously as they went, telling Jonah stories about himself and Anan, the things they had done, and about the events leading up to his return from Jerusalem where he had been bargaining over the price of a wagon full of fine cloth.

"That merchant, Jonah, was as stubborn as a mule with something to lose. You would have thought I was asking to buy his eyes off him. But I got the wagon and the cloth for a rather reasonable amount." He shook his head slowly. "I should have stayed behind with Anan. I could have helped him through his ordeal. He is a sensitive boy, you know, never shows it though."

"If you, had come with us," Jonah panted, "you might not have made it back. Not everyone escaped easily from the Assyrians."

"Why don't you tell me about your journey?"

"Maybe later, if you don't mind."

"Alright. Last year, I went to Israel," and the merchant was soon off again, chattering on just like his son. Nonetheless, the one-sided conversation helped pass the time, and soon the sun began to set. Jonah was near to fainting by the time the first stars began to appear in the dull blue sky, and still the merchant showed no signs of stopping for the night.

"I hate to slow you down," Jonah puffed, "but I need to rest." Jonathan halted abruptly and Jonah bumped into him. "It's all right if you want to just slow down a bit. I can keep going. I'm just—" He was cut off by a sudden shout.

"Abba! Over here!"

Jonah shook his head to clear it and saw Jonathan running down the road toward a small group of travelers. Recognizing the tall form of his brother, he also took off with an ungainly, stumbling stride. When he drew up alongside the group, he saw Anan wordlessly embracing his father. Their affection and love for one another was plain for all to see. If Jonah had not known Anan was adopted, he would never have guessed. Both father and son spoke with the same smooth speech, could light up a room with one smile, and possessed sienna hair a shade too dark to glow. The only difference seemed to be Anan's forest-green eyes, a stark contrast to Jonathan's soft brown pair.

As Anan stepped back, he caught sight of Jonah. "My friend, I commend you for your audacity in just up and leaving." He chuckled good-naturedly. "Though a little heads up would have been nice."

"Of course, but don't be complaining, Anan. I brought your abba with me." Jonah smiled, and his spirits soared when he glimpsed his own father. Amittai was completely healed. His eyes were clear and void of delirium. His skin was healthy, and he seemed to have made the journey easily. Jonah shifted his gaze from Abba to Anan, then to Jonathan, taking in the reunion. Finally, he met his brother's gaze. But when he saw the anger there, his smile faded.

"Never do that again," Caleb told him slowly. Jonah was surprised at the coldness of his tone. "How could you do that to us, Jonah? We were so worried."

Jonah was about to explain, but discovered that he could find no words to tell his brother exactly why he had left, especially not with Abba, Anan, and Jonathan around. Despite this, Jonah knew that Caleb deserved to know the truth. In fact, they all would need to be told, eventually.

Gesturing, Jonah started them walking, back the way he and Jonathan had come. Once they were under way, the silence stretched uncomfortably, and Jonah dropped back behind the group with Caleb. Amittai saw their need for privacy and turned to speak with Jonathan. Searching for a place to begin, Jonah started, "You told me once that if I felt God's calling to faith, I had His permission to test it."

Caleb frowned slightly, his eyes turning thoughtful. "Jonah, I think it's time you told me about that dream you had."

If the vision had happened before the raid, Jonah might have refused, but since their trials together, he and Caleb and grown much closer, and now Jonah knew he had to try to explain. He cleared his throat, avoiding his brother's gaze. In halting sentences, he recounted the experience, thinking through each word he chose so he didn't leave anything out. When he was finished, he looked up to see that Caleb's eyes were very round.

"The angel spoke...to you?" he asked in awe.

"Yes." Jonah could barely believe the facts himself.

"And so you came here to see if Yahweh would heal Abba and bring him to you?"

"Yes."

"It was risky, little brother. The journey, I mean."

"You sound just like Zillah," Jonah told him.

They both broke into laughter, a sound that caught the attention of the group up ahead. Amittai turned around to fully face them and smiled. Jonah grinned broadly. Then he realized that the mention of his sister had not brought him pain.

He felt guilty that he should feel so little grief after such a short amount of time, and he said so to Caleb.

"She would want you to be happy, Jonah," was all his brother said. They fell silent, each deep in thought.

"I suppose we could be happy with them, don't you?" Jonah gestured to the trio ahead of them. Anan was talking with his father, and from time to time, they would laugh. Amittai joined their gaiety, the effects of his illness seeming to dissolve in the face of joy.

"Yes, we certainly could."

Chapter Five

The weeks following their arrival at Jonathan's home were peaceful and pleasant. Tekoa had been built on a ridge, surrounded on three sides by a deep valley. The road entered it from the west where there were only rolling hills. Jonathan's home was also west of Tekoa, about a mile away from the small city. As promised, Jonathan had a servant who cooked the meals and kept the house clean. Her name was Haggith, though festive was not a characteristic one would use to describe her. Her slouched figure, shuffling gait, and white lightning streaked hair seemed to belong to a woman twice her age, though her demeanor was far from wizened. The day after the Sabbath, all five of them left the house to go to the market. Jonathan brought his cart of cloth to sell, and Anan went along to help him. Amittai and Caleb had found work as shepherds, guiding flocks through the narrow valley as they grazed. Jonah assisted a group of carpenters who were mending the walls. Jonah's job was to carry messages and supplies for them back and forth across the city's walls. He also tended the governor's own pack-mules, feeding and caring for them when they were finished hauling for the day.

Amittai and Caleb split off from the other three and headed toward the valley to begin their work. Jonah turned and headed for the north gate of the city. Jonathan and Anan set off toward the market. When Jonah reached the gate, he turned to mount the steps to the top of the wall and accidentally bumped into a man coming down. "Oh, I'm sorry."

The man stopped. He glanced down at Jonah from a scowling face, but then he smiled, and it seemed friendly enough. "It's no problem."

Jonah continued to the top. There he met the foreman who was waiting for him.

"Time to earn your keep, boy." The foreman handed him a parchment. "This is a list of supplies we need by the Sabbath. I need you to deliver this to our head engineer at the south gate."

"Yes, sir." Jonah turned and trotted happily along the wall. He was gazing down at the emerald green hillsides when he bumped into the same man again. "I'm so sorry, sir! I did not look where I was going," Jonah stammered, embarrassed to have blundered into someone for the second time that day.

"Is your name Jonah?"

"It is."

41

"Come with me."

Jonah hesitated. It was probably wiser to beg the man's pardon and continue with his duties, but an urgent curiosity caused him to follow the stranger. Perhaps it had something to do with the man's plain, patient golden eyes or his gentle demeanor paired with simple brown hair that curled ever so slightly around his head, giving him such a kind appearance that Jonah could see no harm in following him. They descended the north gate stairs and headed for the market square. Once they were in the square, the man halted, gazing around as if waiting for something. After a moment, he relaxed, then turned to Jonah as if to say something, but once again he stiffened, and suddenly he began to quiver as if attempting to restrain a great wave. He turned to face some booths where merchants were selling oils, cloth, and other home necessities.

"*Woe to you who are complacent in Zion,*" he cried, his voice clear and strong. People began to stop what they were doing and stare. "*You lie on beds adorned with ivory and lounge on your couches. You dine on choice lambs and fattened calves. You strum away on your harps like David and improvise on musical instruments. You drink wine by the bowlful and use the fine lotions, but you do not grieve over the ruin of Joseph. Therefore you will be among the first to go into exile; your feasting and lounging will end. The Sovereign Lord has sworn by himself, the Lord God Almighty declares: 'I abhor the pride of Jacob and detest his fortresses; I will deliver up the city with everything in it.'*" The entire square had fallen silent. People watched the man with fixed concentration, some out of curiosity and some out of fear.

A blind man emerged from the shadows, his arms outstretched. "Yahweh Himself has declared this judgment upon us! What shall we do?"

The man, obviously a prophet, turned to face the blind man, his eyes shining with something that appeared to be respect. "*Seek good, not evil, that you may live. Then the Lord God Almighty will be with you, just as you say He is. Hate evil, love good; maintain justice in the courts. Perhaps the Lord God Almighty will have mercy on the remnant of Joseph.*" With this last declaration, the prophet sagged as if exhausted by the effort of his speech.

Another man, a merchant, strode up to the prophet, placing a hand on his muscular shoulder. "Amos, it is good to see you. We were

42

worried for your safety after Amaziah of Bethel ordered you to stop prophesying. King Jeroboam will likely arrest you if you return to Israel. Stay here in Judah where it is safe."

"Thank you for your concern, my brother, but I cannot stop prophesying where I am called any more than I can stop my heart from beating."

"I see. And what did you say to Amaziah in response to his challenge?"

"The challenge to stop prophesying?" Amos laughed, golden eyes squinting. "I told him that *I was neither a prophet nor the son of a prophet, but I was a shepherd, and I also took care of sycamore fig trees. But the Lord took me from tending the flock and said to me, 'Go prophesy to My people Israel.'*" His voice was tinged with awe.

"So, you will not stay here?"

"I must prophesy to God's people, in Israel, though also here in my hometown. *I saw the Lord standing by the alter, and He said: 'Did I not bring Israel up from Egypt? Surely the eyes of the Sovereign Lord are on the sinful kingdom. I will destroy it from the face of the earth. Yet I will not totally destroy the descendants of Jacob,' declares the Lord. 'In that day I will restore David's fallen shelter, I will repair its broken walls and restore its ruins, and will rebuild it as it used to be.'*" Once again, Amos finished and sank wearily onto the stones.

Jonah watched in fascination. "You are Amos the prophet? My family has heard of you before, but I thought you stayed in Israel."

"Yes, I am Amos. And you are Jonah ben Amittai, if I am not mistaken."

Jonah took a step back, suddenly suspicious. "How do you know my name?"

"The message which Yahweh gave to me extends to you as well. 'Go prophesy to My people, Israel.' You have been called; you have been chosen."

"But I've just become a man."

"Yes, but Yahweh does not see you as your age. Yahweh wants you to be His prophet, to speak His word to Israel and maybe even to other nations, other peoples."

"Well, as long as I don't have to prophesy to Assyria." Jonah had meant that as a halfhearted joke, but Amos answered him seriously, his patient eyes harboring no dishonesty.

"You just might have to."

"I have the choice of where I go and do not go."

The prophet did not reply. Instead, Amos patted Jonah's shoulder and then disappeared into the crowd.

Chapter Six

The moon's soft glow flickered between the close-knit branches of the trees. Jonah leaned his back against a trunk, closing his eyes in thought. The night air did him good, helping him to relax after a long hard day. At the age of thirty-seven, it was hard for Jonah to say if field-work had become more or less difficult with the passing of time. The rows of wheat rustled softly nearby. Harvest time was nearing, and soon they would reap, be paid, and have a merry celebration. Anan would be returning from Samaria, and the household would enjoy his jovial company a while before he headed off again, this time, for Moab.

Always on the move Anan was, even more than his father. As a farmer, Jonah was well rooted in Tekoa. He couldn't leave even if he had wanted to, and he did not. Each morning, the sun rose brightly just for him, and the sky was a brilliant blue. Even when it was not, the clouds seemed to wave as the wind rustled the neat rows of date palms. Working beside Caleb and his father, Jonah could think of no better life.

Yet the pain of losing his beloved sister refused to leave. It had dulled to an ache for a while, then dissolved, at least for the most part. There were moments when he heard a certain sound and he turned, ready to see her striding up the road, her hands on her hips and a reprimand on her lips. He rubbed his coal black beard with a callused hand. Zillah's soft voice singing a distant melody drifted through his mind. With a pang, he realized just how much time had passed. In fact, she probably wouldn't even recognize him. He had a full beard, muscular build, and height to rival his brother's. "It is hard enough to put meat on your bones when you eat full portions." The memory of his sister's words, sharp as if it had been only moments ago, struck Jonah like an unexpected blow. He needed relief.

Pushing himself to his feet, Jonah stumbled off in the direction of the well, a small community source that awarded cool, clean water. As he neared, he heard the soft rubbing of the ropes being pulled upward. He slowed his steps, trying to keep the crunching of his sandals on the ground to a minimum. No one should have been up at this hour, especially not hauling water. Soon he could see the dim outline of a small figure pulling and straining at the ropes. A few moments later, Jonah could identify the figure of a small boy. The boy was very short, with short blond hair, and sunburned skin. Every bone of his body seemed to poke out like sticks in a goatskin. Jonah had never seen the boy before, and when he noticed the heavy sack strapped to the wiry shoulders, he supposed the boy was traveling.

"Do you need any help?" Jonah lowered his voice, keeping it soft.

The boy turned sharply to face his addresser. His hands moved to his thigh, reaching for a dagger most likely. Jonah took a step back, preparing to speak, but things happened far too quickly. The bucket, full of water, pulled the rope back down into the well with a deafening zip that ended in a splash. The sound startled the boy so that he jumped. At the same time, his hand was clasped on the dagger's hilt and he brought it up in one quick motion, unaware that as his arm came back the blade came with it.

"No! Stop!" Jonah raced forward.

The boy stumbled away from him, tripped over a stone, and began to fall backward. Time slowed to a crawl as Jonah reached out his arm to grab the knife away. He missed by a hairsbreadth, the keen edge brushing his calluses. He stepped forward to balance himself, extending his arms out like an overweight bird trying to become airborne. Just then, an earsplitting scream cut through the night.

"You shouldn't have scared him, sir. Or he wouldn't't've injured himself." Lydia, the closest thing to a physician in the area, bent over the unmoving form. "He's lost a lot of blood." She lifted a strip of linen from a basket on a shelf, placing it near the marred shoulder.

"How bad is it, Lydia?" Jonah paced behind her, trying to keep his frayed nerves intact.

"At best, his arm may always be weak." She stopped and looked down at the boy. "But I think it will heal."

"At worst?"

"I may have to remove the arm, but of course, that is worst case. That will only be necessary if it becomes infected."

Jonah turned his back to her, heading toward the back window of the small home. Resting his palms on the ledge, he shook his head. "You are right, Lydia. I shouldn't have scared him. I should have left him alone."

"Abigail!" the boy cried abruptly. The voice, thin yet desperate startled them both.

"Lie still, boy. I need to clean your arm." Lydia stroked the small forehead. Reaching over into another basket, she retrieved a small jar. She placed a cloth over the jar's mouth and tipped it upside down for a moment. Then she took the cloth and held it under the boy's nose. Jonah watched the frail body grow limp. The boy was soon fast asleep.

"Are you certain it will heal?"

"Yes," she replied, confidently.

Jonah glanced at the bloodied fabric clinging to the boy's arm and winced. As if she saw his doubt, Lydia turned to fully face him. "The blade entered with a great deal of force, but it was also very sharp, so the wound is fairly clean. It almost went the full length of the blade, right in the middle of his arm too. It looks as if he turned and the blade twisted. The injury's across from his heart, right here." She pointed to a spot about six inches below the top of the bloody shoulder. "Nonetheless, he will recover, as long as the wound is kept clean." She sighed at Jonah's deepening frown. "You should go home and wait, sir. I will send someone to fetch you when the boy wakes up."

Jonah nodded dumbly and stumbled outside. For a moment, he stood in the dark stillness, unsure of what to do. Moving slowly to the side of the house, he peered in the window. After one glance at Lydia bent low over the boy's shoulder, red stained cloth in hand, he took off, running full out toward Jonathan's house. The sound of his sandals slapping hard against the dirt, his tunic flapping behind him, his labored breaths, and the hammering of blood through his brain filled his ears. His heart pounded so that he could feel the movement in his chest. Suddenly, Jonah halted.

He was back years ago. In his mind, he was once again running through the fields after hearing that his sister was indeed dead. He had eventually fainted from exertion on someone's doorstep. The kind stranger had taken him inside and laid him in his own bed.

The following morning, the man had asked around and eventually discovered that Caleb, Amittai, and Anan had been searching for a boy meeting Jonah's description. The man had deposited Jonah at his own house in the early afternoon. There he had stayed, curled in a corner until the other three occupants returned from their searching. Caleb had been especially upset, but nothing said or done could make Jonah acknowledge any of them. It had remained that way for several days until hunger had made Jonah rejoin the world he had been trying to leave.

But the most vivid memory of that day was his vow to avenge the death of his sister. Even now, years later, he still tried to escape from the dull ache of loss, retreating in his mind to an empty, blank void. In the void, there was nothing but silence and peace, but the silence was deafening and the peace, temporary. He had begun to run again, still deep in thought. His feet retraced the familiar path from the area near the well back to his house. His house—Jonathan had opened his home to all three of them, never asking for anything in return, though Amittai had insisted on paying him a small portion of what he made for simply staying in the house. Even that had not lasted long, and soon all five of them were living as one family.

"Jonah?"

Caleb's sunny voice crashed through Jonah's thoughts. It took him a moment to realize he had entered the house without awareness of opening the door or stepping from dirt to stone. Footsteps echoed as Caleb descended the stairs. He stopped short when he saw his brother, standing slump-shouldered in the middle of the main room.

"What's wrong?" Caleb demanded.

Jonah stared past his brother into empty space.

"Caleb? Is Jonah finally back?" Amittai came down, drawing up just behind Caleb. "Oh no."

Jonathan, overhearing, pushed past them on the stairs. "It's not Anan, is it?"

"Anan?" Jonah shook himself. He had to gain control before they all panicked on him. "No, no it's not Anan." He broke off again, staring into nothing.

"He is clearly very upset about something." Caleb turned to head back up the stairs. "Best to leave him alone. There will be no convincing him to talk when he is like this."

Three thuds repeated each other as six feet ascended the stairs. Jonah hardly noticed. He was thinking about the boy and what he could do to help him. Surely there was something. Anan...Anan. The name rang in his mind. Anan was adopted. He shook his head. He could never be a father. Besides, the boy deserved two parents. Jonah knew what it was like not to have a mother. If he adopted the boy, he would be taking away the possibility. A soft knock made him whirl. He swung the door open so hard it went as far as it could go and made a crash like thunder, shaking the house. A servant stood wide-eyed in the doorway.

"Lydia sent me to—"

He broke off when Jonah shoved him aside, running back toward the well and the home just beyond it. He knew what he would do. He would ask the boy what he wanted. And if the boy already had a family, then what? But something in Jonah knew that the boy had no one in the world that cared about him. What sort of child walked with a sack on his back to nowhere? The kind of child that he had once been.

The boy was sitting up when Jonah entered. He lay back against a pile of cushions, eyes closed. Lydia sat nearby in a chair, watching the figure pensively. When she saw Jonah, she stood. "He hasn't said a word since I woke him, but he's fully awake and his mind seems clear."

Jonah nodded. He crossed the room to the bedside, his eyes riveted on the white cloth blotched with red that covered the boy's wound. "What is your name?" He spoke the words slowly, unsure if the boy was in shock. The eyes opened, revealing two enormous amber spheres.

"Benjamin." He blinked several times, then stared at Jonah—assessing. "You're the one who was chasing me." Benjamin's breaths came in labored gulps. He seemed utterly exhausted.

"Benjamin, I was not chasing you. I was just..." Jonah waved his hand helplessly in the air, unsure of what he had intended to do. "I was just wondering why a young boy like you was drawing water in the middle of the night."

"Why was a man like you lurking in the trees in the middle of the night?" The question, innocently placed, had no answer.

"Isn't there someone waiting for you somewhere, Benjamin? Do you have any family?"

"Do you?"

"I have a brother and my father lives with us."

"No mother?"

"No, she died. Do you have a mother?"

"What was she like?"

Sensing Benjamin's attempt at a one-sided conversation, Jonah asked again, "Do you have a mother, Benjamin?"

"No."

"A father?"

"No."

"A..."

"Don't you get it?" Benjamin shot to his feet, his body trembling with rage. "No father, no mother, no brothers, no sisters..." He halted. In his eyes, Jonah recognized the same empty gaze that had often filled his own. "At least, not anymore," the boy finished.

"Abigail?" Jonah remembered the name.

"Yes."

Lydia hurried over and fussed over Benjamin, insisting that he lay back down.

He struggled weakly. "I can do it. It's not like I'm paralyzed or anything. It's only a knife injury." His dry and flat tone put barely recognized emphasis on the *only*. The shriveled humor reminded Jonah of himself. He recalled a time when he had overheard Zillah talking to his father: *"Jonah is just Jonah, Abba. There's nothing to be done about it."* It was true. He had never been lighthearted like Caleb or witty like Anan. He was simply Jonah, and he had to be Jonah.

"I lost a sister too," Jonah said. The boy met the disclosure with silence. "Her name was Zillah. After Ima died, she was like a mother to me. When the Assyrians came—" Jonah fought to press down his welling grief. "Through the confusion, I only saw her and Abba go down. I never knew what happened until quite some time later."

Benjamin, his eyes staring at nothing, continued for him. "When you found out, you felt guilty, even though there was nothing that could have been done." Jonah gazed at the boy, seeing him in a new light.

"It must be hard." Jonah said, though it seemed a stupid statement to make. The boy had no one and nothing, of course it was hard.

Benjamin was straining to remain focused on Jonah, and was puffing like a pack-mule, his body rigid against the bed linens. Lifting himself onto one elbow, he spoke distantly, "The very one I had relied on for so long was gone, and there was no way to bring her back."

"You'd best get some rest," Lydia soothed, bent low over the dying flames of the fire. She poked them with quick sharp thrusts before adding more wood. Sparks flew as she did this and their reflection glimmered in Benjamin's eyes.

"I don't need to rest." The statement seemed to rejuvenate Benjamin. He pushed himself into a sitting position and locked his gaze on Jonah. "You think you are so much like me, don't you?" he accused, his amber eyes glowing with anger.

"Well, we have both lost a sister and mother and—"

"I have shed no tears over my mother."

Jonah could not stop his quick inhalation of surprise. "Why not?"

"She was considering an apprenticeship for me so she didn't have to pay for my food anymore."

"You cannot know that was her motivation."

"I heard her say those very words herself." Benjamin lifted his chin in defiance.

"At least you had one. What happened to her?"

"She sent me to be apprenticed, and I finished it. When I came back, she was gone. Abigail said she up and left one night, took all the money and everything."

"But she is still alive."

"She would want me to consider her dead. She could have cared less about Abigail and the rest of us. All she cared about was money. Abba couldn't give her the amount she wanted, so she convinced him to divorce her. Then she married somebody else, someone rich."

"So, your father is still alive too?"

"No, the divorce never happened. He had a riding accident on his way home last year. My mother couldn't wait for her mourning to end."

"I am sorry. What happened to Abigail?"

"Why should I tell you?"

"Because I told you about my sister. And believe me, it wasn't easy."

Benjamin pondered the words a moment, then nodded. "I had two sisters and four brothers. Only Abigail was older than me."

Jonah glanced over at the boy, curious. "How old are you?"

"My apprenticeship only lasted three years, I hated it, and my master knew it. I doubt either of us could have lasted a fourth year. I started when I became a man, when I was twelve. It has been a year since so figure it out."

"You're sixteen?" Jonah could not believe it. The boy before him was much too small to be a man.

"After my mother abandoned us, we all left for Jerusalem, hoping that we could find a job in such a big city. My youngest sister and brothers did not survive the journey. Abigail and I managed to reach the city, but she caught the fever soon after arriving. I have been traveling ever since." Benjamin looked down at his hand resting in his lap. When he lifted his gaze, his eyes sparkled with moisture. "My sister's name was Ruth and my brothers' were Abiram, Nathan, Oded, and Jonah. All five of them, six including Abigail, died."

"Your brother's name was Jonah?"

"Yes. Why?" It was only then that Jonah realized he had failed to mention his own name.

"My name is Jonah."

Benjamin met his gaze. "You do not seem anything like him."

"Perhaps that is good."

The boy nodded, then yawned. Despite all his determination, it was obvious he needed to rest.

Jonah looked deep into the amber eyes, taking a deep breath and searching for the right words. "I am going to go home soon, but first I need to ask you something. You have no family, and it is obvious that you are simply wandering around."

"I don't wander..."

"Let me finish. You have no family. Would you like one?"

"I do not need charitable adoption or pity."

Jonah straightened to head for the door. What he said next was laced with anger, though mostly at himself. "Well the least you can do is let me take care of you after the accident that I caused."

"To ease your guilt is that right? You are such a pity-party."

Jonah wheeled to face the boy. "If you had been through what I have been through, you would be a pity-party too!"

Lydia moved to try and calm him, but he ignored her.

Benjamin snorted in disdain. "What you have been through is no different than my trials. And you still have family, you have a home, you have a life! What else do you want?"

"I want the Assyrians to pay for the damage they've caused!"

They were both shouting now. Lydia had given up on trying to quiet the waters and sat huddled in her chair.

Benjamin's eyes smoldered. "You have to stop living in the past and learn to live with it! You've still got a future, unlike me. I'll bet you have a fine job, a fine family, good friends. So, stop your whining."

"That's it. You clearly do not need my help, and I no longer want to help you either." Jonah balled his hands into fists and stomped toward the door. There he halted, frustrated with himself for acting like a two-year-old, wishing for his brother's patient disposition.

Benjamin took his hesitation for something else. "Don't worry about me. Go on and get out of here! But keep this in mind, Jonah!" Benjamin waited until Jonah turned to face him. "You have a brother." His voice was low, calmer now, yet still hard. "You have a father too. But if you waste away your life puttering around like a storm cloud and living in the past, it will be as if you lost them too. So, do not take them for granted. If you do, it will be too late when you finally realize how foolish you were. Be thankful for what you have and stop being so bent on taking revenge for what you've lost!" The door slammed shut on his last word.

Jonah stormed down the path, blinded by rage. The audacity of such a child to accuse him of being ungrateful.

"Jonah, get back in there."

Jonah froze. "Caleb, what are you doing here?" He heard footsteps, and a moment later, his brother stood before him, blocking the path.

Caleb pointed at the house. "Get back in there and talk to the boy."

"Since when do you tell me what to do? I have been a man for years now, you have no right to control me."

"Stop acting so childish, Jonah. I speak to you as your brother because you yourself are not seeing clearly. That boy needs you, and you need him."

Jonah met his brother's gaze, his anger barely controlled. "I can see well enough. He doesn't need me, and I certainly don't need him."

"Actually, you do." Caleb took a deep breath, his tone pleading for Jonah to be reasonable. "Do you realize what a perfect match you are? How much you need someone like Benjamin that shares your hurts? How much he needs someone like you to guide him? Do you realize how dark and hateful you have been since that year? Do you have any idea how it has affected Abba or me?"

"Look, I know I have been a little irritable lately. And I'm sorry if I have shut you out, but can't you see that there is nothing I can do for Benjamin?"

"All he needs are some caring people in his life and a roof over his head."

"He can find that elsewhere."

"Maybe, but he cannot easily find someone who has been through the same things he has."

"And why do I need him?"

"Because you are both broken for the same reasons. You could heal together once you become a little less animus. Besides, the boy has nowhere else to go, does he?"

"I'll think about it." Jonah tried to push past his brother, but Caleb wouldn't budge.

"No, Jonah, you need to get back in there and talk to him, or else you'll both let your anger fester all night, and there will be no hope for reconciliation tomorrow."

Since Caleb wouldn't move, Jonah stepped around him and flounced down the road toward home. Caleb stared after him with the slightest trace of a smile. There was no doubt in his mind that Jonah would be back. His little brother could not resist a challenge.

"What are you doing back here?" Benjamin glared at the figure in Lydia's doorway.

"I was wondering if you had reconsidered my offer." Jonah leaned his shoulder against the doorjamb. He had tossed and turned all night with his brother's words floating through his mind. In the morning, his conscience had prodded him until he finally relented.

"I didn't think the offer still stood."

"I was unsure as well, but it does." Jonah entered the room during the momentary pause. It was clear that the boy wanted to accept. His eyes glistened with tears, and it was plain to see that, for all his words of denial, he was touched.

Looking away, the boy rubbed his shoulder and Jonah thought for a moment that he would refuse because of the accident. In the end, the boy turned his gaze back to Jonah. "I will consider your offer."

It was the sort of moment that Jonah supposed he would later consider to be a turning point in his life, but for the moment, he was unsure what to think. Was Benjamin really a good match for him? Would they actually help each other once they got to know one another better?

"I will give you time to think." Jonah tried to keep his tone flat and unreadable, wary of showing either excitement or lack thereof. He turned without another word and calmly left the house, though his mind raged in turmoil.

Chapter Seven

Jonah bent low over the ground, sickle in hand. The winter's crop of wheat was finally ripe, and the workers had gathered to reap and then sow. Benjamin was two rows to his right and had been working twice as fast since dawn that morning. In another hour or so, he would pass Jonah and move to a different part of the field. The boy was incredible for being as thin as he was and with an arm that was still not quite strong enough to do heavy labor. He could cut with one arm, lay down his sickle, tie the bundle, pick up his sickle, and work faster than half of the other laborers that were twice his size. At the age of nineteen, Benjamin was still as thin as a reed and had grown only a few inches taller. Jonah however, could not have been more blessed than to have him has a member of the family.

Just as Caleb had predicted, Benjamin and Jonah were a match made by Yahweh Himself. Caleb's lovely wife agreed. Amittai had been overjoyed to see his eldest married. Atarah was certainly a good match for his brother, and though they all got along just fine, Jonah found every excuse he could to keep away from her. Now that they had a little one running around, she kept at home quite a bit, but she occasionally chose to visit Tekoa, making the short journey from Aczib where she and Caleb lived.

Aczib was another choice Jonah would never have made, but

Caleb had his reasons. The town rested comfortably in the Shephelah and crops grew well there. Atarah absolutely adored her home, and Jonah wished she would stay there permanently. Caleb seemed to understand Jonah's dislike of Atarah, but Jonah could never truly explain why. She was very pretty, he had to admit. Her dark brown hair set off her dark blue eyes, and her tanned skin was smooth and coppery. But her energy made him want to sit down anytime he was in the same room as her. She talked like even Anan rarely did, jabbering on about the goings on in her town and the latest news from Israel. Outgoing was a word that barely scratched the surface of her jubilance, and it always bothered Jonah.

Worse than the constant forced conversation and worse than her overly enthusiastic, extremely optimistic view on the entire world was her unexplainable and unshakable faith in Yahweh. She could always find a way to turn even the darkest things and show the light of Yahweh in them. She called Benjamin's accident a blessing that had brought him to Jonah. She called Jonah and Caleb's trials a test of faith that had built their character. Overall, she positively bugged him like an unrelenting fly.

Amittai would have also liked to see Jonah happily married, but Jonah wouldn't even consider the notion. He was happy where he was, yet he was careful to hide the real reason—that if he got close to anyone they would die or be severely injured...like his mother, and his sister, and Benjamin. He felt incurably cursed.

Sweat drenched his tunic and the faint breeze that caressed his skin felt lukewarm. Time passed, and Jonah was still deep in thought, darkly ruminating about his life, the past, the present, and the completely unpredictable future. It took him quite some time to hear the small shofar horn that announced that the day's work was at its end. Amittai was the last to reach home, Benjamin, the first.

Haggith was fussing over the boy's sunburned skin when Jonah entered. "A long day of work, sir, does your skin no good," the servant chided him.

Benjamin, who had long since given up arguing, murmured.
"I am sure, Haggith."
"And you, Master Jonah." She turned her accusing green eyes on the newest arrival. "A man has been looking all over town for you. Of

course, I told him you weren't home and to wait a while for you to return. He is in the neighbor's barn right now. If you want me to have him beaten and thrown out of town, let me know and it will be done right away."

Jonah's eyebrows lifted in surprise, partially from the announcement and partially from the fact Benjamin could hardly contain his mirth.

His son mouthed the words, "She hasn't stopped talking about it."

"I think that a beating can wait, Haggith. I will go and see what he wants." Jonah stepped back through the doorway and headed down the path to the nearest and only barn. Dusk had settled, and the sun's blaze had softened to an aura of warmth and tranquility. Because of this, it seemed strange to Jonah when a sudden brightness hit his eyes.

"Jonah."

He fell to his knees as the light touched him with incredible power, yet as gently as a breeze. In his mind's eye he thought he could see winds picking up the dust around him, swirling it into an impenetrable cloud—a protective one. The voice rang in his mind and enveloped him. He wished the feeling could last forever.

"Jonah," it called, sweetly and softly, like an embrace.

"Yahweh," Jonah whispered, barely able to move his lips. He felt paralyzed by the magnitude of love that seemed to sweep him along, like a river, a current so powerful he had neither the ability nor the will to fight it.

"Jonah, *go to the great city of Nineveh and preach against it, because its wickedness has come up before me.*" And then, as soon as it had come, the light was gone. The warmth and love Jonah had been basking in a moment before disappeared. He stared blankly at his feet, feeling stripped and empty.

"Yahweh!" Jonah stood, looking around at the familiar trees and the solid ground that surrounded him. He fell to his knees again, his body trembling as if he had the fever, tears streamed down his face. Yahweh, the God of his nation, the God of his father had spoken to him. Had called him.

Jonah opened his eyes, and he reeled a moment upon seeing Amos standing before him, a smile lighting up his typically impassive features.

His beard and hair were flecked with gray, and the wrinkles on his face were more pronounced, but overall, he looked the same.

"Amos, what are you doing here?" Jonah's tone held no hostility, only pleasure. He had hoped to see the old prophet again someday.

"I intended to visit you at your home and speak with you, but I had a complication." Amos laughed a moment then continued, "I have come to confirm Yahweh's call for you to act. He has seen the wickedness of the Assyrians in Nineveh. He desires to see what is in their hearts—if they will repent or if they are truly corrupt."

"Yahweh wants them to live? To repent?" Surely, Yahweh simply meant for him to merely warn the Ninevites about their impending and unavoidable destruction.

"Yahweh loves all people, Jonah, but as for Assyria, He has and will use them as an instrument of judgment, but there will also come a time when they too will be judged." Amos's quiet eyes dulled a shade with an emotion Jonah could not place. "I cannot say for sure if this is the time or not."

Jonah could not imagine why Yahweh would even consider relenting His wrath against the Assyrians, but at the moment, he needed to digest this information on his own. "Will you join us for the evening meal?"

"I would be honored."

They enjoyed pleasant conversation for the short walk back. Jonah told Amos about Benjamin, about his past with Anan, and his first vision when he was young—although always excluding his lack of faith and bitter attitude toward God. When they entered the house, there was no more time for talk as Jonathan and Amittai bombarded the prophet with greetings and questions. Jonah had told them a little about Amos's prophecy in the Tekoa's market square, and of course, they wanted to know all about his reasons for coming.

In his understanding way, Amos had told them about Jonah's call to prophesy excluding any details, and said that he had merely come to confirm it. He did this so eloquently that they seemed satisfied. The evening passed smoothly and the conversation was pleasant, yet if anyone had paid close attention, they would have noticed that Jonah had a peculiar tension about him. As it was, they simply invited Amos to stay the night, and each of them rolled out their sleeping mats, but not all of them slept.

Jonah tossed and turned as the moon slipped silently across the sky. He thought of his visions, the one years ago and the one that very day. He pondered Amos's interpretation of Yahweh's intentions and His willingness to forgive if the Assyrian's repented. Jonah was certainly willing to prophesy to the Assyrians if he knew they would be annihilated, but suppose they were not? What if they repented, and Yahweh showed mercy and kindness? Could God forgive a people such as the Assyrians? Jonah knew the answer, though he refused to admit it to himself. If he prophesied to Nineveh, they would repent, and he knew Amos would agree with him, and Amos knew the ways of Yahweh much better than he did. If the Ninevites repented and returned to God, Jonah knew they would be spared. He simply could not afford to allow that to happen.

The following morning, Amos left with many hearty farewells and a sack of supplies sent with him for his journey along with gifts of money and small trinkets, which had been practically forced upon the humble prophet. He had said very little to Jonah in the presence of the others, yet he had cast the occasional glance his way, with knowing eyes.

"It is a blessing that your son has been called to be of service to Yahweh," Amos had stated during the morning meal. Amittai had agreed whole-heartedly, though Jonah sensed that the words had been more for him than for his father. With the words of both Amos and Yahweh following him around that day, Jonah planned what he would do.

Amittai and Jonathan expected him to leave immediately to begin his commission, though they did not know where he was bound for—and perhaps they assumed that no one did. Jonah knew he would have to leave, and perhaps it would be good as well. He could settle the matter of Yahweh while aboard a ship to another part of the world. Yahweh would have to prove Himself. If He really wanted to force Jonah to act, He would truly have to force him. Jonah would never, in all the years of his life, prophesy to Assyria at the risk of their repentance and God's unrelenting grace and forgiveness. Jonah had seen the hand of God in his own life. He knew it was only because of Yahweh that he had ever escaped from the Assyrians, and only by His intervention that he had met Anan and now had a good home, family and job. He knew that it was Yahweh that gave his life purpose, and meaning.

He was a prophet; he had been called. But this one duty, his first, he would have to refuse. He was not safe in Judah. If his brother found out through Amos or eventually wiggled the information out of him, Caleb would and could literally pick him up and carry him to Nineveh. Jonah couldn't afford to allow that to happen. He had to leave as soon as possible. It was because of his determination and readiness that his entire day's hopes and ideas were shattered when a messenger came, sent by Haggith most likely, to inform them that Caleb, Atarah and their little one were at the house and waiting.

Jonah, Amittai, and Benjamin barely had time to wash up after work before they were practically attacked by the curious little fellow with enough questions to exhaust even the most verbose individual. Atarah was not far behind with her jubilance and prattling. It was somewhat of a relief to Jonah that Benjamin disliked it as much as he did, though likely for different reasons. It made him feel less callous.

"Uncle Jonah." Elon, the spitting image of Atarah and her bothersome personality, tugged on Jonah's tunic, trying to get his attention.

"Yes, Elon?" Jonah gave him a smile that lacked any amount of cheer.

"If you are Abba's brother, why don't you get sunburned when you're outside too long?" The question stung. Jonah smiled again, though he was certain he looked more like a wolf at that point.

"Well, Elon, my mother didn't sunburn when she was outside, so I suppose I got it from her."

"Oh." The boy rubbed his chin a moment. "Uncle Jonah?"

"Yes?"

"I asked why the sky turned pink before nighttime and Simeon told me it was because Yahweh ate little children and spread their blood along the sky. Is that true, Uncle Jonah?"

"No, Elon." Jonah smiled more genuinely. "Yahweh doesn't eat little children. You cannot believe everything your friend Simeon says."

"Then why does the sky turn pink?"

"I'm not completely sure."

"Oh. Uncle Jonah?"

Jonah considered turning around and stalking off, but he turned tolerantly toward his nephew. "How can I help you?"

"Ima wants me to make my bed every morning, Uncle Jonah. Even on the Sabbath. Is that lawful, Uncle Jonah?"

Jonah chuckled. He could easily see the true purpose of the conversation. "You would have to ask your Abba. He probably knows more than I do."

"Oh, alright...Can I ask another question, Uncle Jonah?"

"Sure, but it will cost you five shekels." Jonah mumbled, wishing that Elon would pester Benjamin instead. The boy looked up at his uncle, his brow creased with confusion. Jonah sighed. Even with Caleb and Atarah as parents, Elon didn't understand humor yet. "Go ahead and ask your question."

"If Yahweh is so good, why doesn't He make everyone good too?"

Jonah sighed again and adopted the same statement his father often used: "How would I know the ways of Yahweh?" It didn't work.

"You can guess."

"Why don't you ask your Abba?"

"You don't know, do you?"

"Not really, Elon. I would have to think about it, long and hard."

When the boy finally wandered off, Jonah decided it would be safer not to be alone. Atarah's shrill laughter almost made him change his mind. She had a whoop that seemed a mixture of a war cry and a jackal in pain. With a sigh of resignation, he pushed open the door and stepped inside. Benjamin had apparently managed to escape and was nowhere to be found. Jonah realized that he was less likely to be so fortunate.

"Jonah!" Atarah leapt up from her seat and hugged her brother-in-law fiercely. "You have become even tanner since I last saw you. Surely Bithiah has taken notice as well."

Another good reason to leave, Jonah thought to himself. Ever since Atarah had married Caleb, she had been determined to match Jonah to her sister Bithiah. In truth, Bithiah was fair and lovely, though she was so much the mirror of her sister that Jonah often wondered how their parents had ever managed. Caleb's father and mother-in-law were quiet, reserved, and humble.

"No, I do not think she has, Atarah."

"Well she has not had the chance to see you in such a long time. It is no wonder!" She was now hopping up and down with excitement, her hands clasped firmly together with delight. "We shall set the two of you up to go and visit the market together." After making her declaration, she continued to stand before Jonah, fairly vibrating with energy.

"Well, Atarah, I'm not so sure..."

"Nonsense. Bithiah told me herself you were a 'noble figure.'"

"I think Jonah would prefer to avoid such interactions, Atarah," Caleb, lounging on a cushion in the corner of the room, remarked. He was clearly amused with his brother's discomfort.

"And why is that?" Atarah trotted over and plopped herself down beside her husband. "Jonah is already forty. In a few more years, he will simply be too old and..."

"Atarah, I do not think he ever intends to marry."

"Oh, I see." She paused a moment, considering. She seemed to take the topic and set it into a "for later" section of her mind before beginning on a new topic altogether. "How is your work faring, Jonah?"

"It is going very smoothly. We are nearly done reaping the grain."

"Caleb is almost done as well. I have been gathering and sorting melon seeds for this summer. Elon has been ecstatic over the prospect. Aren't you, Elon?" She raised her voice to reach the figure peering around the doorframe.

"Yes, Ima, I love melons."

Jonah coughed lightly, seeing his chance to escape. Stepping out of the door, he glanced at the sky as if trying to estimate the time. "Oh, I'm sorry. I have somewhere to be."

"My little brother has an appointment in the middle of the day?" Caleb teased. "Where are you off to then?" Jonah glanced around to make sure Benjamin was not nearby.

"Benjamin has been wanting to own a box of ivory. Don't ask me why, but it has been his heart's desire for a while now. I intend to ride down to Joppa where they have the foreign trade and find one for him. He will be turning twenty soon and perhaps it would be a good gift."

"All the way to Joppa?" Atarah stood, her hands gesturing in confusion. "But it is so far, Jonah. Almost fifty miles. And what about your commission?" Amittai had clearly told them the news.

"On horseback, it should only take a couple of days there and another couple back. And besides, I think it would be worth it.

63

Benjamin deserves something nice every once in a while for putting up with me. I can start my work as soon as I am back." Jonah smiled, he felt confident that he had his brother's approval. He turned and headed upstairs, lifting his chin a fraction as his confidence grew.

Removing a sheet of parchment, he cut off a small bit and wrote a quick note. Tucking this into his tunic he headed back down to where the food was stored. Haggith, though irritable and pessimistic, was very particular about having things organized. She kept each day's flour in a separate, pre-measured bag. That way all she had to do was pour it out, put water in it and some spices, knead it, and then bake it. And so she also knew when they were low on flour and how many more days' worth they had.

Counting three bags, he carefully untied the third and placed the note inside, then he tied it back and headed back upstairs. He could not bring too much with him without arousing suspicion, and he was at the mercy of whether or not Caleb mentioned his trip to Benjamin. He figured his brother would assume it was a surprise and keep quiet, but he still had to hurry. He snatched up two fresh tunics and shoved them into a bag, then he added all his personal savings before tromping downstairs again. Walking over to a shelf, he removed an empty goatskin and filled it with water from a jug. He added to his bag some dried fruit, dried meat, and leftover bread.

He called a hasty farewell to his father and brother, informing them that he would be back in a few days. Though he knew it could be months or even years before they saw him again. How could he know what happened to those who deliberately ran from God? The nearest keeper of horses, Zedekiah, was out behind his home sifting grain. The chaff fell easily through the woven screen and the kernels bounced with vigor as he shook them.

"Shalom." Jonah greeted him.

Zedekiah straightened, a broad smile working its way across his face. He was built much like the horses he owned, stocky, muscular, and hard-working. "Jonah ben Amittai, I haven't seen you around in ages."

"Nor I you. I fear I am in a bit of a rush. I was hoping that you could loan me one of your horses for a day or two."

"A horse? of course. In fact, you can take one for free as long as he's back before the Sabbath."

"That is very generous, but quite unnecessary."

"Nonsense." The man waved a large calloused hand. "Abiel needs the exercise. I have been too busy reaping my grain to take him out much. You would be doing me a favor. Where are you off to?"

"Down to Joppa. I will be sending him back."

"Of course. That's just fine." He set down his screen with care and led the way into the barn. Three nickers and a whinny met them as they stepped inside. "I have two mares and two stallions," Zedekiah announced proudly. "And one of my mares is pregnant. Her foal is expected in another two or so months."

"Will you keep the foal?"

"Perhaps. It depends if it is black or not." He laughed at the expression of bewilderment on Jonah's face. "My daughter Rachel has been determined to own a black horse. 'It can have a little white, Abba,' she told me, 'but only a little.'" He continued to chuckle as he proceeded down the alley between the stalls. "Ah, here's Abiel." He gestured to a tall, handsome stallion with a coat the color of sand. "He is docile as a lamb, but he loves to run. Though I have to warn you that he is currently out of shape." Zedekiah retrieved a rope bridle with a rawhide bit and snatched up a leather saddle. Abiel hardly seemed to care at all as he swung the saddle lightly onto his back, tightened the attached girth, and put on the bridle. "Now just watch that he doesn't get too fast on you. He hasn't traveled enough distance to know how to pace himself."

"I cannot thank you enough."

"Oh it is no problem, just please have him back by the Sabbath."

"Absolutely. Shalom."

"Shalom, my friend." Jonah used the stall's railing to mount Abiel, and his bag held to his back by two cords swung as he did so. He turned the stallion out toward the open road and urged him into a gentle canter.

Chapter Eight

Dust swirled up around Jonah. Abiel's hooves thundered and echoed through the air. The rolling, rocking and soothing gait made Jonah feel weary. His back ached from holding the bag, and his stomach grumbled from the careful rationing of his supplies. Abiel, however, seemed to be having a splendid time. His ears perked forward, and his eyes twinkled jovially. For his supposed lack of stamina, he did quite well for his second day on the move. Jonah hoped to arrive in Joppa that very evening. He and Abiel could then get a good night's rest before parting ways the following morning—Jonah to Tarshish and Abiel back to Zedekiah.

The stallion seemed to sense the urgency and increased his speed, the gentle rocking slipping into a quickened roll. Jonah smiled despite himself as the wind roared past him and filled his heart with exuberance. Trees, shrubs, and buildings alike flew past in a blur of brown and green. The leather saddle was warm from his body and the gentle sun heating it throughout the day. Abiel's sandy coat shimmered like a mirage. Jonah's body rocked back and forth in a lulling motion, and he kept eyes focused intently between Abiel's ears. The slender shining neck came up toward him and then back down. The wind changed pitch as he rocked.

Not a soul in the world would have suspected anything amiss, yet there was. It was indeed a queer feeling of insecurity, of apprehension, and of lurking danger. Abiel snorted, his eyes rolled back and his muscles began pulling and straining.

They had stopped moving. At first, it had been an almost imperceptible slowing, which had soon become a slow and gentle halt. Jonah nudged gently with his legs, unsure of what the problem was. Abiel turned his head, the dark eyes casting a warning glance at his rider. Something was most definitely wrong.

Jonah glanced around. He saw no bandits or hostile travelers, no stalking lions, and no growling wolves. The wind breathed down on them gently, innocently. It was then that Jonah looked down and saw the cause of Abiel's panic. Of four hooves, none of them were visible. A mixture of gray and brown ooze had seeped up a quarter of the stallion's legs; its level steadily rising. They were caught in quicksand.

"Good boy, easy there," Jonah crooned. Abiel snorted again, his shoulder quivering. *Smart horse,* Jonah thought to himself. Quicksand was a danger that every traveler faced when traveling along the Great Sea's sandy coast. Of those who had encountered it, few had lived to tell the tale. Fortunately for Jonah, his father had been one of those surviving travelers. However, according to Amittai's recollection, his horse had been young and frightened. In the end, the horse had struggled so much that he could not even swim out of the quicksand. Amittai had managed to escape by some miracle, but regretted that he had been unable to save his mount.

Jonah determined to do both. He checked around, trying to define the edge of the pit. From what he could tell, the nearest edge was to his right. Reaching down with his foot, he tested the thickness of the sand. It was on the thick side, barely thin enough to swim in. He lifted the pack off his back and threw it over to the ledge where it landed with a thud. Sliding gently into the ooze, he held fast to the reigns and beckoned Abiel to swim with him.

The horse complied in a most docile manner, acting as if he were swimming in a muddy pond rather than in a pit of quicksand. Jonah, however, had difficulty keeping down his swell of panic as the sand seeped into his clothing and surrounded him. The smell of mud and salt was so overpowering that Jonah felt nauseated. The sand was half way up his neck, and he still had a short way to go. A moment passed, and the sand crept even higher up his neck, making odd sucking sounds as he fought against it. The ledge was a welcome sight, and he gently tested its thickness. It held. He pulled himself up and breathed in the fresh clean air around him. Pushing himself onto solid ground, he backed as far away as he could and gently tugged on the reigns.

Abiel continued his slow progress both forward and down. The sand now covered his back, though it was difficult to tell since both horse and quicksand were the same hue. Once at the ledge, Abiel began to hoist himself onto it. The crack that followed startled them both. A split, resembling a lightning bolt, shot along the crust toward Jonah. Moving cautiously to the side, he urged Abiel to try again. This time, he managed to get one hoof up, though the other punched through. Amazingly, the stallion, by putting all his strength into the effort, levered and wiggled his way onto the ledge. He walked cautiously up to Jonah, his hoof occasionally punching through the crust, but overall, holding both of their weight.

Jonah decided to take a more cautious route until he was sure they were clear of the quicksand. Looking down at his clothes, he laughed aloud. His tunic had turned from a light brown to simply a lighter brown. His skin, however, felt pasty. Looking over at Abiel, it was hard to tell any difference. The sand colored stallion tossed a sagging mane and dribbled mud all over both of them. He was so glad to be alive that he felt unreasonably giddy and knew that he eyes must have sparkled. Permitting a smile to spread on his face, Jonah bent to retrieve his sack before taking Abiel's bridle and gently leading him around the quicksand pit.

After a while, he realized there was no reason to guide the stallion since the horse followed as readily as a dog. Jonah smiled and strode on ahead, keeping a good ten feet between himself and his horse so that he could gauge where the crust was the thickest. Abiel understood the danger and followed Jonah's every turn—a most brilliant horse indeed. The sun dried their skin, coat, and clothes alike until they resembled stiff hedgehogs meandering around on an endless stretch of sand.

Up ahead, Jonah thought he could see some green dots on the horizon. He strained his eyes, trying to decide if what he saw was just a figure of his imagination or something much better. As he continued, his hopes soared higher and higher. The green dots were accompanied by little humps no bigger than a pinhead from where he gazed upon them.

Abiel began to fidget with excitement and, fearing losing his mount, Jonah dusted the dirt off the saddle and lifted his leg to place it into the stirrup. The long leather strap dangled tantalizingly close. He strained and tried pointing his toe, then flexing it. After some time, he managed to catch the strap with his foot and slip it into it. Then he seized the leather pommel and swung his free leg behind him, gaining the momentum that carried it up and over Abiel's back. Nonetheless, his leg was screaming by the time he settled himself in.

"I think I've pulled every muscle in my body trying to get on you, Abiel," Jonah muttered. The stallion angled a knowing glance at his rider. Jonah lifted the reins with a sigh and clucked. He was rewarded with a jarring trot before, finally, a gentle rolling canter. He was more cautious this time, forgoing his longing to enjoy the ride, and instead watched the ground ahead for any depressions or changes in hue, but he saw none.

They thundered into Joppa a few hours later, Jonah barely able to halt Abiel before he rode right through the market. The first thing he needed to do was find a place to stay the night. Thankfully, it was neither the Sabbath nor a holiday, so most of the inns were open and had plenty of vacancies. Jonah found one that seemed safe and comfortable and, after tying Abiel firmly to a post outside, entered the inn. The dimness of the interior left him unable to see for a moment.

"Friend, welcome. Please come in; have a seat." The innkeeper, a plump red-cheeked man with strange, pale blue eyes, beckoned to Jonah.

"Oh, no thank you. I have only come to rent a room for the night."

"No wine for the weary traveler?" The innkeeper shook his head as if Jonah had made a grave mistake.

"I am neither weary nor a drunkard." Jonah's tone reeked of irritation.

"I see, and you aren't suitable to be a prince either, more like one who has been rolling in the mud all day. Since you clearly are above my lowly standards, why don't you go and find another inn. There are plenty." The man turned away from Jonah a moment, examining his hands. Then he added in a tone meant to beguile, "None, however, have the same pleasures as mine." He smiled slowly, watching Jonah as the statement hung in the air like bait.

"What do you mean?"

"He means vile dancers and witches and deceitful fortune tellers," a man muttered from the corner of the inn. He was sagging low over a cup of wine, a tangled and overgrown beard hanging down to his knees.

"No need to listen to him. He's a regular, meaning he's a drunkard." The innkeeper laughed, the sound eerie and haunting in the dark room.

"I believe I will take your advice and seek out another place to stay."

"Aye sure, but you won't find any dancers as good as mine no matter what he tells you."

"I could care less about dancers and witchcraft," Jonah said.

Suddenly the innkeeper seized Jonah's wrist. He stared intently at Jonah's palm, his gaze boring into Jonah. "Witchcraft you say? No, it is not witchcraft, but true and holy. But holiness is not something you seek, my friend."

Jonah reclaimed his arm with a violent jerk. "What nonsense are you spouting?"

"To run from the gods is the worst of sins, my friend, but never fear. It takes very little to appease those like Asherah. Only a little worship—"

Jonah swung his arm, fist clenched, with as much force as his could, catching the man in the jaw. Due to the innkeeper's great bulk, he was practically immovable. "Have you no child either? For surely Moloch requires no less than a human sacrifice."

"I won't listen to any more of this!" Jonah raged, his teeth clenched and his fists raised. "You fool, scoundrel, I worship none other than Yahweh, the God of Israel." He turned and fled the inn, the innkeeper's laughter pursuing him.

"Aye, so he says. Then tell me why it is the God of Israel he is running from." The entire assembly in the inn roared with drunken laughter.

Abiel gave a snort of surprise when Jonah opened and then slammed the inn's door. Taking the stallion's bridle in firm yet trembling hands, he led him down the street. If he had known how vile Joppa was, he would have sought out a different port, but as things were, he was where he was.

Another inn, a few streets over seemed more inviting. Jonah retied Abiel to yet another post and swung the door open. There was more light in this one, but it was also more crowded. To Jonah's relief, the laughter that rang through those sitting around table was clear. He could hear no slurring or hysteria in their voices. The innkeeper that greeted Jonah was a tall and big boned figure. His head was bald, and he wore enormous gold hoops in his ears that dangled and clanked with each step he took.

"Shalom." The man's voice held a quality that was strangely soft. His eyes were small and squinting, but his tone seemed friendly enough.

"Shalom, I am seeking a place to stay the night."

"How many?"

"Myself and my horse."

"How long?"

"Just one night."

"And I am assuming you desire to wash your clothes before the morning?" The innkeeper's eyes roved over Jonah's muddy garments with amusement. Jonah nodded sheepishly. "Very good, are you willing to work for rent?"

"Certainly."

"There are a few baskets in the back. Down the road is a large pile of soil, dumped there by those building us a large mikvah. I have a warehouse down the road that is also full of soil, the result of leveling a hill. The soil needs to be removed. Workers will be removing the mikvah's pile the day after the Sabbath. I need you to remove half of the soil from my warehouse and dump it on the pile. It should take you about four or five hours."

"That sounds very reasonable. May I go ahead and put my horse away?"

The innkeeper nodded. He pointed to a man leaning against the wall in a far corner. "Jaala, get your hide over here and assist this man. He has a horse that needs to be stabled for the night. The horse will need feed and water as well."

"Yes, Master." The man straightened and approached Jonah, giving a small bow of his head. He gestured toward the door. The air was cool when they stepped outside, and Abiel's nicker broke through it with ease. "He's a fine one, sir. Were you just passing through or intending to sail?"

"I will be setting off to Tarshish at dawn."

"Will he be staying here?"

"No, he has been borrowed and must be returned to his owner before the Sabbath."

"My services are available."

"Thank you." Jonah untied Abiel and stroked his neck.

"Right this way, sir." The man, assumedly the groom, led the way toward a stone building near the back of the inn. He led Abiel into a large straw-bedded stall, then fed and watered him. When he was finished, he gave the stallion a pat and turned to leave.

"Would you show me to the warehouse?" Jonah asked.

The groom stopped and turned respectfully. "Of course, sir." The groom headed out the back of the stables and lifted the baskets. He then strode up a small stone walkway toward a large wooden building. There were slits in the walls at the top for ventilation, but no apparent windows. A single wooden door served as the entrance and exit and the groom swung it wide. As expected, a monstrous mound of soil confronted Jonah. Four or five hours work for sure, six if he did not hurry.

"May I be of any more assistance to you, sir?"

"No, thank you." The groom nodded, left the baskets for Jonah, and then sprinted out the door lest he be missed by his master. Jonah stood a moment, gazing at the dirt. With a sigh, he lifted one of the baskets by its handles and set to work.

"A thousand sorrows, sir, but I cannot take on any more passengers," apologized the burly captain. Copper highlights tinged his plain brown hair and eyes.

"Surely just one more would not overcrowd your ship." Jonah was sick and tired of searching for a ship that would carry him to Tarshish—the destination that was absolutely the farthest Jonah could ever get from Nineveh. The irony of his decision struck him every time he thought about it. To sail as far as he could from God's calling, to refuse it so vehemently was terrifying, yet hilarious too. "To run from the gods is the worst of sins." The innkeeper's warning tone and shrieking laughter jarred Jonah back to the present, back to the captain who was speaking to him.

"...possible, but it would likely displease my other passengers as their quarters are already tight as it is."

At that moment, a giant of a man ran up to the captain and touched him on the shoulder with urgency. "Sir," Jonah heard him mutter, "one of the passengers spotted a rat in the hold. Of course, one rat is far from uncommon, but the man is as fastidious as they come, finicky as a governor. He demanded that we remove the vermin from the ship." The man shook his head in frustration. "Catching a single rat on the *Midnight Runner* would be nearly impossible. I told him this, and he said that he refuses to ride on an infested ship. He demands a refund on his payment before you leave port."

"So be it. Pay him back. He will receive what he deserves in due time. He will not reach Tarshish for another eighty years if he is determined to sail on a ship without rats. Especially one that leaves from Joppa. Oh, and do keep an eye on the vermin population." The captain turned to Jonah. "And as for you, you have your chance to board the *Midnight Runner*. Will you take it?"

"With ecstasy, my good Captain...?"

"Captain Chenaniah."

"With ecstasy, my good Captain Chenaniah."

In a matter of minutes, Jonah had paid the fare and was being led up the ramp by the giant man whose name, Chenaniah had informed him, was Oz, his name meaning strength. It suited the man. Oz was no thick-headed person, however. His eyes watched every movement of the crew, and his gaze swept the scrubbed decks and traveled out to sea where the sun hovered over a vivid blue horizon. Jonah followed Oz across the deck and down into the quarters below deck. On a typical day, Jonah would have frowned at the shabby, crammed area he was to call home for the next month. Today, however, he was simply too exhausted to consider the place to be anything but luxurious.

Oz seemed to understand for he said, "You should get some rest after arguing with captains all day long." The big man laughed, his voice echoing off the walls. "We weigh anchor at dawn."

The *Midnight Runner* drifted gently on the rippling sea, pulling eagerly at her heavy rock anchor. The southerly wind brushed past her, ready to take her away. Were it any stronger, the captain would have been forced to wait another day. The small, motley crew, though tough from years of sailing, could not row the craft any great distance. The

Midnight Runner sat high on the deep blue waters. Coils of rope lay sprawled on her decks, and the odd bird squawked in the hold. The crew worked to bring in the final loads of supplies as Captain Chenaniah bellowed out orders.

Below deck, Jonah sat up and looked around in momentary confusion. Where was he? Then he remembered. He was off on an adventure, a stupid one indeed. He stood and paced in the tight quarters. Four paces forward, turn, four paces back. He shouldn't be there. He should go home. Perhaps he could even speak with Amos. Jonah was convinced the prophet understood his plight. Amos would go to Nineveh for him; Jonah was sure of it. Or was he simply trying to convince himself? Above him, the sun peeped cautiously over the horizon, streaming rays of pink stretching out toward Joppa. Jonah heard Chenaniah give the order to weigh anchor. It was too late. He was off to Tarshish.

Chapter Nine

Haggith shuffled out the back door of the house, impatient to start the day's work. Hens clucked in the yard, and a rooster crowed for all he was worth, which was, of course, very little. A single goat bleated pitifully in its pen, and a flock of sheep could be seen in the distance, making their usual rounds behind their shepherd. Haggith gripped her bag of grain protectively as the chickens sped around her in circles. Young chicks cheeped noisily as they raced to catch up to their parents. Haggith swatted irritably at the fowl, continuing her slow trudge toward the nesting box. The henhouse, carefully built, allowed the chickens to come and go as they pleased to lay. The eggs had to be collected each morning and evening to ensure that foxes wouldn't steal them. The chickens retreated up into high bushes and acacias each evening; also wary of foxes.

Inside the hen house lay four pleasant looking brown eggs and one odd light-brown egg covered with lumps and spots. Haggith collected them all with equal appreciation and scattered some grain around the house as a "thank you" to the hens. After depositing her prize inside the house, she returned to the yard, carrying a bucket over to the goat pen. An, the goat, grunted a greeting and poked her head through the wooden fence, eager to empty her bulging udder. Haggith's hands worked gently and quickly, and the milk squirted into the bucket with vigor. She had always considered An to be an odd name for a goat, but there was no reason for her to question the master's decisions. What was the name of a goat to her? Better to leave some questions unasked. An turned a solemn brown eye to watch her work, small ears twitching this way and that, catching every sound. Haggith patted the rough hair on An's head and lifted the bucket. Taking care not to spill any, she hobbled back toward the house, leaning heavily to counterbalance the milk.

Master Jonathan was in the main room going over his numbers, scrolls littered the floor, and the air was thick and musty. He tended to talk aloud when he did this, often without even noticing, and Haggith did her best to hide her mirth at some of the things he said.

"That stubborn man could have easily handed those over for a shekel or two," he mumbled as she entered. "But no...no, he had to go and charge me ten shekels for a mere basket of them. A single basket, and a small one at that. And to think I paid those ten shekels. How the man wormed it out of me, I will never be able to say. He didn't even use the typical tactics. There were no complaints of stealing food from his children or of robbing him blind. I bet he has no children with an attitude like that. Such deceit I have never seen in my life..." He trailed off, scratching away with renewed determination and indestructible focus.

Haggith let the corner of her mouth tip in a hint of a smile. She set aside the milk and began untying the day's flour sack to make the bread.

"I would bet my house on the fact that that man could sell the fruit right back to a fig tree. And I am not a betting man...except for the time I accidentally made a bet aloud. Goodness, was that ever a crazy day. They had me dancing a donkey in the market when I told them that surely there was no way my son would ever eat a raw fish. I said I would dance in the market if he did, and all the other vendors know I would rather do a lot of things than dance. Hah, and of course, Anan himself had to overhear that comment and convinced me to raise the stakes to dancing a donkey. I sure wish he had looked more disgusted than he did when he ate that raw fish. In fact, I bet he enjoyed every bite!" Jonathan threw his hands up in the air, launching his writing stick across the room.

He seemed not to notice Haggith and merely retrieved another writing stick and resumed his work. Haggith's slight smile had given way to a smirk, and in the end, she found herself fighting laughter. She remembered that day, clear as the sun. She could still see in her mind's eye Master Jonathan pulling hard at the donkey, trying to dance to the tune his son was humming with all the vendors jeering and laughing. Of course, only herself and two others had witnessed how the fish had been deftly hidden into a fold of Master Anan's tunic rather than down his mouth. But of course, it was not a servant's place to tell on her own master. Master Jonathan had found plenty of ways to get back at his son after that event. Haggith forced herself not to think of an example; she had work to do. Still, she sputtered, smirked, and sputtered again.

"Haggith?" Master Jonathan had finally noticed her.

The elderly woman turned respectfully toward him. "May I be of assistance, Master?"

"Not at the moment. There isn't a chance you were laughing, is there?"

"Likely not, Master."

"I see." His mouth curved though as he resumed his work. And she knew she had been caught. The silence was shattered as Master Jonathan began to laugh. Haggith, despite her best efforts, laughed as well. And soon they were howling.

Haggith fumbled with the bag of flour, pouring it out onto the kneading board. She continued to chuckle as she sifted the flour through her fingers a moment, but then she stopped as a slip of parchment was revealed in the sifting flour. Unfolding it, she saw it was a note. How odd for it to be in the flour bag. Perhaps some careless worker had dropped it in with the grain. Her eyes scanned the note and she gasped.

Master Jonathan turned toward her. "Haggith, what...?"

The parchment slipped from her hand as she fell backward onto the stone floor.

"Lucky, so very lucky," the physician mumbled as he dabbed at the servant's forehead with a cloth.

"More like a miracle." Jonathan bent over Haggith, frowning slightly. "She is not in the least bit frail, but a fall like that should have resulted in a head injury. Good thing I left those cushions where I did."

"What caused the incident, do you know?"

Jonathan considered the note he had read just moments before. It pressed stiff in his palm. "No, I have no idea."

At that moment, Zedekiah entered, without knocking. His face pale and drawn. "I saw the physician ride in. I hope you do not mind my dropping in, Jonathan."

"Not a problem. It was only a small incident. Haggith fainted."

"Fainted? That woman?"

"It is somewhat of a mystery."

"Is there anything I can do?"

"Actually, there is. Would you send word to Caleb?"

"Jonah's brother? Of course, but—"

"Haggith was going to fetch him this afternoon for a visit. We have something to discuss."

"Right away. Anything else?"

"No, thank you, my friend. Shalom."

"Shalom." Zedekiah turned and left, closing the door softly behind him. The physician continued to watch Jonathan even after the conversation had ended, his eyes keen and forehead creased in thought.

"I am a healer of the body, not of the mind like some. Though there are some things that do not escape my notice," he told Jonathan carefully.

"Such as?"

"You lied to your neighbor."

Jonathan stood quickly, a little too quickly. "If I may say so, that is none of your business."

"Of course not, sir. Is there anything I should know though? Anything relating to this poor woman's incident?"

"Yes." What was he saying? This had to be kept a secret. The note was a private matter. "Yes, but I fear it would be unwise to tell anyone. It involves a close friend of mine. And I would not wish to make the matter public."

"Very well." The physician stood as well, seeming satisfied. "She needs to rest a day or two, but after that, if she feels up to it, she may continue with her normal tasks. Though I would recommend that she take it easy. No long trips to summon relatives from other towns." The man let his statement settle a moment before gathering his things.

Jonathan showed him to the door and paid him. The physician mounted his horse and turned sharply toward the city. He clucked noisily to his mount and sped off, slowly disappearing until he was only a speck on the horizon. Jonathan sighed and went back inside. He crossed the room and sat next to Haggith, the note clutched firmly in his hand. The day crawled on slowly as the lonely figure watched and waited.

Chapter Ten
Nineveh, Assyria

The delicate silk slipped easily through her fingers. The fabric was so light she could have easily thought it air. "How much?" she heard herself ask, but she should not have. It was foolish to purchase such a thing.

The man lounging at the back of the booth stepped forward. His arms folded across his chest. He named an outrageous price, and she found her chance to slip away. This was no place for an urchin like herself to be, but she could not resist the market. Father would likely find out and there would be a punishment, though in the end, she typically found the reward higher than the penalty.

"Marbita!" She spun at the voice. No one should know where she was! She scanned the crowd and heard her name again. A boy appeared before her a moment later. His Assyrian eyes were lighter than what was common and his tanned skin clearly showed the years he had spent in the sun. Her eyes widened when she recognized him, and she glanced about nervously for a moment.

"Shammi?" Marbita stared at her younger brother. Shammina should have been training. Why was he in the market?

"I need to talk to you, Marbita." He gazed at her with a hopeful expression, fully aware that she could easily tell Father who would be furious to find he was not training. However, he also knew that she had a soft spot where her brothers were concerned—especially since she hardly ever saw them, all six being away and working hard to become soldiers. Shammi, however, was her main weakness.

Shammi was the second to youngest, and though Marbita would never admit it, he was her favorite. They had always been inseparable from the moment Shammi was born. If it had been any of the others, she would have said no, but not with Shammi. Marbita sighed, nodding consent and followed him through the market.

She knew right where they were headed before she even approached the immense walls. Shammi was taking her to Rabil's home—the sort of place where people were fortunate to emerge alive. She considered stopping him and demanding that he find another place to talk, but his stride was determined. There was no turning back now. The door swung open with the softest touch and the darkness they stepped into was complete.

A building that was part of the walls was not permitted to have windows that looked out to the surrounding countryside, only in at the city. And Rabil didn't even have those. No torches were lit, and there was no hearth. The only way one could know whether Rabil was home was by the raucous snoring emitting from a corner of the building. A stench hit them hard as they entered. Wine? Rotting food? Just plain uncleanliness?

Marbita however had been here before. She knew what it was. Rabil was an absolute madman, a brute at best. Death was his obsession, which was one reason why he used to be an army general. Now that he was no longer fighting, he had to find some other outlet for his fetish. He killed rats. There were plenty to be found near the market and in the dark cool crevasses in the walls.

Rabil's home, though, was more than just a home for rats. Vegetables littered the floor, purchased by Rabil, but not for himself. These were intended for a darker purpose. Rats could be heard, not seen, running across his floor, over his sparse furniture, and around his sleeping mat. Marbita and Shammi stood and listened a moment. Rabil lay still on his mat, but he was awake. A moment passed, one breath, two breaths. A swish was followed by a grunt, then a sharp squeal. Rabil had accomplished his goal. A heartbeat later, the squealing stopped, and though unseen, a rat lay dead. Rabil tossed its carcass into a bucket where it landed with a sickening plop on top of a pile of others. Marbita was unconsciously backing toward the door when Shammi stopped her.

"General Rabil?" he said.

Another sound, the sound of a man turning. "Hey there, boy. You're the one they call Shammina, right?"

"Yes, sir."

"Ah yes, you're the one I like. Only boy in the area with respect enough to call me my proper title."

"Yes, sir."

"What did you want, boy?"

"I have come to make a proposal."

"Have you now?"

"Shammina!" Marbita stepped between them, momentarily finding her tongue. "What are you..."

"A moment please, General." Shammi stepped back out into the sunlight. Marbita almost ran over him in her attempt to escape. He led her to an empty booth at the edge of the market and sat down inside.

"Shammi, what are you thinking? The only proposal you should ever make with Rabil is to exit his house in functioning condition."

"Marbita." Shammi held his hands up a moment, thinking. "I want to be a soldier very badly."

This statement took her by surprise. She knew it was true, but what did that have to do with anything? "I know."

"And I want to fight Egypt."

"Egypt? Shammi, no one has ever conquered Egypt before. And Assyria has no intention of trying."

"So?"

"So, you are downright out of your mind."

"What if I could just go right into Egypt? I could assassinate Pharaoh." His bright eyes were wide with excitement.

Marbita saw that she had some work to do to push this dream out of his mind. "You can't murder Pharaoh without soldiers to back you, Shammi."

"Why not?"

"What does this have to do with Rabil?" Marbita leaned back against the wall of the booth, watching her brother with an inquisitive gaze.

"General Dorar refuses to let me study Egyptian battle tactics. I must know how they fight in order to fight them. If I could learn how to be a soldier under Rabil's instruction—"

"Absolutely not!" Marbita was on her feet now. "Shammi, you must promise me you will have nothing to do with that man. He is dangerous, do you hear me?" Her voice had risen to shouting and it took tremendous effort to bring it back down to a whisper. "Father will skin you alive if he hears you have quit your training with General Dorar."

"Would you tell him?"

Marbita sighed. She sank back down onto the ground in front of her brother. "No, I would not tell him."

"Alright, then what reason do I have not to ask General Rabil to train me?"

"Shammi, you know how I feel about you spending time with Rabil. I know how much you idolize the general, but it is far too dangerous to spend time around him. He is extremely unpredictable and—" Marbita halted. Shammi's eyes spoke far more than words ever could. "And you already know all this, yet you have made up your mind to ask him." Shammi nodded, his lips curving into something akin to a smile. "If you have already made up your mind, why did you drag me into all of this?"

"Because I need your help."

"My help?"

"I need you to get me back into the house without being recognized." At the confusion on his sister's face, he pressed on. "I need you to help me disguise myself as a girl."

"I'm sorry, Shammi, I don't understand how—"

"And as a girl," he cut her off, "I can come and go from the house as a friend of yours. You and your friend like to go to the well and to the market together and you see her quite often. I can find a place to hide at night and stay in the house because, determined as I am, I am not feeling so good about the idea of sleeping at Rabil's. During the day, I can train with Rabil, and at night, I can sleep at home, hidden away."

"And what about your meals?"

"Maybe I could meet you at the well every day and you could bring me food."

"You've thought this whole crazy thing out, haven't you?" She sighed at his twinkling eyes. She wished could shake him from his naiveté. "That's asking a lot of me."

"But you'll do it, right?"

Marbita let her gaze linger on his face a moment. The handsome young features brimmed with hope. "You have only recently become an adult, Shammi. You are only thirteen. Are you certain Rabil will accept you?"

"You can be certain," said a voice.

They both started, and swung their heads upward to see Rabil lounging lazily against the booth appearing less of a towering menace than before. His bloodshot eyes rested with surprising warmth on Shammi.

"I will teach you, boy," he said.

Marbita looked over to her brother, saw the glow in his eyes, and she knew that if there had been any hope to change Shammi's mind, it was gone now. He would become a soldier, a ruthless soldier. He would take on a bloodlust under Rabil's direction, and she was helpless to stop it.

Father was uncommonly cheerful when Marbita entered the house that night. Mother was also there, sullenly stirring a pot of broth in the corner. She forced herself to clear her mind of thoughts of Shammi. She needed to keep her senses clear and her wits at their sharpest when she was near Father. He, like Rabil, was dangerously unpredictable.

"Evening, Father," she greeted him.

The solid wall of his back moved, and he faced her. His face was set in its usual impassiveness, but his eyes smiled. "And to you, Marbita. I spoke with my brother just before you arrived."

"Did you, Father?"

"I did." His gaze cooled and then hardened on her face. "He had much to tell me." The black eyes shifted to where Mother sat stirring. "I brought back grain from the market. The old bins should be emptied and cleaned." Marbita noticed the slight slurring of his words. He had been drinking. Mother rose obediently and shuffled toward the back door. Mother always shuffled everywhere she went. It was a constant reminder of Father's easily raised ire. "My brother informed me that he was in the market earlier today."

Marbita's senses came alert, though she tried not to show it. "Was he?"

"Yes, he was. And he told me that he just happened to see a young girl of your appearance wandering aimlessly among the stalls and booths." In an instant, he had seized her wrist and twisted her arm painfully. "What a waste, I told him, that a girl should dawdle away her time in the market, wandering aimlessly. And in a way, it reminds me of someone else who used to do that quite frequently."

Marbita winced, knowing it would make her seem submissive. "I confess it was me in the market, Father." He slowly released her arm, though his body was still tense, waiting for her to continue. "I only spent a moment there, Father." She formed the lie carefully, aware that one wrong word would only get her into more trouble. "I was looking for some cloth with which to make new garments. The old ones are becoming worn." The admission was apparently satisfactory.

"My brother told me he saw you enter a booth selling cloth. Did you find anything worth remembering?"

"No, Father, the cloth we ourselves make is more cost-effective."

"I see. So, there will be no reason in the future to spend time in the market?"

"Likely not, Father."

"Very good. Now go and sleep. Tomorrow I expect the house clean by noon. I have a friend who intends to pay a visit, and I do not wish him to think that I house a vagrant."

"Yes, Father." Marbita turned and walked up the stairs. She tried her best to keep her eyes low, her steps quick. But the fire inside of her refused to be smothered. Her shoulders straightened and her chin raised, even if only a fraction. In her peripheral vision, she saw her father watching her with a menacing gaze. Surely, nowhere in Nineveh was safe. Peace and happiness here, she knew, were nonexistent. Not long after she lay down on her mat, she heard footsteps.

Mother emerged through the doorway, her eyes dark with worry. She knelt by Marbita's mat a moment, turning her wrist to see the already reddening mark. "It will swell and ache for a while," she said quietly. "You will survive it though. You cannot lose a fight until you lose your hope." She let her gaze rest on Marbita's face a moment. "I know it is a battle to find joy in this place, but even your father will smile for a good reason once in a while."

Seeing her mother, ivory skin glowing in the lamplight, black hair hanging in a canopy, Marbita wished with all her heart that she could tell of Shammi's new ideas, that Mother would be reunited with her son from time to time. She'd give anything to make Mother's lovely mouth curve in a smile, to hear her musical, tinkling laugh, to see her wide eyes fill with joy, and to prove that Father had not after all managed to separate Mother from her beloved children. He only permitted Marbita to stay so she could help Mother cook and clean.

Mother caressed Marbita's hand for a moment before she stood. Squaring her shoulders, her face cleared of all emotion. It was a necessary thing in Nineveh, among the Assyrians. Hiding your emotions was to hide your weaknesses. And no Assyrian was allowed to be weak. Mother turned, and for a moment, Marbita saw the limp she worked so hard to conceal in a shuffle. Marbita knew that beneath the thin swaying garment was a crooked leg, a punishment, a curse. Like a shepherd, Mother had said—Father had thought the action of laming her was like being a shepherd. Sheep that wandered were not safe, so a leg had to be broken. Marbita closed her eyes. She knew that no amount of crookedness in her body could keep her from flying. Flying with hope, flying towards love, flying toward freedom. And she was determined that nothing Father did would ever kill her hope. For it was true; if she never lost her hope, she would never lose her fight for freedom.

Chapter Eleven

Many years have passed since being captured by the Assyrians, but I have not forgotten. Neither Amos nor I told you of my destination, where I have been sent to prophesy; it is Nineveh. The message I am to declare is of destruction, but I am no fool. The healing of Abba and our escape from the caravan has proven to me that Yahweh is merciful and loving. There is little doubt in my mind that the Assyrians will repent. And when they do, Yahweh will forgive them. There is no changing Yahweh's mind, so I believe that if the message is not delivered, then the Assyrians cannot repent. And so I am bound for Joppa to find a ship that will take me to Tarshish. Do not try to contact or find me. I do not know if I will return.

Jonah

"He says he is no fool, though I doubt the fact." Caleb leaned against the wall, arms crossed stubbornly across his chest.

"Ah yes, Master Caleb," Haggith, said softly, sitting propped up by cushions and watching the scene before her. Benjamin, Amittai, Jonathan, and Caleb all stood staring at each other. All had different opinions, and all were determined to have the others see things his way.

"Fool or no, who wants to go to Nineveh?" Benjamin asked, his arms also crossed.

"But surely Jonah cannot simply run from God," Amittai interjected, his skin slowly paling.

"He can, and he just did," Jonathan muttered. "The only issue is that he will not get away with it." Turning to Amittai, he added, "I can't even imagine what you are going through, I have seen my sons struggle, but to watch your child go through spiritual battles must be ten times harder. Even now, with Anan gone, I feel like my days are empty."

"We should have pressed him for more information." Caleb scanned the faces of the others, daring them to object. "If he had told us where he was going, I would have known if he was headed in the wrong direction—seeing as Tarshish is on the other side of the world!"

"That's for sure." Benjamin widened his eyes dramatically. "And I'm sure that once you caught him sneaking off somewhere else, Abba would have just turned around and marched off to Nineveh."

Suddenly, Caleb turned sharply on him. "You sure do enjoy contradicting me don't you, Benjamin? I encouraged Jonah to adopt you for the benefit of all of us. Do you know who it's helped? Only..."

"Please, may I get a word in edgewise here?" Amittai cut in, his tone frustrated. "My son has made a mistake, that is clear. What are you doing standing around here arguing about it though? This will not help." He angled a pointed glance at Caleb. "There is nothing to be done."

"But pray," proclaimed a new voice.

They all turned, surprised.

Amos nodded courteously from the doorway. "If I may enter?"

"Of course, come on in." Caleb unfolded his arms, his shoulders slumping a little.

"We shall pray for Jonah," Amittai declared as he greeted Amos.

"Hold up a second." Benjamin's stance was defensive, his eyes hard. "In the note, Jonah said that neither he nor Amos told us of his destination." All eyes turned to Amos, some with surprise, others with mistrust.

"I..." Amos looked down at his feet, his face flushing slightly. "I knew that Jonah was upset about his commission. I also know what it feels like to be commissioned by Yahweh to do something you despise. When I first met him on the wall in the city, I could feel his pain just by looking at him. That was years ago, and it is hard to say if it has decreased or merely multiplied. When he was just a boy, his eyes were dark with anger and regret, but most of all, he burns with hatred. I told him about his call to be a prophet, and do you know what he said?" Amos let out a laughing breath. "'Well as long as I don't have to prophesy to Assyria.' I told him that he just might have to, but I do not think he believed me at the time." He sighed, then eased himself down onto a cushion. "I know that Jonah hates the Assyrians, and I know he is hurting. I also know he is angry at God, more than anything else."

"But Jonah is far from losing his faith," Amittai said hopefully.

"Yes, he still has his faith. More precisely, he still knows there is a God. To him, Yahweh has turned into a monster, one that only loves his enemies and is ever punishing him. Jonah has decided to run. He will bend himself—trying to live without God. It will not be long though before he breaks. And when he does, God will be there. Which is why we must pray. For hard as it is, Jonah must come to the end of himself in order to find himself. Jonah must learn that, when it comes to Yahweh, His love, His presence, there is nowhere for him to run."

"He will try though," Amittai said sadly.

"Yes, he will try."

* * *

The ship rocked gently on the endless sea, its sails full of wind and the decks glistening with mist. Captain Chenaniah watched his crew at work with an air of satisfaction. His men consisted of Greeks, Hebrews, Moabites, and the odd Egyptian. They had all come a long way since the beginning of their ventures. The Hebrews and Moabites were known for fishing from time to time, but sailing on open water in a large ship was something entirely different. The river loving Egyptians were accustomed to floating up and down the Nile with the current, trading, transporting, and sometimes fighting. Now the Greeks, they were the seasoned sailors Chenaniah had always dreamed of having in his crew. He himself was a Hebrew. He'd loved the water ever since before his birth. A voice called to him, breaking through his thoughts.

"Captain? Captain?" Oz, now beside him, looked down at him with concern.

"Oh uh, sorry. What is it?"

"Storm on the horizon."

"Storm?" Chenaniah gazed out across the azure horizon.

"Coming from that way." Oz pointed a burly hand off to Chenaniah's left.

He turned his eyes toward it. Indeed, a black line headed swiftly in their direction. He observed how fast it was advancing and his pulse began to quicken.

"Rouse the whole crew; get all hands on deck," he ordered. With a few giant strides, he took hold of the tiller, his knuckles turning white as he gripped it with apprehension. No storm should advance that quickly. No storm should have come at all.

Kleitos heard the call before any of the others. At first, he could not understand what was going on. It wasn't his shift; it was his time to rest. A moment later, he was standing in his quarters, feeling smaller than his six feet of height, his heart racing. Storm? A storm on the clearest day he had seen in months? Up on deck, chaos reigned. Men raced from stern to bow, hearing orders, some obeying, some too confused to comprehend. Seasoned as they were, they had been caught off guard and confusion replaced the drilled crew they should have been. Darkness had fallen, though it was still midday. Bolts of lightning could be seen in the distance. Kleitos watched, counted the seconds between each blast. One, two, three, crash! One... Screams! His head jerked. The water, once calm, was now roiling and waves were beginning to build. The ship lurched sideways. More screams—no, cries. Kleitos tried to hear over the escalating wind.

"Leviathan! It's a leviathan!" a voice shouted. Kleitos raced to the side, leaning over the rail, staring hard at the water. A great bulk passed beneath the ship. Boom! Crash! The thunder answered, and the *Midnight Runner* shook. Another lurch and Kleitos felt his feet swept from beneath him. The ship shuddered as if it also feared the mysterious creature that threatened to ram its hull again.

Kleitos stood, gazing around him in surprise. It had only been a few moments and suddenly the sky was black as night. Without warning, sheets of rain pummeled the ship. The torrent was so fierce that the water on deck rose above Kleitos' ankles in a matter of seconds. He gasped and stood frozen, unable to resist his terror. Never in his thirty years upon these waters had there been a storm like this.

He was not alone with his fears. Almost every crewmember around him was calling out now—some for their lives, some to their gods, others for their families. The crew tossed cargo for all they were worth, but Kleitos' limbs refused to obey. Some of the men were so panicked they had resorted to bailing; a waste of effort on a craft like the *Midnight Runner*. A wave rose high to port. In a rush of adrenaline, Kleitos leapt toward the door that led below decks, but he was too slow. Water crashed into the *Midnight Runner* like a hammer. Kleitos shut his eyes tight, wrapping his arms around his head as he was rammed into wooden objects, ropes, walls. He lost track of the way up. Was he resting against the deck? The rail perhaps? His lungs burned with the effort of restricting oxygen to his body.

A moment more would have been too long, but he was fortunate. The water drained away from his bruised and beaten body, and he gasped for air. He stood, wondering if it was an injury to his head that made him think the world was sideways. He glanced up and cried out in horror as the entire port-side of the ship lifted clear of the waves and seemed to be falling on him. A wave, at least three times larger than the previous pushed hard against the *Midnight Runner*, threatening to capsize her. The men were trained to lower the sails, and lighten the ship; capsizing was a rare concern for a ship like the *Midnight Runner* even on the Great Sea and there was little to nothing to be done!

"Great goddess Leucothea! Have mercy on us!" The plea reached Kleitos's ears and he knew instantly who it was. Captain Chenaniah, Hebrew though he was, was entirely willing to call upon any god in a situation like this. And the fact that the captain, his captain, had given up hope was too much for Kleitos to bear. The entire crew began to fall into despair. The ship was now at a sixty-degree angle, and Kleitos slid helplessly toward the starboard rail.

"Take a deep breath and hold on tight!" Captain Chenaniah called.

Kleitos swore with feeling. If those were his beloved captain's last words, he would—he smashed into the starboard railing hard. The air was knocked out of him and he lay gasping as the water continued to rise. Then, the strangest thing happened. The great leviathan rammed hard into the *Midnight Runner's* stern, causing her to shoot forward across the mountains of water. All the men on deck groaned as they slammed into yet another wall of water, but the ship stayed level...or was it? A heartbeat passed as she hovered in the air. Kleitos curled into a ball, waiting for death to claim him. The *Midnight Runner* crashed down with a tremendous boom into the roiling waves.

* * *

Shammi was nearly unrecognizable when he left the house later that afternoon. Marbita had seen to that. His short hair would be allowed to grow, and his masculine tunic had been exchanged for something more feminine. Marbita had been afraid at first—afraid that Shammi was making a mistake, afraid that she had made a mistake, but overall, she had been terrified that Father might find out. Now, however, she was not. When she had seen Shammi's glowing features as he came in through the door, the way he held his chin high, his shoulders back, she knew she would do anything to see her brother this happy every day. She remembered her resolve of the previous night. Nothing Father did would get in her way, nothing. The day crawled on slowly as she awaited evening, the time when she would go out to draw water from the well.

"Marbita?" Mother peered around the doorway at her as she ground the grain into flour.

"Yes?"

"Have you seen your uncle?"

"No."

Mother turned with a sigh and shuffled out of the house. Marbita turned back to her work, her eyes blazing. Her uncle, the man Father looked up to, modeled after, took advice from. If it hadn't been for her uncle's suggestion, Mother would still be able to walk and run freely. If it hadn't been for her uncle's observation yesterday, she would not have a swelling and aching arm.

After a time, she had enough flour for the next few day's worth of bread. Or as her brother called it, stone mud. It was true that the rough, grain kernels yielded an odd colored flour, much like the color of mud, but it was all they could afford. They were the scrapings, the leftovers. And perhaps it was also true that to keep it preserved Marbita and Mother often made the bread in a sort of hard, thin wafer. But Shammi hardly ate anything. Her brother was the epitome of picky. The bread had to be just the right consistency, and the soups had to contain just the right amount of spice. The water for, goodness sake, had to be lukewarm, but not too warm. *He will marry someday,* Marbita thought to herself. *He will marry and his wife will beg to be divorced because he will never eat a single morsel of what she fixes for him.*

Marbita smiled and then looked up and out the window. The sun barely hovered over the horizon. She concealed her gasp with a light cough and ran out the back door to fetch the large water jug. Hoisting it onto her shoulder, she trotted off toward the well, fearful that she would miss Shammi. When she arrived, she saw that the usual line was nonexistent. It was far too late for any sensible people to be out drawing water. She took several deep breaths before stepping toward the well and lowering her jug.

"You come late, dear friend."

The voice was so familiar. Yet when she turned, she hardly recognized the speaker.

"Sherah, I fear I could come no sooner." It felt strange, using a girl's name to address her brother.

"Did you bring anything for me?"

Marbita smiled. Shammi's tone and the look in his eyes practically spelled hunger. He sagged heavily against the well, his mouth tipped in a frown, but his eyes were alight with eagerness.

"Yes," she said, laughing. Marbita extended the previous day's bread, carefully wrapped along with a handful of dried dates and a small goatskin of water that would never be missed. "When I dribble the water on my wrist, it is not so cold that I flinch, but it is also not so warm that I do not feel its coolness," she told him, smiling.

"So, you finally figured out how to get the right temperature." He smiled back as he tipped up the goatskin, drinking deeply.

"I apologize that there was nothing lying about but stone mud." She leapt back with a small squeal as water splattered her face and neck. Laughing, she withdrew the quarter filled jug and, without a thought, dumped it on Shammi. They both laughed, throwing back their heads and enjoying the sensation of unguarded joy. Marbita could not remember the last time she had laughed, and Shammi likely hadn't had a free moment to enjoy life either. It took quite a while to stop the laughing, and when it ceased, they still shook with mirth. Marbita's hands wobbled as she tried to lower the jug back into the well. Suddenly, she burst out again, and they laughed until their sides hurt and they moaned, unable to breathe.

"I take back all the positive things I've said about laughing," Shammi managed to say between gasps. "It is, in fact, quite seemingly unhealthy."

At this, they began again, and Marbita found herself on the ground pounding the well with her fists. They waited for the laughter to subside. Then they embraced and parted ways. Shammi went to Rabil's for evening training, and Marbita went back home with a jug full of water. Her heart soared with every step, and her hopes were more optimistic than ever as she awaited the following morning and the answer to her questions concerning Rabil.

* * *

Jonah lay in his quarters, his eyes flickering beneath their lids as he dreamt...

Zillah bent low over him, her sweet scent calming his fraying nerves.

"It's alright, Jonah. Everything is alright."

"Where is Mama?" Jonah's voice quivered, his whole body quivered.

"It's alright, Jonah. Just be careful of the water."

"Water?"

"The water is everywhere, Jonah."

"What water, Zillah?" Jonah sat up, watching his sister in confusion. She smiled, her hand stroking his back in languid motions as she always did. But something was wrong. Why was everything roaring? Why was everything wet? Jonah shivered, hugging his blanket close. Suddenly...no it couldn't be! Why was he hugging Zillah's blanket? Why was he at home, in the corner, remembering...

"The water is everywhere, Jonah." The voice beckoned to him. He turned, but nothing but blackness greeted him.

"Zillah? Zillah?" The house was empty. Where was Mama? She said she would be all right, she was only feeling a little warm. Jonah began to cry. Caleb was captured. Abba was bleeding. Jonah was falling, falling from where?

"She's dead, Jonah," Abba told him.

"Who, Abba?" His gazed darted about in confusion.

"Both of them."

"No, they're here, Abba."

"The water, Jonah, be careful. It's not safe." Zillah was so close, but he couldn't see her.

Chapter Eleven

"Jonah, wake up!" Caleb was bent over him, his hands and feet shackled, yelling, screaming at him to get up. But Zillah was there ...Zillah was nearby. He couldn't leave her...

"Are you deaf?"

Jonah sat upright with a jolt, sending waves of pain down his neck. His vision went black for a moment as all the blood rushed from his head. "The water..."

"So you know?"

Jonah blinked. Captain Chenaniah was standing over him, his eyes staring distantly. "Know what?"

"The storm. The ship nearly capsized. *How can you sleep? Get up and call on your god! Maybe he will take notice of us so that we will not perish.*"

"My god?" Jonah murmured distractedly. His God was Yahweh, but Yahweh wouldn't save him. He had run from Yahweh.

"You heard me! Pray or we will all die!" The captain turned and left the quarters, going from spot to spot checking for men, making sure they were praying.

Jonah had barely gotten his scattered mind together when a copper-headed Greek strode up to him, his bright blue eyes as cold as the sea in winter. The man seemed bewildered to see him. "You aren't one of the crew. You must be a passenger," he grumbled in surprisingly competent Aramaic.

"I am." Jonah rubbed the sleep from his eyes, blinking them hard to keep then open.

"We are casting lots in the captain's quarters."

"You're doing what?"

"Casting lots. You know, seeking answers from Fate...that sort of thing. Then we'll know who is to blame for this calamity."

With no will to argue, Jonah stumbled after the man, his mind still foggy. Casting lots? These men must be a step beyond superstitious. To trust a name pulled out of dozens, asking the universe for answers when all else fails. The air inside was thick, and there was an uncomfortable dampness that clung to the skin, making one feel just wet enough to wish they were dry.

"For those who do not know me, my name is Kleitos. I am Greek, and I am part of Chenaniah's crew. Let's gather all the names now."

95

A piece of parchment was found and the crew and passengers lined up to have their names written down. Jonah followed the man in front of him up the line, his mind and body not truly cooperating as he would have hoped.

"Your name?" Kleitos asked him impatiently.

"Uh..."

"Clod doesn't even know his own name," he grumbled to the man beside him, who laughed mirthlessly.

"My name is Jonah, Jonah ben Amittai," Jonah managed to say.

Kleitos scribbled it down and the man behind Jonah pushed him aside. The parchment was cut so that each name was on its own piece. Then Kleitos requested a bowl.

"There aren't any," a man from the crowd replied.

"What do you mean?"

"We threw over everything. There isn't a pot, bowl, jug, box or bird cage left on board."

Kleitos cursed and Jonah couldn't stop the wince.

"Just heap them on the table," Kleitos mumbled to the man beside him.

The man obeyed, piling the scraps neatly into a mound. Together, they mixed them thoroughly. A blindfold was placed over Kleitos' eyes and he reached for the pile, fingers sifting through the scraps. He withdrew one and lifted the blindfold. Despite his doubts about the whole idea of the situation, Jonah found himself holding his breath, much like everyone else in the room. Kleitos opened his mouth to read, and the men leaned in, prepared to catch the name.

"Jonah ben Amittai."

A collective breath was released, though one man was not the least bit relieved. The name was repeated, the crew and passengers glanced around, wondering who the mysterious culprit was.

Fearing a quarrel that could easily end badly, Jonah slowly raised his hand. "I am Jonah," he breathed.

"What was that?" Kleitos leaned toward him.

"I am Jonah," Jonah declared. All eyes turned toward him.

"*Tell us, who is responsible for making all this trouble for us? What kind of work do you do? Where do you come from? What is your country? From what people are you?*"

Chapter Eleven

Kleitos' questions struck Jonah all at once. He stood for a moment, arm hanging foolishly in the air. Jonah lowered it, thinking. He considered not saying anything, or perhaps lying. Did he know why the storm had come?

"*I am a Hebrew.*" The sound emerged from his mouth. He had not requested it. He had not permitted its use. What was happening to him? "*And I worship the Lord, the God of Heaven.*" Jonah tried to stop the words. They were a lie. He was no longer a follower of Yahweh. "*Who made the sea and the dry land. I am fleeing from His presence.*"

A gasp emerged from the crew.

"*What have you done?*" Kleitos asked him, incredulous. "*What should we do to you to make the sea calm down for us?*"

Jonah shut his mouth tight, his lips whitening. His body trembled, and he felt he might explode. The words shot out in an instant. He could not catch them, and they were not his own. "*Pick me up and throw me into the sea and it will become calm. I know that it is my fault that this great storm has come upon you.*" Jonah clamped a hand over his mouth. What was he saying?

"We could never throw you overboard," Kleitos exclaimed. "The God you serve would curse us for taking a life that rightfully belongs to Him!"

"I agree." Captain Chenaniah stepped up next to Kleitos from the crowd. "Gather all the men and the oars. We will try to row to land."

For the rest of the afternoon, though it was hard to tell the time, the men rowed to no avail. Though the oars dipped into the water and the men pulled, though the captain shouted at them, and though each man cried out to his own god, it was no use. It must have been midnight when they gave up hope. Not even a speck of light shone down from the sky, not a single star, not even the moon was visible.

Kleitos set down his oar and scooted out of the bench. He approached his captain with downturned eyes, fully aware that the ship could tilt at any moment and fling him into the wall. "Captain, we can't."

"Can't what?" Chenaniah bellowed, his face red with anger.

"We can't. I mean we won't make it to land. We have tried every direction. We're sitting ducks in the middle of this storm."

97

"Idiot! Why can't we move?"

"Captain, the current comes from one direction and the waves come from all directions. The wind is howling out there so that the ship is never truly flat on the water. Half of the oars are in the water, half are out. Captain, it is impossible."

"Are we not the crew of the impossible?" the captain roared. His fists clenched tightly, his jaw set. "Have we not perused these waters for over thirty years? Haven't waves bashed this crew upon the decks of the *Midnight Runner* a hundred times before? How can a storm dishearten you so?"

"We have traveled far over the years, Captain, but this storm is like none I have ever seen before. The ship has nearly capsized at least three or four times."

"Well, it ain't capsized now!"

"No, Captain."

"So why can't you row it to land?"

"Like I said, we're being pushed by current, wave, and wind in all different directions." Kleitos looked down at the floor. Chunks of wood that had been broken off from the mast and ripped out of the decking by the leviathan's charge were lying here and there on the ground below decks so they would not fly around and cause more damage.

Suddenly Chenaniah seized one and threw it at Kleitos with all his strength. The sailor was quick, but not quick enough. The wood hit him square in the chest and sent him staggering backward.

"Kleitos, get this miserable ship and her crew on a piece of dry land!" Chenaniah seethed through clenched teeth. He whirled and stormed up the stairs, leaving his men to gape behind him.

Kleitos should have seen it coming. He'd ducked, but Chenaniah had surprised him. The wood stuck fast in his chest—piercing his skin. He cried out in agony and fell backward. Some of the crew reached to catch him, and they laid him gently down and took hold of the wood.

"No! Leave it!" Kleitos's voice was barely audible. It hissed out like air through a tiny hole. They didn't listen to him. With slow, careful movements, they removed the wood. It took four of them to hold Kleitos down while a fifth pulled out the shards. Kleitos could vaguely hear himself moaning in pain. A moment later, his ice blue eyes closed and he felt nothing.

Jonah, sitting at an oar at the very back, witnessed the scene unfolding. He knew what was going to happen next, and for some reason, he did not fear it. Though it had not been his words that had urged the crew to throw him overboard, he knew it must be done. Suddenly he laughed. Heads turned to stare at him, but he didn't care. God had put those words straight in his mouth. He did not bother to wonder why.

It was just as well though. He would die when they threw him overboard; he would die and he would win. He wouldn't have to prophesy to Assyria. He would simply die and someone like Amos would have to do it in the end.

The only disconcerting factor was that Yahweh was still there. He had yet to escape God, though he had run, run right into a storm in the middle of the sea. He still had not managed to get away. He saw the men whispering, stooping over Kleitos's still form, casting glances in his direction. His earlier aura of peace vanished in a flash. His heart thudded wildly as they came toward him.

"You said you were running from your God?" one of the men asked.

"I am."

"And he has found you."

Jonah started to say no, but he knew that was wrong. "Yes, He has."

"We must throw you overboard or else your God will kill us all."

Jonah said nothing. His limbs began to tremble as he faced death. Should he say something? Would they listen? The man grabbed his arm and pulled him to his feet. The crew half guided, half dragged him up the stairs.

On deck, the *Midnight Runner* was a sorry sight. Her sails were shredded past recognition, her decks were beaten and dented. Jonah felt himself walking crookedly as the deck leaned first one way then another. Water splashed over them as waves broke on the battered structure of the *Midnight Runner*. When they reached the rail, Jonah felt his knees grow weak. The waves rose to the height of hills. He had to look up to see the smallest one. One crashed into the *Midnight Runner* from the other side and they were thrown against the rail.

"Quickly now, or we will be washed away!" one man cried. They lifted Jonah, and he kicked at them instinctually. It was difficult to go willingly to his death, even though he thought he'd made peace with the grave not long before.

One of the sailors cried, *"Please, Lord, do not let us die for taking this man's life. Do not hold us accountable for killing an innocent man, for you, Lord, have done as you pleased."*

The men began to sob with fear and Jonah long to curse their ironic stupidity. They weren't the ones being thrown into the water. A moment later, they released him over the side of the ship. Air swirled around Jonah for a moment, cool air blasting against his face and body. He was terrified, but after an instant, his fear vanished. He was drifting. No, he was flying.

The impact of striking the water brought him to his senses. This wasn't a game; he was going to die. Fear trickled back into him as he tried to keep above the waves. He swam as never before, desperately, yet with little hope. The side of the ship was too slippery to hold, so he swam away from it. Perhaps there was land nearby, maybe just beyond that wave, just beyond the one behind that. Water crashed over him from behind. He felt himself being dragged under by its force. He fought for air, fought for life, and fought the water. His lungs burned; his whole body burned. He shivered, his teeth chattering from fear. He curled himself up in an attempt to stop the shaking, and he began to sink.

Wake up, he told himself. *Swim or die.* He forced his body to uncurl, though the water struck him hard. He began to swim, but he was spinning. Which way was up? He stopped a moment, felt the direction in which he was sinking and swam against that pull. His eyes were shut tight. Was there air above him? Or was the water endless? His need for oxygen slowed him down. He was getting tired. Maybe he could just rest a moment.

Then he understood. Zillah was waiting for him. Zillah was just beyond the water. He forced his body to move. He would find her just over the water. Mama would be there too. Mama could swim. She was on land just beyond the water. Jonah broke the surface with a gasp.

He gulped air for several moments, relishing the feeling of it filling his lungs. When he had survived this, when he saw Mama and Zillah later, beyond the water, he would never take air for granted again. Water splashed in his face, he wiped at it in frustration. The Assyrians were fighting him. They were trying to take him. They sent the sea a message...wait. *What's wrong with me?* He rubbed irritably at his eyes. *Mama's gone, Zillah's gone, and the Assyrians are far away. Survive Jonah, find land.* He began to swim again, over wave after wave.

Then, without warning, he was lifted high into the air. He fell back down with an ungainly smack. He stopped for a moment to rest, but then he cried out. To his left, a wave had built up. It was higher than any mountain he had ever seen. He couldn't even see the top of it.

"Yahweh!"

Dark water enveloped him, swirling. He could not fight it. It merely flew past him. He could not escape. The water was everywhere.

Chapter Twelve

The house was positively bustling with activity when Benjamin returned from the fields. At first, he could not imagine what was going on until he heard laughter. *For the love of sanity, couldn't that woman leave him well alone?* Atarah was often immune to the glares and discomfort of others. Benjamin was sure of that when he opened the door. She rushed forward, a ball of energy and liveliness. She was always like this, but today, she seemed even more vibrant than ever.

"Ben, oh Ben!" She threw her arms around him and hugged him tightly. "Imagine your father up and leaving you like that."

"I can take care of myself," Benjamin muttered, though it made no difference.

Atarah, deep in her own thoughts, narrowed her eyes, then frowned; all of her energy and jubilance draining away. "Poor child. Jonah should have just come to us and we could have helped him work out his problems." She sighed, sniffing a little. A moment later, she straightened her shoulders and turned, calling out to the little boy in another room. "Elon, child. Come say hello to your cousin."

Two feet puttered into action, and soon Benjamin was confronted by another sea of energy. "Cousin Ben, pick me up! Cousin Ben, will you play tag with me? Cousin Ben where is Uncle Jonah?"

Atarah stood back smiling. She likely assumed that Benjamin enjoyed the attention; he did not. Neither did he like being called Ben.

Though his preference had never been consulted in the matter. Hoping for some relief, he turned his full attention to Atarah, ignoring Elon who soon gave up and wandered off. "How are things in Aczib?"

"Everything is splendid. Caleb has been working like a mule, and with another little one on the way..." She looked in surprise at Benjamin's startled face. "Oh, you didn't know?"

"No, I did not." He forced a smile.

"The midwife came by yesterday to make sure everything was going smoothly." Her smile, which always seemed painted on her face, widened. "She said it is likely to be a girl." Atarah clasped her hands in front of her expectantly. Benjamin sighed inwardly. He supposed he should smile and congratulate her, but he was really hoping for some food and a long nap.

"How wonderful."

Her smile wavered for a mere moment at his dreary tone. "Caleb was hoping for a girl. And he was so sure that Yahweh would answer his prayers that he decided on a name ahead of time, just in case."

This caught Benjamin's attention, though he could not have said why. He waited for her to continue, every muscle tense for something, anything.

"We are going to name her Abigail—it means my father is joy."

Without warning, Benjamin felt the bonds holding his emotions together snapping and falling away. Moisture gathered in the corners of his eyes, and he stepped back sharply.

"Ben, what is it? Have I offended you in some way?" She reached a hand forward, and Benjamin noticed for the first time that she was wearing a vibrant red headscarf.

Images of his sister caught him off guard. Abigail had loved red, the color of the sunrise and sunset, the color of the birds and flowers. He turned and raced up the stairs. Atarah's words filled with confusion as they drifted after him, "I don't understand. Caleb, what did I say?"

"I don't know, Atarah," Caleb answered, his tone turning bitter. "Benjamin is the mirror character of Jonah. Just leave him be. He will tell us if he wants to."

Benjamin knew that he would have to explain later, but at the moment, he could not. He sank down onto his mat, the memories, buried deep in his mind, rushed forward and he felt his senses fading.

He lay down on his back and closed his eyes, opening the door to his carefully stored away past.

He had not dared to recall his mother, his father, or his siblings since sitting by Jonah in Lydia's home. They had remained sealed in the past—not forgotten, but never mentioned. Jonah and Lydia were the only ones who knew his story, though neither had had reason to mention it. Benjamin longed to return for just a while. He stirred, forcing his limbs to move. He closed the door to his room, hoping it would discourage anyone from entering. Then he returned to his mat and allowed himself to fall back in time.

Mother was arguing with Abba. It was far from unusual. They often quarreled, and Benjamin had learned to shut their words out of his mind, but tonight he could not. They were so close, and even though he covered his ears, he could not blot them out.

"He is my child as much as yours," Abba was saying. Benjamin knew what they were discussing. Mother wanted to send him off to be apprenticed.

"So are Abigail and Ruth..." Mother began to list the names.

"I know, but Benjamin is my eldest son."

"Which is exactly why he needs an education."

"Why can't he stay here and work with me?"

"Because I'm tired of having that boy around the house."

"He isn't just a boy." Abba had raised his voice. This surprised Benjamin. Abba was very soft-spoken.

"He is to me. Send him to be apprenticed, Reuel, and it will be your decision. Otherwise, I could just have them all apprenticed—the less mouths to feed the better. We don't have enough around here as it is."

"There is enough to live. I've just about had enough of your desperate need for a grand house and a grand life. You knew when our fathers arranged our marriage that I wasn't very rich."

"My father pressed me to agree. My discontent was never taken note of."

"Please, Miriam, please just learn to be content with what we have, can't you?" Abba's voice was thick with emotion.

"The answer is no, Reuel. I am taking the boy tomorrow morning, and if you decide to stop me, then I'm leaving."

Benjamin's heart began to race. He waited for a protest from Abba, but he must have run out of words. Abba needed to assume the authority and tell Mother what to do since he was the head of the house, but he never did—not even when he knew Mother was wrong. Benjamin wondered what it would be like if he had a hard and strong father that would say no to Mother, but then things would be different. He did not want to trade his Abba for another. Still he could not fight off the panic, he was going to be apprenticed, he was being forced away from his father. He wanted to work beside his abba, he wanted to stay.

"Abigail?" Benjamin turned his head, searching for his sister in the dark.

"Yes?"

"Will you hide me?"

"Benjamin..."

"Please, Abigail. I don't want to leave Abba and the others."

"I...I can't Benjamin. I'm sorry..."

A knock jarred Benjamin into wakefulness. He blinked and angled his head to see the door open. Haggith entered with a bowl of stew in her hands. "You missed supper," she said. As she came to him, the silence stretched uncomfortably. "I'm sorry that Mistress Atarah offended you." She set down the bowl, her eyes searching his for a moment. "Will you tell them why?"

"That's no business of a servant."

She jerked slightly, but then her face resumed its usual impassiveness. "Very well, Master Benjamin." She left him, closing the door behind her.

Benjamin pushed away the bowl. He had no appetite. All he wanted to do was go back and relive the past. But when he closed his eyes, it would not come, so he simply turned over onto his side and slipped into a dreamless sleep.

* * *

Jonah didn't realize that he had passed out, but he was not surprised. Perhaps he had gone under and fainted from lack of air. His head throbbed, his body ached, but overall, he felt unharmed. He smiled to himself. He was alive, and he had not died in the storm. His mind felt groggy, and he felt somewhat feverish... Suddenly, he jerked.

Something was very strange about his surroundings. His earlier feeling of peace vanished. The ground beneath him felt slimy, and he tried to recoil from it.

"Hello?" The sound that emerged from his mouth was barely audible. "Hello?" He stood, and felt the ground shudder beneath him. The world suddenly tilted. "Help! Is there anybody here?" He slid slowly along the slimy floor, something brushed his skin and he felt a burning sensation that made him gasp. The stench that filled his surroundings hit him like a blow as his slide built up speed. The burning sensation struck him in the leg and he moaned, struggling to fight the panic that threatened to overtake him. The pitch-black space around him increased his feeling of helplessness, and he felt like weeping.

Where were people? Wasn't there anyone who could get him out? A deep rumbling began from somewhere above him. It grew and the slimy floor beneath him shook. He was thrown forward, but he fought the motion, scrambling to his hands and knees as the ground moved convulsively. Was he imagining the intensifying heat? Was he going mad? The air was so thick, almost too thick to breathe. It crushed his lungs and he struggled for each breath. Why was everything so hot? He touched his forehead and what he felt made his heart race. He began to spin as the rumbling grew, and the world around him echoed and swam in his delirious mind. When he tried to stand, the heat stole the strength from his limbs. Finally, he could take it no longer. With a final gasping breath, he collapsed onto the slimy ground and fainted.

* * *

Benjamin woke the following morning with a massive headache. He rubbed at his temples, squeezed the skin between his forefinger and thumb, and even went downstairs and dumped a jar of cool water over his head. Nothing helped.

"Oh good, you're up." Atarah's cheery voice startled him.

He wheeled. "I thought you and Caleb left last night." There was a pause in which he thought about the tone of that sentence, but he didn't have the energy to soften it.

"We were going to, but I wanted to make sure everything is good between me and you. I mean, I did not expect or know..."

"Everything is fine," Benjamin lied. "You can go home. There's nothing wrong."

"Oh yes, I can see that."

"I just need some time alone."

"Of course, Ben. After all that has happened regarding your father and with whatever happened yesterday..." She stepped forward to embrace him, her eyes sympathetic.

He stepped back. "Nothing happened yesterday." They both stood still, watching each other.

"If you say so, I believe you." She placed a hand on his shoulder, her touch motherly and Benjamin forced himself not to pull away. "You know that if there is anything wrong, you can always come to Caleb and I."

"I don't know about Caleb. I think he is rethinking his call to encourage Jonah to adopt me."

"Nonsense!"

"He nearly said so himself." Benjamin's lips twitched in a smirk. "Apparently, I'm not helping as he had hoped."

"He's just upset, Ben. However, I do apologize for his behavior. I think he feels the distance growing between himself and Jonah and feels the need to blame it on someone. He's upset that his only brother choses not to come to him with his problems." Benjamin nodded, then gently stepped out of her reach. Atarah sighed and turned to go into the house. "I suppose Caleb, Elon and I will just go home then."

"Aunt Atarah?" She stopped, turning. Benjamin swallowed hard. He had called her back, he had to say something. "Abigail is a lovely name."

"Do you think so?"

"I do."

She smiled and headed back to the house. Benjamin knew he should explain, but not today, maybe another time. He began to walk with no particular destination in mind, just placing one step after the other and looking down at the ground. He stopped when a pair of hooves appeared beside his feet. He looked up to see Zedekiah's stallion, Abiel, watching him with curiosity.

"Hi, Abiel." He reached out and stroked the horse's velvet nose. Abiel nudged him, pressing his shoulder against Benjamin, begging for a scratch. Benjamin obliged, noticing how much sand came off along with the hair and dirt. "Been rolling have you?"

Abiel turned his left eye toward Benjamin, the look hilariously similar to that of a human. "You have no idea," it seemed to say.

"Abiel! I have been searching across half of Judah for you," Zedekiah complained, coming up behind Benjamin.

"I thought you kept him stalled at this time of year so he doesn't go raiding the farmer's wheat fields."

"I do. Ever since your father rode him down to Joppa, he has been determined to spend his time out of his stall." Zedekiah chuckled. "And as you can see, he has been doing a fairly good job of it." Benjamin held his tongue, knowing he should not tell Zedekiah of Jonah's reasons for riding to Joppa. "The man who brought him back said that your father was doing quite well, though they were both positively coated in sand when they arrived at his master's inn. A strange tale if you ask me."

"Coated in sand? Why would they have sand on both of them?"

"Don't ask me, son." Zedekiah laughed, his eyes twinkling. "Though if you did pressure me to answer I'd say they got themselves stuck in quicksand."

"Quicksand?"

"That is, unless your father enjoys rolling in mud along with Abiel here. And Abiel is usually a very clean stallion, doesn't like being dirty."

"Quicksand," Benjamin murmured to himself in disbelief. "And the man said that my father looked all right?"

"Yes, he did—just sandy." Zedekiah took Abiel's reins and called a farewell over his shoulder.

Benjamin grunted a vague response, but he wasn't really paying attention. Something deep inside his mind was stirring; his memories were returning. He walked over to an acacia and sat beneath its sparse shade. Closing his eyes, he allowed himself to drift a moment before his mind cleared.

"Benjamin, she's gone." Abigail choked on the words, a wave of golden hair peeping from beneath her red headscarf.

"What do you mean, Abigail?" Benjamin fought hard to keep his eyes open. He was exhausted from his journey home, but he was also excited. He was finally rid of his miserable master. After three years, he was free. His mind wandered to thoughts of spending his days working beside Abba as they had always wanted to do, but Abba was gone.

"Benjamin, are you listening to me?" Abigail took hold of his shoulders and shook him.

"What, sorry."

She let out a frustrated sigh. "Mother is gone."

"She is?"

"She left just this morning."

"Doesn't she do that frequently?"

Abigail shook her heard at his confusion. "You heard that Abba died?"

"Yes, a messenger came and told me."

"Well her mourning was over last week."

"And?"

"And she has had the eye of some handsome rich man from the next town over, and she intends to marry him."

"So soon?" Benjamin set down his bag before sitting down beside it.

"Yes, have you listened to anything I've been trying to tell you?"

"No, I'm sorry, Abigail. Start over please."

"You know that she was just about ready to divorce Abba before he died?"

"Yes, I know."

"Well as soon as he did, she practically strolled around looking for someone to marry."

"She can't very well do that when she's in mourning," Benjamin said through clenched teeth. "That sort of audacity should upset the whole town."

"Well it did, but you know Mother. She doesn't care about other people. She just wants money. And she found it in the form of a certain Kenan. He is extremely rich, I hear, and apparently he likes her enough to marry her."

Benjamin sat aghast for a moment, absorbing the information. To request a divorce from one's husband was a very uncommon thing, but to marry immediately after, when she had no real reason to was unprecedented.

Abigail continued, "On top of that, she took all the money that Abba had saved up."

"All of it?"

"Yes."

"But how could she? Oded and Jonah are not even ten years old yet. She didn't leave anything at all?"

"No, Benjamin. You know how she is; she doesn't care about us. We are on our own, and I need your help."

"Of course."

"We need to go to Jerusalem."

"The capital of Judah?"

"Yes. It is very big, Benjamin. There are lots of people, and I'm sure we can find somewhere to work. Then we can build a home outside the city and maybe farm the land."

"What about them?" Benjamin gestured to the room where his sister and brothers slept.

"They will come with us."

"But it is so far, Abigail."

"Where else can we go? What else can we do? We'll never make it here living under Mother's reputation's shadow. You are the oldest male in the house, Benjamin. That makes you the head of the house. So, make up your mind. Which is easier? Staying here and starving or going to Jerusalem and looking for work?" She was yelling at him now, her amber eyes shining like two spheres of fire. "What would Abba say, Benjamin? You were his favorite. What would he tell you to do?" Her voice cracked and she broke off, watching him through a film of tears.

"I...I suppose we have to go to Jerusalem. We need to gather a light load of provisions. You and I can carry them, and we should leave in a couple of days. We'll need the time to prepare. Besides, I need to recover from my journey."

"At least her leaving coincided with your return." Abigail wiped her eyes and embraced her brother. Then she turned and headed to bed. Benjamin remained sitting for a long time, ruminating. Just this morning, he had considered himself a beetle beneath his mother's sandal. Now he was the head of the house. He was the only thing standing between his family and a life filled with uncertainty. He had to be their support and their leader. In a mere two days, they would leave and make the long journey to Jerusalem—to a new home, and with luck, a new beginning.

Chapter Thirteen

Day and night were impossible to distinguish in his dark slimy prison. Jonah lay unmoving, he felt a crawling sensation over his entire body. It felt like tiny creatures swarming over him. His stomach turned in revulsion at the thought, but he lacked the energy to sit up, even to open his eyes. He tried to fit the pieces together in his mind, to figure out where he was, how he had gotten there, and how to get out. He assumed that he was still in the water and on some sort of vessel because of how it went and up and down. He noticed that the transitions were smooth, as if the water were now calm. He repeated that last bit to himself again. *The water is calm.*

The sailors had thrown him overboard to calm the water, and now he was stuck. But what was he stuck inside of? Pressing down his fear, Jonah reached out a hand and lifted a fistful of the creatures. They squirmed, a heap of little legs and small bodies. They were tiny sea animals of some sort. He had heard of great swarms of small sea creatures that fishermen encountered. They turned the water pink. Jonah strained his memory to recall what they were called. Krill, that's what it was. And the animal that ate krill was...he sat up, dropping the handful of krill. The sounds, the movement, the stench, the burning liquid, the slimy walls and floor. He was *in* a sea creature. He was inside a whale!

Jonah used his new-found adrenaline to stand. The heat threatened to force him down, but he fought it with all his strength. He was inside a whale! He was going to be digested! He was currently being eaten! Panic pressed hard at his lungs, making it difficult to breathe. How had he managed to get himself into this mess? His mind asked the question, but he knew the answer. He was running from God, what did he expect? A blessing? He felt himself sinking, sinking in trepidation, sinking in despair, and sinking in krill.

Jonah wondered how much longer he had to live. If God were punishing him, he would die inside this fish. Jonah thought of exactly how hungry and thirsty he was. He felt as if he had missed about four or five meals. It could very easily have been inaccurate, but it gave him an idea. His thirst made him think of times in Gath Hepher when the water was low and he had drunk nothing for two or three days during famine times. The wells would dry up, and they would have to dig their own. He knew that he could not survive for much more than a few days without water.

He felt the slime on the floor and walls. The burning sensation met his hands and he drew back quickly. He knew that it was remotely different from water and that there was nothing inside the whale that he could drink. He could always eat the krill, but he wasn't hungry enough for that. The heat would likely make him even thirstier, and Jonah wondered if it was even worth trying to stay alive. Maybe he could find a way to hasten this torturous death.

Yet a small niggling feeling made him hesitate from traveling down that road. It was so minute, yet it was there. It was an if...if he could survive, if he could escape, if by some miracle he was spared. Jonah let his muscles go weak, and he collapsed onto his knees on the stomach floor. He was so tired. If he just closed his eyes, perhaps he would go to sleep and never wake up. Jonah pushed hard at the thought. He had to stay alive. But the heat was so oppressive, so intense. Jonah felt his body swaying and he fell backward in a faint.

When Jonah awoke, his senses were in a muddle. His mind felt foggy, his only thoughts were of the heat and his thirst. There were less krill now. Most of them were likely digested, farther down inside the whale. Jonah wondered how long it would be before he too was digested, before his life ended as it inevitably would. He closed his eyes and lay back down, ready to pass out from the heat again, but a voice deep inside was calling. The sound built until it seemed that it truly echoed off his ears.

"What about them?" Jonah pushed at his conscience. He didn't want to care about them. All he wanted to do was leave, to enter the dark realm of death. Unwanted thoughts of his family seeped into his mind, but he tried to ward them off. In the end, he lost the battle, and allowed the thoughts to drift through his mind unhindered. He remembered opening the door on a glorious morning, just after Benjamin's accident, to see the small boy on the doorstep. All Benjamin had asked was if he could come in, and now he was Jonah's adopted son, willing to call him Abba.

"Will you call me?" This voice was different and it affected Jonah even more than the first. He knew whom the voice belonged to, though his heart still did not believe.

He whispered the name, "Yahweh." His past visions shot to the forefront of his mind of Yahweh's encouragement when they were in the Assyrian camp and of Yahweh's call to action to prophesy to Nineveh.

Jonah thought about the events leading up to his imprisonment inside the whale. It had all started because of a mere thought—the thought that Nineveh might repent, that they might be forgiven. But what if they weren't? What if God actually meant to destroy them? If Jonah missed the opportunity to prophesy of the destruction of the Assyrians, he could never forgive himself. His mind swam. There was a risk either way. When or if he prophesied, they might repent and they might not. Jonah knew he had to try. But first, he had to get out of the whale.

Searching the stomach had been pointless. In the dark, it was impossible to tell if there was a way out. There was now only one hope, only one place to go. Jonah fought his weariness and raised himself onto his knees. He closed his eyes, not to the darkness around him, but to the bitter darkness inside of him. With a mere glimmer of hope to cling to, Jonah let his heart pour out as he prayed.

Time passed quickly as Jonah lost himself in his misery and hopelessness. He had been banished from God's sight. But even inside this stinking whale, Yahweh was present. He would rescue Jonah; He was willing. The whale went through a series of twists and turns, and

Jonah was tossed around accordingly, but it did nothing to stop his mind's flow. Half an hour later, Jonah felt his prayer coming to a close.

"Salvation is from the Lord," he finished.

The whale began to move, violently it seemed. The krill scurried around him, desperate to escape. Jonah felt himself pelted by the creatures as his world spun round and round. Liquid hit him hard. He felt it tearing at his skin. Acid, not surprising for a stomach, but why was there acid now? He felt himself being pushed along by the liquid. Though he fought it, it was like fighting a wave. He slid along a tube-like tunnel, full of slime that coated him from head to toe. He felt sick to his stomach and extremely dizzy.

"Yahweh, help me!"

The liquid entered his mouth, his skin burned like fire. He threw up, his body convulsing as he shot up the passage. A moment later, he hit a hard surface with a smack. Unsure of where he was, he pushed himself up onto his hands and knees. Battling hard against unconsciousness, he looked around. At first, all he could see was white light after complete darkness. Slowly, colors began to form, then shapes. He was out of the whale. He was on dry land. Jonah let out a shout of joy, though it was little more than a croak.

He was absolutely parched. Drinking salt water would be a foolish choice, and he fought to restrain the urge. He heard a splash and turned to see the whale off to his right, rolling itself away from the sand, flopping on a giant scale to get back out to sea. Jonah watched it and marveled at the streamline body, powerful tail, and large gentle eyes. A while later, it submerged, then its back became visible above the surface. It blew a great stream of water into the air. Then it dove, tail slapping the water, sending a wave that pushed the waters of the Great Sea up onto the sand on which Jonah lay.

He struggled to stand, unable to contain his elation. He was alive. He was out of the whale. Yahweh had heard his prayer and answered it. He moved farther up the beach, back behind a large dune covered with coarse grass and began to dig. Eventually, he was rewarded with a tiny puddle of water, a while later it became a large pool. He stuck his head down inside and drank deeply, digging out the sand and grit when it slid back in. The water was pleasantly fresh, despite the slight salt tint. He splashed himself with it, swiping at the slime that was evaporating on his skin; leaving behind a smelly film. With his thirst quenched,

Jonah crawled on hands and knees up the beach. He found a clump of bushes and slid beneath them. The sun beat down, but to Jonah, it felt like a cool breeze after the furnace that was the whale's stomach. Closing his eyes, he relaxed and fell into a deep restful sleep.

* * *

He was waiting for her, as usual, beside the well. Marbita couldn't help but smile at his appearance. His hair had begun to grow, and he was now accustomed to wearing the girl's clothes. Beneath the folds of cloth, however, he was becoming more muscular than he had ever been. Shammi had always tolerated his training. Now, however, it was clear that he loved it. Sure, life was difficult enough without having to worry about staying concealed, but that was the fun of it.

"Marbita, you are always late."

"I know, Sherah," she said, using his fake name. "Father has chores for me to do though."

Shammi lowered his eyes a moment, thinking. "Things must be difficult for you...now more than ever."

"I will not deny the fact." Marbita would not allow him to think that she was not sacrificing much for him. Nonetheless, she noticed her hard tone and tried to soften that statement. "It's been worth it though. Seeing a good friend has been a blessing." It was a deadly game they played, yet they did it with the utmost ease. If Father or General Dorar ever discovered where Shammina was, both he and Marbita would be killed. Every able-bodied male had to become an Assyrian soldier, and it had to be under the instruction of General Dorar.

"The teacher has changed considerably." Shammi avoided using Rabil's name in public areas.

"Has he?"

"He drinks less and is more...stable."

"That is good, Sherah." Marbita smiled as she lowered her jug into the well. Things were going very well with Shammi's training. He was looking more like a man than ever, with a thick muscular build. And he was both quicker and stronger than before. Marbita could not imagine why she had ever considered that anything serious could go wrong.

"I enjoy my learning very much, Marbita."

"That is good to hear." She hoisted the now full jug onto her shoulder, preparing to head home. "Oh, and here is the cloth you requested, Sherah." She unslung the pouch from around her neck and passed the hidden food and water to her brother.

He took it rather reluctantly. "I hate to burden you with my requests, Marbita." Marbita stopped a moment and looked deep into her younger brother's eyes; seeing a solemnity in them that hadn't been there before.

"It is no trouble." She watched him disappear into the crowd. Just another cloth-clad figure in a city full of thousands. Marbita shifted the heavy jug into a more comfortable position and began to walk back home. It was good to see her brother in healthy condition and in fairly good spirit. He would be returning home that night as well.

Mother was busy cleaning the house when Marbita entered. She lowered the jug onto the table and watched Mother a moment, noticing that she stood painfully on one leg. "Has it grown worse, Mother?"

"There is nothing to be concerned about, Marbita."

"But the physician said the break was not clean."

"It's fine, child. Now help me clean before your father gets home. Then I'll have even less trouble."

Marbita rummaged around the boxes before she found a decent rag and dipped it into her mother's bucket. The floors were so dirty that even after cleaning a mere few feet the water had turned dark brown. She leaned over the bucket and frowned, Mother in her youth frowned back at her. Marbita remembered the years when their home had had proper floors, but that was a long time ago. Ever since the plague that had ruined the empire's economy and snatched away her beautiful and only sister...

"Who is coming tonight, Mother?"

"Your uncle."

"Not again."

"Hush, Marbita, unless you want your tongue cut out."

"Why must he come tonight?"

Mother sighed and set down her rag. "We are women in Assyria, Marbita. We are given no right to ask why."

"Then I shall find some place to live where I can."

Mother smiled and smoothed a dark strand of hair away from Marbita's face. "Such fire in my daughter; they can never put it out." Her smile faded slowly, and she returned to work. A comfortable silence resumed as they scrubbed the stone floor, aware that the sun was steadily sinking lower on the horizon.

When Uncle Ador knocked, Marbita thought it always sounded like thunder. When her uncle spoke or walked or fought, he always sounded like thunder. Tonight, he was especially frightening because Shammi would be coming home. Marbita usually had time to warn Shammi beforehand, but tonight she would have to make sure he never entered the house. Father was no fool, but at least he was drunk most of the time. Uncle Ador, on the other hand, was sharp as an arrow, and deadly as one too.

Her uncle entered with his powerful stride and soldier's stance. His appearance fit the appearance of a god of death or war, and she wondered if Assur, the god of war and Assyria, was a constant presence in Uncle Ador. For his black eyes, black hair, imposing stature and icy calm made her shiver just to look at him. Marbita heard her name called and she rushed forward, head lowered and her posture submissive.

"Answer your uncle, girl," her father ordered. "He was inquiring if Shammina has been found."

Marbita's mind began to race, and she was grateful that her head was down. "Uncle Ador, I have not heard any news of Shammina."

"Why are you lying to me?" Her uncle spoke slowly, but his voice was hard as stone and his gaze equally cold.

Marbita felt her heart skip a beat. "I can assure you, Uncle, that I am not lying."

In an instant, her wrist was seized in an iron grip. Uncle Ador's narrow eyes watched her with suspicion. "Where is Shammina?"

"Uncle Ador, I tell the truth. I have not seen my brother."

Her wrist was released and Uncle Ador stepped back. "She's telling the truth, Nineel."

Marbita exhaled as slowly and cautiously as she could. Any visible sign of relief would have revealed the truth. Uncle Ador was an Assyrian. He knew how to manipulate the mind using fear. Every Assyrian soldier learned to. It was part of their warfare.

"You are dismissed." Father waved her off, and Marbita retreated without hesitation.

She mounted the stairs and stepped into her room, nearly running into Shammi in the process. "Sham...Sherah, you come at a bad time," she whispered, her heart racing.

"I heard. Are you all right?"

"Of course. Come with me." She led Shammi to the storage space in the corner of the room where the mats and cushions were kept. Just like every night, he wormed his way to the very back, and she concealed him beneath a pile of blankets that they would never use. He was used to roasting each night in the little closet, and she wondered if she could somehow find a better place for him to sleep, but tonight was too risky.

An instant later, Mother was by her side and Marbita gave a small start. "Mother, are our duties over already?"

"They are discussing something downstairs, Marbita. Nineel told me to stay out of the way."

They stood for a moment, and Marbita thought that she could hear a tiny movement from the closet. She removed her mat and her mother's and unrolled them in the opposite corner, hoping that Shammi would be able to remain silent. The house was especially dusty after shifting around the dirt during cleaning. The small sneeze startled her, but she reacted in time.

"Oh! Excuse me, Mother."

Mother watched her for a moment as she lay down on her mat. Marbita turned to the wall in time to hear another sneeze.

Then Mother came close and stood over Marbita, watching curiously. "Are you ill, Marbita?"

"No, Mother." Another sneeze sounded. Marbita rubbed her nose. Her acting didn't cut it. Mother's eyes went wide and she scanned the room. "I'm not catching a cold, Mother," Marbita told her, though her voice was far from steady. Yet another sneeze resounded from the closet, and Mother rushed over, pulling out mats and cushions. "Mother, what are you doing?" Marbita rushed forward without thinking, panic causing her body to act without her willing it to. She arrived too late.

Shammi sat in the corner of the closet, rubbing his nose and smiling sheepishly. For all her work at disguising him, Marbita had hoped that he would only ever be seen from a distance. His hair was long, and his tunic feminine, but he looked the same otherwise. Being this close, it didn't take too much imagining for Mother to put the pieces together.

"Shammina," she whispered, reaching out a hand to lead him out. He came with lowered eyes. Neither of them knew what Mother would do next. She had not seen him since he had left for training and there were tears in her eyes. She embraced him a moment before turning to Marbita. "You have to tell your father the truth." Marbita stepped back, shaking her head.

"No, I can't, Mother. Why do you think I've hidden him all this time?"

"I know he's your brother, Marbita, but he is not permitted to be seen outside of the training grounds without permission from the General."

Marbita took a deep breath and decided to gamble. "He has permission, Mother."

"Then why is General Dorar looking for him?"

"General Dorar is no longer his commanding officer." Mother raised her eyebrows. Glancing from Shammina to Marbita. "General Rabil is."

Mother gasped, taking hold of Shammi's shoulders. "What are the two of you thinking? Rabil is a madman!"

"No he's not, Mother!" Shammi blurted. "He's the father that Nineel can never be." Marbita squealed as the smack resounded in the dim room. Shammi swung his head away from Mother, a red mark showing where her palm had struck him.

"I am ashamed to call you my children. Rabil is the essence of scum in Assyria." Mother hissed through clenched teeth. She turned to leave the room. "I will explain everything to your father. It is better for him to hear of this while I am there to bargain with him. I might be able to convince him to let Shammi return to his training alive. But as for you, Marbita..." She let her gaze fall on her daughter. "You must leave."

"Leave?"

"You said you wanted to already."

"But, Mother..."

"There is no argument I can make for you, Marbita—none at all. There is no way for me to convince Nineel to let this go where you are concerned. He will not let you live." Mother reached for the door, but a moment later, she crumpled to the ground as clay shards flew in all directions. Shammina dropped the broken jug. Marbita screamed. A

119

moment later, they heard feet pounding up the stairs. Uncle Ador and Father were coming.

Shammina grabbed Marbita and dragged her to the window. "Climb out, Marbita. Now!"

Marbita fought to gain control of her shaking limbs. For a moment, she dangled on the ledge before falling the remaining seven or so feet. She tried to let her knees spring when she landed, but still she fell over. Shammina followed an instant later, and soon two heads stuck out the window. She felt herself hoisted up and pushed down the alley that backed their home.

"Run, Marbita! You know where to go!"

And Marbita ran. She ran through the alleys and across the market square, down more alleys, and around the darkest and most dangerous streets in Nineveh. She ran until she came to the wall, the wall where Rabil lived. Refusing to let herself think, Marbita swung open the door and stepped inside, shutting it softly behind her. To her surprise, Rabil was up. A small lamp cast enough light to see his dark face.

"General Rabil, it's me, Marbita."

He turned toward her, and she saw that Shammi was right. His eyes had lost their crazed look, and the floor was clean. No rats scurried in dark corners. No food lay scattered on the stones.

"Marbita, what are you doing here?" His voice was the voice of the kind, and not of the mad. "What's wrong?"

Marbita pinched her wrist to break her shock. Surely the man before her was not the same Rabil that had slaughtered rats to satisfy his blood-lust. "It's Shammi; he's been found out," she managed. "My father and my uncle are chasing him, maybe attacking him." In an instant, Rabil was on his feet and out the door. Marbita wondered if she should follow, but decided against it. What good could a girl do in this situation? So instead, she sat down on a low cushion with her heart thudding violently in her chest.

The corners of the house still lay in dark shadow. Nonetheless, the transformation was quite noticeable. The smell that had once occupied the windowless room was gone, and so was the sense of lurking danger. Marbita heard shouting outside. She stood, prepared to run or fight. The door swung open, and she got a glimpse of the scene outside.

The four men appeared to have come down the alley, Rabil and Shammi in the lead, Father and Uncle Ador in pursuit. Shammina slowed and turned to face Father, Father struck a blow to him and Shammi moved to return it, but got a second blow and staggered backward. None of them drew a weapon, but Marbita they did not need one in order to kill. Rabil, hands balled into fists, pushed Shammina behind him and out of the way. With a cry of rage, he began to swing at her father, his eyes dark and deadly. Her father returned blow for blow and shouted, "Shame! Shame!", with each breath he took. The main cause for fear though was the man who had opened the door.

Her uncle who had opened the door, saw her in an instant and moved toward her, dark eyes glittering. Marbita was trapped. She knew she could never get around him and out the door. She also knew he would not let her live; that was unless he grew a conscience, which was as likely as Assur turning from a god of war to a god of peace. Outside, she saw her father go down beneath a melee of flailing fists and curses. Shammina kicked him one moment, and shook his head the next, as if unsure of what to do. Rabil however, pummeled Father relentlessly. Angered that he would show no compassion for his son, and Marbita realized that Shammi was right. Rabil had become the loving father to Shammina that Nineel never was. Shammi stepped away from Father's slumped form and caught sight of Uncle Ador. He spun and rushed through the doorway to defend her.

From nowhere, her uncle produced a knife and turned on Shammi, his eyes glittering malevolently in the light streaming through the doorway. Time slowed to a crawl as Uncle Ador took up a fighting stance, his hand moving, the blade coming closer to Shammina. In a burst of adrenaline and determination, she leapt between the two of them. Uncle Ador's blade was mere inches from Shammina when she did so, and she felt its coolness touch her neck and pierce the skin. Shammi was her little brother. She had to protect him.

She felt something warm flow down her neck and over her shoulder, but she felt no pain. Marbita crumpled to the ground and rolled over onto her back, then panicked in the realization that she was vulnerable. Uncle Ador stood rooted to the floor, blinking in surprise. Shammina saw the opportunity to strike and she distantly heard the blade clatter to the ground before they locked arms, wrestling for it. The blade was just lying between them, easily accessible. If Marbita had been listening, she would have heard Rabil shout Shammina's name and his footsteps as he raced toward them. But as in a dream, she rolled over, shot to her feet and leapt for the knife. It was the wrong move. Neither Shammi nor Uncle Ador had expected her to go for the knife, and with a slur of curses Uncle Ador kicked at her savagely. Shammi released his hold on Uncle Ador and flung her across the room to safety. The knife lay on the ground for an instant before Uncle Ador swept it up, aimed, and threw it. Marbita lay her head down on the cold stone floor as the world went black.

Chapter Fourteen

Jonah opened his eyes cautiously, fully aware that he was not under the bush anymore. He vaguely recalled being lifted and moved. He blinked. He was in a house. A small one at that, but a house nonetheless. Rolling his head to the side, he was mildly surprised to be staring into the soft eyes of a sheep. The sheep let out a small startled bleat and trotted away. A minute later, he heard footsteps.

"Took you long enough to wake up." A man with wispy mouse-brown hair and eyes entered Jonah's peripheral line of vision.

"Wh...where am I?" His throat was parched, and his tongue felt very large.

The man noticed this and lifted a dipper to Jonah's lips. "You're in my house," he stated. "My name is On."

"On?" Jonah asked. He remembered Jonathan's goat An, and smiled.

"O-n he says," the man muttered mockingly. "What be your name, O' wise man who balks at the name On?"

"Jonah."

"J-o-nah." The man shambled out of Jonah's sight a moment, and then returned with a thin piece of bronze. "Listen, Jonah, you're pretty lucky that you look the way you do. Otherwise, I would have just left you there on the beach."

He raised the mirror to allow Jonah to see himself. Jonah felt his jaw fall open a moment. His skin was white as flour. In addition, he was almost completely bald.

"Ya look like someone boiled you for a year," On remarked, laughing. It sounded more like a cackle, but Jonah smiled anyway. It was good to see another human being. "Now pay attention to what I have to say. I'm getting a good ways up in age and don't have enough time left to waste being a nurse and feeding the needy. So as soon as you can walk, you're leaving." He crossed his wrinkled, vein-lined arms, showing an unmovable front. "Alright?"

"That sounds reasonable."

"Good. Because I have to be somewhere in a week, so hurry up and get better so you can be out of my hair." The man cackled again. "Though I don't have much hair left anymore." Then he left, and Jonah dozed.

The next thing Jonah knew, he was drenched from head to toe. On stood over him with a jug of water tipped down, a clear sign of what was happening.

"Is there a problem?" Jonah asked irritably. He had just drowned in the ocean, been swallowed by a whale, stayed in the whale's stomach for at least a couple of days, and now he was in the kind and gentle care of a man named On who didn't have the decency to let a person sleep.

"You were a moanin' and screamin', and I was worried the neighbors might think I was killing somebody."

"Moaning and screaming?"

"Something about big fishes."

"Oh."

"Speaking of fishes, what is a boiled potato like you doing on the sea shore?"

"I was swallowed by a whale."

"Oh, I actually kinda like you now. You are very funny." When he saw the expression on Jonah's face he stopped mid-cackle. "You aren't joking, are you?"

Jonah's eyebrows went up. "No," he replied.

"Yes?"

"No."

"Pardon?" On started cackling again. "Oh, I thought you were just saying my name backwards." He began to howl then stopped. "So, you were eaten by a whale, uh?"

"Yes."

"And now you're having bad dreams about it all?"

"I suppose."

"Well, I suppose I don't blame you." He watched Jonah a moment. Then his eyes crinkled at the corners. "Can you walk yet?"

"I don't think so." They both laughed then. It felt good. When they stopped, Jonah said, "I can write though."

On looked at him a moment. "You want parchment and ink?"

"If that's possible."

"'Course it's possible. My son's a scribe, but away for the month seeing the world." On grinned as if every young boy took leave to see the world. "I have his stock." On gathered some cushions and propped Jonah up so he could write. Then he rummaged around his shelves for some blank parchment. "There. Ink and parchment. Anything else for the fish food?"

"No."

"Yes?"

"That's all, thank you." Jonah smiled as On shuffled away. Then he turned his attention to the paper. He remembered the dreams On had spoken of. At first, they had been of whales and angry sailors, but those had not been entirely unexpected. Afterward, though, he had dreamed of a city, a huge city with walls so wide that two chariots could ride along it side by side, a city with people, wicked people inside of it. And then there was the voice: "Go to the great city of Nineveh and preach against it, because its wickedness has come up before me." Jonah knew now that the storm, the whale, and his survival in its stomach was all part of Yahweh's plan to send him to Nineveh.

It frustrated him that he could not avoid his task. And this time, he knew, as he had inside the whale, that he must obey. He must prophesy; he was a prophet. And he had to remember the events of his work somehow didn't he? He bent over the parchment and began writing about his calling, then the ship and its crew, and finally he came to the whale. He paused, and then wrote of his desperate prayer. The writing flowed as fluidly as water, and he knew that it was not only his words, but Yahweh's. The feeling was the same as when he had told the crew to throw him overboard. His mouth, his hand, but not his words.

Now that he was writing down his prayer though, he recalled every word, every feeling that had swept over him.

He wrote:

> "In my distress I called to the Lord, and He answered me. From deep in the realm of the dead I called for help, and You listened to my cry. You hurled me into the depths, into the very heart of the seas, and the currents swirled about me. All Your waves and breakers swept over me. I said, 'I have been banished from Your sight; yet I will look again toward Your holy temple.' The engulfing waters threatened me, the deep surrounded me; seaweed was wrapped around my head. To the roots of the mountains I sank down; the earth beneath barred me in forever. But You, Lord my God, brought my life up from the pit. When my life was ebbing away, I remembered you, Lord, and my prayer rose to You, to Your holy temple. Those who cling to worthless idols turn away from God's love for them. But I, with shouts of grateful praise, will sacrifice to you. What I have vowed I will make good. I will say, 'Salvation comes from the Lord.'"

With the final sentence of his prayer, Jonah lowered the parchment with a sigh. He rolled it up into a tight scroll and set it beside him on the mat. Then he slowly swung his legs around until they touched the floor and rolled onto his hands and knees. He lifted himself on trembling legs, working to balance himself after days of being tossed around inside a whale. Taking a deep breath, he put one foot forward. He held his arms out to his sides to steady himself for a moment. Then he tried another foot.

"That don't count as walking, boy."

The voice startled him, and he fell onto the mat.

"Sorry, did I surprise you? I thought you young ones have eyes on the back of your heads."

"Oh, that's fine."

"Well either way, that doesn't count as walking."

"I see."

"Said the blind man."

"Sorry?"

"Never mind." On held out a small platter of food. "Here's some bread so you can walk sooner, and fish so you can take revenge. Oh, and water, but just in case, it isn't enough to drown in."

Jonah smiled as he took the platter and drank from the dipper On handed him. He knew that when he left, which with On's help would be soon, he would never forget this place. He knew that in the years to come, he would always credit his survival after being vomited up by the whale to On. And may he die by the hands of the sea if the generations after him were not taught to remember the man sent to save the prophet of God.

Despite seeming of a crusty disposition, On was more than happy to loan Jonah some money to purchase food and provisions on his way. Which was why Jonah found himself within sight of the great front gates of Nineveh after a several laborious months of walking, following road upon road in a constant eastward course. Jonah felt as if he could sleep for another month and had no intention of ever traveling across half the world again. But, as things were, he knew he would likely have to.

He had seen the hand of Yahweh in his travels over the past days. No robbers had attacked him, no quicksand or sandstorms had threatened him. The worst thing he had encountered was the occasional argumentative innkeeper that was reluctant to trust a bleached Hebrew overnight. During his journey, Jonah had heard God's words echoing through his mind—words of a prophecy: "Forty more days and Nineveh will be overthrown." Jonah felt a mixture of emotions whenever he thought of those words. He wanted them to be true, just like when he was very young and longed for his mother to return from the dead. He yearned for Nineveh to be destroyed. But what if they repented?

As he approached the gate, his mind began to spin, taking in his surroundings with awe. The Khosr river flowed steadily through. Heavy iron bars prevented entrance to the city by the river. The walls were even more massive than Jonah had imagined. Indeed, two chariots or perhaps three could ride side by side along its top. It stretched on for miles to his left and right and he wondered if he would even be allowed to enter such a place. The guard at the gate was clearly intended to represent the face of intimidation. He was a monstrosity in comparison to the people swarming around him, and his muscles bulged as if he were born to be strong. Unfortunately, he appeared too on edge to be effective. Jonah found himself addressed in Aramaic, a language that was more widely known than Hebrew.

"You there, Hebrew. Who are you? What is your business?" The guard's dark Assyrian eyes narrowed to slits as he examined Jonah's face. "I am a prophet of Yahweh, the God of Israel." Jonah felt the power of God surging through him. He was not afraid of this man; he was not afraid of the Assyrians. The guard beckoned to one of his comrades and spoke with him in Assyrian. He gestured at the city, the people around them, then himself.

The second guard, a smaller man than his comrade, stepped up to Jonah. "You will wait here for him to return." Then he nodded at the first guard who disappeared into the very heart of the city.

Ashur-Dan III, Emperor of Assyria, reclined on a couch in his room, enjoying the feeling of air cooling his feverish skin. His servants waved their fans as hard and as fast as they could, hoping to gain some favor in their master's eyes. Ninos, his secretary rattled on beside him, providing the summary of the events he had requested.

"Assyria's population has greatly plummeted since the plague last year, Your Majesty. Then there is the earthquake of last month, the month of Shamash. It was so powerful that the priests are certain it was supernatural, and with the solar eclipse as well, the empire is in an uproar. I have the details logged here, Your Majesty, and..." Ninos stopped, watching Ashur-Dan worriedly. "I fear that I have bored you, Your Majesty."

"No, I was only thinking."

"Of course, Your Majesty. Would you prefer peace and silence?"

"No." Ashur-Dan sighed and gazed about Nineveh's palace. The earthquake had done so much damage to his main capital that he had been forced to move his seat of power to Nineveh, an inconvenience without doubt—although the massive walls and endless luxuries helped to cool his fraying nerves. The recent devastation of the plague, the great earthquake, and the solar eclipse were all things he knew could not be coincidence. No emperor that he had ever heard of had suffered so much during his reign. What had he done that the gods were punishing him so? The astrologers had been in and out of his improvised throne room asking questions about his birth, his life, his superstitions, and reading his palm and future. No matter what they did and no matter how hard they prayed to the gods, the answer was always the same:

Nineveh will be overthrown. No more and no less. It was the only thing he had to go on.

He realized suddenly that his servants had stopped fanning him. He glared at them a moment before noticing that there was a disturbance outside the throne room door. "Have them enter," he ordered the guards at the door. A sentry and a group of the palace guard entered and bowed.

One of the palace guards, a wiry man with sunken eyes stepped forward. "Your Majesty, this sentry here says that a man has arrived at our gates claiming to be a prophet of Yahweh."

"A prophet of Yahweh? Israel's god?"

"Yes, Your Majesty."

Ashur-Dan blanched. He reached out a hand and crooked a finger at the priests and astrologers huddled in the corner. They rushed forward in a tizzy.

The high priest of Assur materialized from the group. "Your Majesty we have not tried praying to the gods of such remote nations as Israel. We assumed that they were powerless."

"Well maybe it's time you tried," he snarled at them. A prophet of Yahweh was outside his gates, requesting entrance. He knew he could not refuse. He knew from rumors and tales all throughout the southwestern Levant that the prophets of Yahweh were notorious for always being correct, no matter how insane their prophecies were. If this man prophesied destruction.... "Permit him to enter and I want to know what he says to the people."

"Yes, Your Majesty." The soldiers bowed and left the throne room.

As soon as the door closed, the priests began clambering for their ruler's attention. "Your Majesty, should we make sacrifices to appease Yahweh of Israel? Maybe if He is preparing to send ruin to us, we can change His mind."

"No, wait and see what this prophet has to say." Ashur-Dan rose and left the throne room, none too confident that he would ever enter it again.

Chapter Fifteen

Ador watched the girl's chest rise and fall with each shallow breath. Nineel, his beloved brother, was gone, killed by his very own son and the old crotchety General Rabil. They had both escaped the punishment they deserved, though he could not understand how. He moved his black, battle hardened gaze back to the girl. He was one of the best generals in the Assyrian army. How had a young soldier who had never seen battle gotten away from him? How had his niece, a mere child, interfered with his abilities? Perhaps he had grown soft. Surely that was the reason he had hesitated in his throw just long enough for Shammina to duck and get away.

When he had returned with the girl to Nineel's home, the man's wife was gone too. Now it was just himself and his niece, a niece he would do well to dispose of. Still, he could not help but admire her audacity in taking part in the fight. It was rare to see such a truly violent female in Assyria. Most of them cowered in fear, and likely they all should, but Marbita was different.

He had seen to it that she was tightly bound with coils of rope, but he was beginning to wonder if the precaution was currently necessary. The gash along her neck was deep, and she had lost a considerable amount of blood. She might never wake up.

Ador stood with a sigh. He was going stir crazy in here. He was supposed to be back with his men yesterday, but he felt the need to wait for Marbita to wake up. At the moment though, she seemed to be far from consciousness, so he left her where she was and stepped outside. The fresh air satisfied his lungs as he took successive deep breaths. It was more than just clean air; it was scented, scented with blood. The very streets of Nineveh ran with it. Death was their very way of life. And since they had been unable to campaign due to a weak and incompetent ruler, their need for blood had become domesticated. The result of the incompetence of his emperor had satisfied Ador's very dream to see Assyria reach her full potential of violence and bloodthirsty power, but what good was the Assyrian spirit if she was too weak to fight?

A sound attracted Ador's attention, and he jogged down the street toward the market square. There he stopped in surprise. A man, white as a ghost, stood in the middle of the market square yelling with all his might in Aramaic: "Forty more days and Nineveh will be overthrown. Forty more days and Nineveh will be overthrown." He repeated the statement over and over as he tromped past crowds of shocked city-folk. He certainly had a haughty air about him.

"What sort of man has the audacity to make such a claim?" Ador asked the stranger standing beside him.

"They say he is a prophet of Yahweh."

"Yahweh? I have never heard of such a god."

"Apparently, everything Yahweh's prophets have prophesied has come true."

"All of it?"

"Yes."

Ador felt his limbs begin to quiver. He was a general in the Assyrian army. He represented a piece of Assyria. Nineveh was her greatest city. If it was demolished.... On sudden inspiration, he rushed back to the house. To his surprise and relief, he found Marbita just as he had left her, and she was also awake. Her eyes went wide when she saw him, but as was her nature, it was only an instant before the fear vanished.

"Who are you?" She demanded as he entered. Ador ignored her and instead, rested his battle-hardened gaze on her own dark one and noted how much fire burned in her eyes. "You can't do anything to me," she hissed.

"I'm not going to. The prophet is." He ignored her expression of bewilderment and untied her. He pulled the girl to her feet and rebound her hands. Taking a hold of her elbow, he dragged her out of the house.

"Where are you taking me, you swineherd?"

Ador felt his ire raising its dark evil head. "I'm taking you to the prophet."

"You aren't taking me anywhere."

He reached out and slapped her hard. She did not lower her head and there was no submission in her eyes. He hit her again and a third time until she at last looked away. Her eyes were so dark, and the fire in them triggered a memory he had tried to forget. Larsa once had that same fiery spirit as well—until he had lamed her, just like Nineel had lamed his own wife. But Larsa had not submitted to him. Instead, she had run away and wounded his pride beyond recovery. To be able to order about a portion of a massive army and not to be able to control one's own wife left him seething. Marbita would soon learn that she had no right to disobey. She was just a girl, a girl in the great empire of Assyria.

It didn't take long to locate the blanched prophet. He did not move very fast as if he were weary and did not wish to waste energy.

"You there, prophet." Heads turned as Ador called out to the man.

"What do you want?" The man turned dark, haunting eyes on him.

"I have come to bargain with your god."

"Bargain?"

"This is my niece, my own flesh and blood. If you were to sacrifice her to your God, perhaps He would look upon us with more favor." The crowd around them began to nod and mumble agreement. Surely human sacrifice would please this Yahweh of Israel.

The white man spat on the ground in front of Ador. "Yahweh does not accept human sacrifice; He detests it."

"I do not believe you." Ador was desperate. He had to get rid of this girl who reminded him so vividly of Larsa. "If you do not take her and sacrifice her to your God, I will do it myself."

The white man looked as if he were about to speak, then he stopped. He looked Marbita over and his mouth twitched. "Very well, I will take her." Ador pushed Marbita forward with relief. The crowd began to cheer as the white man moved on, Marbita in tow, shouting out his prophesy against Nineveh.

The girl watched her new captor curiously. He was as white as a sheep from head to toe, and he was nearly bald. The sight of him both disgusted and intrigued her. And the message he carried was so odd. He was prophesying destruction against Nineveh, which was apparently where they were. She wondered if it would actually happen. The day wore on and she kept her silence, unsure of what her captor was really like. All he had said since he had taken her was, "Forty more days and Nineveh will be overthrown." The words were repeated over and over again.

As the sky began to darken, her captor's voice grew weaker and weaker until he finally decided to look for an inn. She could see no money pouch on him and wondered how he would pay for his stay. In the end, money proved unnecessary. He was clearly a very important man, for as soon as he entered an inn, they offered to allow him and his "human sacrifice" to stay the night for free. Her captor agreed without any argument and they were shown into a room more luxurious than the girl had ever seen.

The man pushed her inside and unbound her hands, watching her with a mixture of pity and abhorrence. "What is your name, girl?"

"My name?"

"Yes."

"I..." She closed her eyes a moment. What was her name? It felt as if it were on the tip of her tongue. The only word she could think of was Shammina. Why was that the only name she could remember? Perhaps it was hers. But Shammina was a boy's name, wasn't it? "I think my name is...Mina." She shrugged a shoulder. It was as good as any name.

"Mina." The man tried the name. "Alright. You can call me Jonah."

"Jonah. That is not an Assyrian name."

"It is Hebrew."

"What are you doing in Nineveh?"

"I am prophesying of its destruction."

"I can see that." They stood in silence for a moment.

Then Jonah asked, "Why are you unsure of your name?"

"Because I can't remember."

He watched her a moment. "If I were to make a guess, I would say it's because of that wound on your neck. It looks like someone stabbed or slit your throat."

134

She touched the wound and winced. "Tried to," she corrected softly.

Jonah sat down on a sleeping mat. "Too bad they failed."

She gave a small start. "I get the impression that you dislike me."

"Not you in particular. I hate all Assyrians."

"Then why did you rescue me from that man?" She thought of the man's words. Apparently, she was his niece.

"Because, well—" He lifted his hands in a gesture of confusion. "I really don't know. And you are starting to make me regret it."

"Am I?"

"Yes. The only reason I'm taking you with me is because everyone thinks you are a human sacrifice for Yahweh."

"And aren't I?"

"No. I told your uncle that Yahweh hates human sacrifice, but he didn't listen."

"Alright." She sat down on a mat up against the opposite wall. "So what reason do I have not to walk out that door right now?"

"Because if you do, they will bring you back."

She nodded in understanding. "So I'm stuck here then?"

"Yes. But don't worry. You'll be dead in forty days."

"Ah." She lay down, wondering how she had ever come to be held hostage by this strange, bleached Hebrew who was so anti-Assyrian. "Why do you hate all Assyrians, Jonah?"

"Because you people killed some of my family."

"I'm sorry."

"No you're not."

She didn't argue with him. At this point, she was beginning to agree. He sure was miserable to be around. Mina closed her eyes. She longed to know what her real name was, and where her family was—other than the man who claimed to be her uncle. Did she have any other? For just like Jonah, if anything had happened to her family, she would also want those who were responsible to pay. She rubbed her neck. And by the looks of things, she likely had enemies.

The next day was no different than the previous. Jonah made his usual grating remarks from time to time, but other than that, all he did was shout out his message. When the sun reached its zenith, they slipped into a bakery and Jonah requested a loaf of bread, which the baker gave gladly. Mina should have been surprised when he did not offer her any, but she was not. So busy was her mind at trying to remember the past that her present hunger seemed entirely irrelevant to her situation. Jonah fell into a conversation with the baker concerning his Hebrew background, and a sudden thought presented itself into her mind. The thought itself gave her peace as she felt her mind slowly clearing, and the fear of memory loss begin to recede into the past. As soon as Jonah stopped speaking, she caught his attention.

"Jonah, if destruction is declared on our city, why don't you pray for us like Abraham did in your Torah?"

"How do you know anything about the Torah?"

"There is an old lady that tells stories in the market. She traveled with caravans as a child."

"I thought I made my opinion clear."

"Yes, but you took pity on me."

He glared at her, his lips tightening into a line. Then, abruptly he smiled. "Of course, I will pray as Abraham did for Sodom and Gomorrah." Mina took a step backward in surprise.

"You...you will?"

"Absolutely; I will pray with all hopes raised that the outcome is the same as it was in Abraham's case." He turned and strode out of the bakery, leaving her to sputter with rage behind him.

Jonah was relieved that he had finally found a way to keep Mina quiet. She was as annoying as Atarah, innocently impudent. The girl trailed after him, shoulders slumped, as he wandered through the streets. The sun was setting low in the sky by the time Jonah's voice had once again become hoarse. He needed to rest up for another day of prophesying. Nineveh was an enormous city. The walls themselves were over seven miles long. Its size gave Jonah new hope. Perhaps God would destroy Nineveh after all, and when He did, a large part of the Assyrian population would vanish from the face of the earth. What a blow it would be for them when their great city, in fact the largest city in the world, was demolished.

It was callously satisfying that every shop or inn Jonah walked into offered him free service. Everyone in Nineveh, it appeared, was hoping that by helping Yahweh's prophet they would somehow appease Yahweh Himself. Jonah found himself, not entirely without intention, wishing that the Ninevites would be wrong. If only he knew for sure that there was no hope at all for them, then things would be easier. As the moon rose high in a twinkling blanket of stars, Jonah lay down on a simple mat, ready for sleep. But sleep refused to come. He tossed and turned, most likely keeping the girl awake as well. And when he finally did rest, he wished he had not, as dreams invaded his mind.

Benjamin lay on his mat in Tekoa, his arms slung out on the floor. Jonah stepped toward him, watching each slow, shaky breath. Was he ill? Jonah knelt beside his son and reached out to gently touch his hand. In an instant, the scene around him changed. He was no longer in the house he knew, but in a different home. The walls were shabby, and the floor was coated thickly with dirt. Yet there was a sense of belonging that accompanied the place. Jonah stood and glanced around. A small boy sat on the floor beside a bag, talking to a beautiful girl with her golden hair tucked beneath a red headscarf. It took Jonah longer than he would have expected to recognize his son. Benjamin was thinner than he had ever seen him, though he was well muscled. His bare arms were dirty, and his jaw jutted out from a thin worried face. They were discussing a trip to Jerusalem and Jonah remembered his conversation with Benjamin that dreadful night of the accident. Benjamin's sisters and brothers had died on that trip. Jonah had to prevent their deaths. In the strange feeling of being absent from oneself that accompanies dreams, Jonah walked between the two.

"Abigail." The girl turned to face him. Her wide amber eyes filled with fear. Jonah felt his heart constrict. The likeness was unmistakable. "Abigail, you can't go to Jerusalem; you won't make it." He reached to take her hand, but she backed away. Fearing that she would disappear, Jonah rushed forward, but as soon as he touched her, the scene around him changed.

It was still Benjamin, Abigail, and himself, but something was odd about the way the girl held herself. Her back was to him, and she stared off into seeming emptiness. Suddenly, she turned and Jonah leapt back in surprise. On her face was the mask of death.

"For him, for him you must return." Her voice made his blood run cold. It was not the usual vibrant voice of the living. It was dry and toneless, though beneath it ran a vein of terrible desperation. She

grabbed Jonah's arm, and her skin was cold as ice. Then, without warning, she fell. Benjamin rushed forward to catch her, and when they came into contact, she returned to a living state. Benjamin bent low over her limp body and heaved loud hiccupping sobs. Standing in the background, Jonah found he could not move to console his son, nor could he do anything about the life that clearly was draining from Abigail's features.

Then she lifted her hand toward him and moved her fingers ever so slightly to beckon him closer. He obeyed. Benjamin disappeared from his mind as he stooped over. She lifted her head and pressed her mouth against his ear. "For him you must return. He is lost and will never find his way back home."

Jonah woke with a start to find himself back in the house in Tekoa. He glanced about him, checking to make sure everything was as it should be. Everything was, except Benjamin was gone. Recalling Abigail's words, Jonah hurried out of the room. He searched the house, the yard, the surrounding fields. But to no avail. Benjamin was gone.

A moment later the scene changed yet again. Now all thoughts of Benjamin and Abigail fled his mind as he was confronted by the girl. Mina she called herself. She stood before him, a smirk on her lips.

"Jonah, the reluctant prophet, doesn't want us to repent."

"No, I don't," he growled. What was she doing here, invading his dreams?

"I can help him you know."

"Help who?"

"Your son."

"You? You're nothing but a vagrant."

She jerked at that comment. Though Jonah was unsure if it was the insult or something else. A look of bewilderment crossed her face and she looked away a moment. "Do you have any sense of morality, Jonah?"

"An Assyrian is preaching to me about morality?" He laughed. "That is hilarious."

"Jonah, we're all humans. Haven't you ever done something bad?"

"Well of course..."

"And what makes you think what I've done is worse than what you have done?"

"Because..."

"Because I'm Assyrian, right?"

"Exactly."

"Jonah, you can't get the people mixed up with the people."

"What are you jabbering about?"

"We are simply people. Yes, we have distinct features, but we are people. Now the ones you hate are the Assyrians. We are Assyrian, but not every Assyrian is as you think. We can be both bloodthirsty fighters and innocent victims of those same fighters. I am not a fighter, Jonah. I did not have anything to do with your losses. The only reason you hate me is because I live in Assyria.

"Think about it, Jonah. We are all people. If you desire to kill us, then you desire to kill your fellow man. To look forward to our destruction is the same as anticipating your son's demise with pleasure."

"You lie!"

"You deny that you want us to be destroyed?"

"No."

"Then why do you say that I am lying?"

"Because I don't want anything bad to happen to Benjamin."

"But you yearn for God to harm people, His own creations. Do you admit that you consider yourself better than us? More deserving of God's grace?"

Shouts outside the inn startled Jonah into wakefulness. He felt in his mind and his body that the dream was incomplete. There was still something left to see, but there was no returning now—not that he wanted to. He stumbled down the stairs and nearly fell upon the midget of an innkeeper in his haste to see what was causing the raucous outside.

"What's going on?" Jonah demanded.

The innkeeper glanced up at him nervously. "Sir, it's a royal decree being announced."

"What is the decree?"

"Read it for yourself. One has to be passed around every part of the city anyway." The man handed Jonah a sheet of parchment. His eyes darted across the scrawled writing with apprehension.

> In Nineveh, by the decree of the Emperor and his nobles: Do
> not let man, beast, herd, or flock taste a thing. Do not let them eat or
> drink water. But both man and beast must be covered with sackcloth;
> and let men call on God earnestly that each may turn from his
> wicked way and from the violence which is in his hands. Who knows,
> God may turn and relent and withdraw His burning anger so that we
> will not perish.

"Rather absurd is it not?" the innkeeper asked as Jonah handed back the parchment. "Can you imagine putting sackcloth on the fowl?" He laughed mirthlessly and strutted off to serve his costumers.

Jonah felt his knees going weak. He staggered up the stairs like a drunken man and burst into their room. Mina sat cross-legged on her mat, watching him intently. Her piercing eyes reminded him of the dream. And when she opened her mouth, he felt chills crawl up his neck.

"I was downstairs earlier this morning. I read the decree. Our emperor hopes that Yahweh will have mercy on us. But I can see by your face that you yearn for God to harm people, His own creations." When he voiced no denial, she stood and confronted him, her eyes, blacker than night shone like ebony spheres. "Do you admit that you consider yourself better than us? More deserving of God's grace?" Still he said nothing, so she continued, "Jonah, you realize that that makes you a reluctant prophet. You don't want us to repent. But Jonah, we are all humans."

Jonah found his voice. "That may be so." He needed to set some things straight between himself and his dreams. "But some humans are too wicked for God's grace."

"Is that true, Jonah?"

He turned upon her angrily, mostly because he knew it wasn't true. God would forgive the Ninevites, but He would not spare this one. He grabbed her wrist and hauled her out of the inn. Because many of the people knew that the girl was meant as a sacrifice for Yahweh, they did not stop him as he dragged her through the street. At first, she trotted behind him, wrenching at her arm and trying to free it. But after a while, she tired of being pulled and began to hit him, yelling at him to let her go. Still the people did nothing. Surely now was the time the prophet of Yahweh intended to offer the sacrifice. Jonah was disgusted at the reason behind their inaction. Though he hated her and all Assyrians, he did not want any blood upon his hands; at least, not directly.

"Pig! Clod!" She spat at him, clawing at his arm to free herself. "Where are you taking me?" Jonah didn't respond. In truth, he was unsure of where he was taking her also. Eventually, they were away from the bustle of people and wandering through back alleys.

Jonah stopped abruptly when he saw a sprawled figure surrounded by a pool of blood no more than a few yards ahead. Red stains spattered the ground and the surrounding buildings. Jonah moved toward the man in disgust. The sort of conditions these people lived in would have repulsed even the lowest of slaves, and terrified the best soldiers in either Israel or Judah.

Stepping closer, they could now clearly see the scene. The man had been hacked to pieces by whom or for what reason Jonah had no desire to know. All of his body parts were detached and his face was contorted in a scream, forever frozen in place. Jonah hurried on, fighting the tightening dread in his chest, dragging Mina behind him.

Maybe Abigail was right. It would be best to get away from this city, especially since God might still destroy it. Jonah felt both reluctance and joy at the prospect of leaving. He took pleasure in the fear and awe that his nation's enemy showed him and would gladly bask in it a few more days before returning home. No doubt the girl would go with him to escape the doomed city if she had the choice, but he would not give it to her. They entered a clearing, in the center of which stood a dried up well. Deciding quickly, Jonah took hold of the rope from the well. One end remained attached to the well and the other end was soon in his hand. He bound the girl's hands with the rope and lifted her over the opening.

She kicked hard at him, cursing in Assyrian. He lowered her quickly into the well, and though she fought him like a wild beast, she was bound and weak from her injury, and her struggle made little difference. Jonah pushed her hard, and she dropped like a stone, feet clawing at the slimy stone walls. There was a plop when she hit the mucky bottom, and Jonah worried that the landing had killed her, he did not want to be a murderer. He heard her let out a grunt and then the sound of smacking as she shifted.

Turning sharply, he scanned the ground and soon found what he wanted. Picking up a sharp stone he began to saw away at the rope connected to the well. The dirty fibers yielded easily, and he watched the rope drop down. Without another thought, he tossed the stone aside and hurried to exit the wicked city.

Chapter Sixteen

Anan heaved a heavy sigh, low over his bowl. Haggith's unique choice of spices was a tremendous link between himself and home and he felt at ease upon breathing in their pleasant odor. How many years had he eaten at this table, in this house? Too many to remember. However, this morning's return had been different than any other over the years. It had been more bittersweet, less monotonous. The news of Jonah had left him shocked for the larger part of the afternoon. Sure, his friend could be a little rash when it came to the Assyrians and their past, but to openly defy the God of Israel was entirely absurd.

Haggith busied herself by being motherly as usual. She fussed over Anan's travel worn clothes and how pale he looked and how he should stand up taller and never slouch. Abba had just recently sent word to Caleb and Atarah, inviting them over to visit with Anan. And Amittai had spent a great deal of time praying upstairs since hearing of Jonah's decision. Benjamin was a mere ghost of the man Anan remembered from his last visit. He never smiled, took very little notice of anyone, and spent large amounts of time in a daze. Anan couldn't help but wonder if Jonah realized the amount of disarray his leaving had caused.

After declaring himself "just fine" for the hundredth time to Haggith, Anan rose from the table and sauntered outside. The sky was a pleasant pink on the horizon, and he let out a soft sigh, relishing the peace and quiet that his home offered as opposed to the city. A sound, that of a human walking, caught his attention. Anan turned to see Benjamin moving toward him. His eyes were glazed over, unseeing. Anan wondered if he should do something before Benjamin walked into anything he shouldn't. In the end, he simply fell in step beside the boy.

They meandered on an aimless path that seemed completely random to Anan, but Benjamin's feet fell with confidence. Jonah and Benjamin were much alike, Anan noticed. Both lived in the past more than any person truly should. They were always ruminating, never completely in the present. Benjamin stopped abruptly, and Anan glanced around, wondering what the matter was. He watched in surprise as a strange expression crossed Benjamin's face and he fell forward. Anan caught him just inches from the ground and lowered him gently the rest of the way. Benjamin's eyes cleared and then widened in surprise at seeing Anan.

"I wasn't expecting to see you," he mumbled. Anan helped him into a sitting position and knelt beside him. The sparse grass bristled underneath them, a dull green shade as the sky darkened.

"Well, I'll admit I was not expecting to see you wandering around in a daydream."

"And I would have continued wandering. I have been reliving my memories, Anan."

"I suppose you are Jonah's son."

"I think I woke up because you were watching me." He gave a small, crooked smile.

"Benjamin, may I be blunt?" The boy nodded, head lowered. "It cannot be good for you to live like this. You have to stop."

"But I don't want to." Benjamin spoke like a young boy rather than a grown man.

"Why not?"

"Because..." He broke off, looking over Anan's shoulder. "Who's that?"

At first, Anan thought Benjamin was making excuses, but when he glanced over, he saw that if it was an excuse, it was a very good one. A towering man mounted on a plain brown horse was riding toward them. When he was about ten feet away, he clambered down and approached them, feet shuffling as if he would rather not have come. His appearance was not that of the ordinary Judean farmer. He looked rougher, almost as if...

Benjamin stood and addressed the man in Aramaic. A wise choice since he hardly looked Hebrew. "Who are you?"

"I am Kleitos," the man stammered. He seemed shaken by Benjamin's bold tone and stance. His strange blue eyes darted from Benjamin to Anan and back again. "I am Greek."

Benjamin took a step forward. "And I'm not interested in your life-story."

Anan rose and placed a hand on the boy's shoulder. Turning to Kleitos, he placed his question with more courtesy than the former had. "What business did you intend?"

"I bring news. I must speak to the head of the household in which Jonah ben Amittai lives."

"That would be my father, Jonathan." Anan led the way inside the house. Jonathan was bent over his scrolls as usual, and Haggith was sweeping dust clouds into the air. The particles drifted throughout the room before the wind picked them up and carried them through the windows on either side of the home.

Abba glanced up in surprise when he saw Kleitos. Rising, he bowed with his head in greeting. "How may I help you?" he asked, also addressing the stranger in Aramaic.

"I am Kleitos a Grecian. Are you the head of this house?"

"I am."

"I bring news of Jonah ben Amittai."

"News?"

"There was an...event out at sea. The entire crew is too shaken to return to the ship and they are returning home for a month. I have a friend here in Judah that I will stay with. I was heading east from Joppa anyway, and I decided that you should hear the story firsthand."

Pounding resounded upstairs and Amittai stumbled down the steps. "News? About my son?" Kleitos glanced from Jonathan to Amittai and back to Jonathan. Clearly unsure of what to do or think.

"Where are my manners? Please, come sit down." Abba offered Kleitos a seat and saw that he was comfortable before inviting Amittai, Benjamin, and Anan to sit. When he lowered himself on a cushion, Anan noticed that he seemed to have aged. Abba had always appeared younger in the way of energy and liveliness. But an air of unease had settled over the gathering.

"I am a sailor on the ship, the *Midnight Runner*, the captain of which is the Hebrew Chenaniah." Kleitos crossed his legs and worried the edge of his ragged tunic. "Jonah was a passenger on board. We hardly paid him any notice for the first while. Then the storm came." He looked down at his lap, his fingers moving more rapidly. "The ship nearly capsized several times. The sails were torn to shreds, and almost everything on board was damaged. Many of the crew were injured and we were desperate to find land." His hands were now close to shaking and he clasped them tightly. "We are, you could say, a bit of a superstitious lot. Having come from many different places in the world and having worshiped many gods in our youth. So, we saw no reason not to trust in fate. We drew names to see who had caused the storm to come upon us. For it was undoubtedly the worst storm I have ever seen. We drew Jonah's name, and many of us were surprised. We barely knew the man. When we asked him what we could do about our situation, he told us to throw him into the sea—"

"No!" Kleitos jumped at Amittai's voice. "My son is not stupid, Kleitos. He would never say such a thing."

Anan reached out a hand to help a fuming Amittai back down onto his cushion. "Let him finish."

The older man grumbled as he resettled himself.

"We said we could never do such a thing, and Captain Chenaniah would hear nothing of the sort." Kleitos's voice was considerably less steady, and they all stiffened in apprehension. "We tried to row to land, but the sea was so rough that we made no progress. The captain was furious and hurled a sharp chunk of wood at me. I was unconscious after that, but when I recovered, the crew filled me in on the rest of the details. They said that they had taken Jonah and, seeing no other option, they threw him overboard."

"No!" Amittai shouted. Benjamin's jaw fell open and he was as pale as a ghost. Jonathan and Anan also blanched, and they heard Haggith gasp from the other side of the house.

Kleitos's entire body quivered with tension. He was likely afraid they would tear him to pieces, and Amittai likely would have if Anan had not helped calm him down a second time.

"See, he is not finished! Let him finish," he soothed.

Once everyone was finally calm, Kleitos continued. "Before the storm reached its peak, a monstrosity of a creature had been ramming into the ship from time to time. The crew watched as Jonah fell into the water, but a few moments later they lost sight of him. Then they spotted him father away from the ship. And the creature, a giant thing it was, swam up and—"

"I've heard enough." Kleitos fell silent as Amittai stood and stormed toward the stairs. A moment later he returned, fists clenched. "What happened?"

"The creature, the monster, it ate Jonah." Amittai went limp and fell in the midst of the group. "But then the sea calmed," Kleitos stammered on in alarm. "It calmed as soon as the monster ate him, and we tried to row back to Joppa. The winds were unfavorable, and weeks went by with hardly any progress. Finally, the captain ordered us to row for the nearest land. We anchored the remains of the *Midnight Runner* and half of the crew walked back to Joppa to find a boatwright to repair the ship. The other half stayed with the captain on the *Midnight Runner*. The crew and I felt guilty about what we had done, so they told me to ask around Joppa until I found the inn at which Jonah had stayed while they returned to the ship. I talked to the innkeeper, and he directed us to his servant who told us where Jonah lived. The servant said he talked with a man who knew Jonah. His name was Zedekiah."

"We know Zedekiah," Anan managed to say. "Thank you for relaying this information."

"I am so sorry." Kleitos rose and turned toward the door.

"Please, won't you stay the night? The journey to Joppa is a long one. Surely you wish to rest up." Anan glanced at Haggith, making sure she seemed composed enough to handle a guest.

"I hate to be a burden."

"It is no trouble," Anan assured the man. Even Benjamin nodded in encouragement. In the end, Kleitos relented and Haggith saw to it that he was properly set up for the night.

When Jonathan found his voice, his smiled weakly at the group. "I dare say, I've seen enough people pass out lately to think I had bred a new type of fainting goat."

* * *

Mina fumbled around in the dark bottom of the well. The stuffy air smelled slightly of mold, and she fought the urge to gag. She wondered if she could somehow worm her way out of the filthy and soggy rope. Fortunately for her, the blanched prophet had bound her hands in front instead of behind. She placed her hands before her and began sliding them back and forth as fast as she could, her palms flat against each other. Her wrists began to ache, but she felt the rope tightening with the tension, and since it was moist, it gradually widened. The knot tightened, but it also gave her a tiny bit of slack. Now that it was not as tight, she took a deep breath and yanked her right wrist toward her with all her strength. To her amazement it pulled free, leaving a bright red mark on her free wrist and hand, but she did not mind.

She pushed the rope off her other wrist and stood up. Her body ached from the fall and she felt bruised, but otherwise unharmed. Stretching out her arms, she found that each palm came into contact with a wall. Pressing her back against one, she extended her legs. The muck oozed around her as she tried to shimmy up the slippery sides. It was barely small enough for her to fit snugly. With her feet braced on one side, her back on the other, she began to inch up toward the circle of light above. Her heart gave a leap of triumph when she saw how far she'd come. It would only be a matter of time before she was free.

Mina felt her mind drifting idly toward thoughts of her tightly closed past. Her memories were a little clearer now. Shammina was not her own name, but that of someone she knew, someone close. And her uncle was a man to be feared. Another name formed itself in the recesses of her mind: Rabil. A soldier? The light was so close she felt as if she could reach up and touch the rim. Only another two or three feet to go. Her muddy bare feet clung to the stones, and her body groaned with the exertion. If only the well had been built a few inches smaller.

She was about to poke her head up through the top and look around when she stopped herself. This was the darkest, most vile part of the city. A young girl didn't just stroll down the street without expecting trouble. She remembered the dismembered man and shuddered. Mina inched up a tiny bit more and very cautiously peered over the edge of the well.

What she saw made her have to stifle a gasp. A merchant was trudging along the alleyway toward the opening in which the well stood, seeming perhaps a little lost. His steps were careful and his eyes were wide and watchful, and not without good reason. Another man was watching the merchant from the lee of a warehouse. This other man wore a dark cloak, but still she could see he was unshaven and his clothes in tatters, but he was built like a soldier. Mina had seen the combination before.

It was illegal for an able-bodied man not to fight in the army. So many mothers had sent their sons to fend for themselves in the areas where even soldiers who guarded the city did not dare to patrol, perhaps in hopes that they would live better lives if they stayed near home. Such assumptions were often misplaced. These boys usually grew up as thugs and hoodlums. They became the very definition of evil in Nineveh's streets. Mina was certain that life in the army would be easier than killing in one's own city for a living, but perhaps she was wrong. After all, females and males had different mindsets on such matters.

The merchant seemed to be completely unaware that he was being stalked, and Mina could not resist the thought that she should warn him. But then she would be putting herself at risk too. Was such a thing worth her life? There was still a chance the merchant would come away shaken and poorer, but unharmed. Though she braced herself, she was still surprised when the man leapt out of nowhere and tackled the merchant. It was then that she wished she had called out.

"Tell me where you hid it," the attacker growled.

The merchant, seeming quite stunned, muttered a few words that Mina did not catch.

"Liar! I know you stashed it away. What of the bargain?"

"You did not hold up your side either, Layth," the merchant spat. He pulled his arms beneath him and heaved. The other man, Layth, was smaller, and though he tried to wrestle the merchant down, it was no use. They stood and confronted each other, muscles tense to fight. From her position, Mina could see the profile of the attacker and his rare green eyes were startlingly evil.

"You said you would deliver him within a week's time. How did you fail?" Layth asked, eyes blazing with anger.

The merchant leaned forward irritably. "I already told you, I lost track of him."

"But what about the gold? Why didn't you deliver that either?"

"Because you did not return her as promised."

Layth grunted, shaking his head in frustration. "So neither of us did our work correctly. Except for the fact she would have been returned if you had done your job."

"But you assured me that, even if I failed to bring the boy, the trade would go through."

"Rabil, I'm sick of your games." Layth's lower jaw moved forward as his tone filled with menace. "Either get it right or don't get it right. But don't expect me to work miracles if you don't complete your task."

Mina's eyes widened. Rabil...she knew that name. It now occurred to her that the merchant did indeed look familiar, though she could not entirely place the memory.

"Just return the girl to me, and I will give you the gold." Rabil appeared to be on the defensive, on the verge of pleading.

"You know he won't agree to that. You must bring the gold first, and he wants it yesterday."

"I can't trust you to hold up your end either," Rabil spat. "Do it my way or say goodbye to the gold." Layth threw off his cloak and set his jaw. The merchant also removed his bulky outer garment and took up a fighting stance.

"You're coming with me, Rabil. He will not wait for the gold. And since you will not tell me where it is..." The man angled his head in the tone of a shrug, no more needed to be said.

Rabil, unaffected by the threat, shook his head. "You aren't taking me anywhere until I know she's safe."

As if on cue, both men drew daggers.

"You haven't lost your gall, Rabil, have you? You know I could kill you if I was missing both arms."

Rabil shrugged in the same dismissive manner the man had. They began to circle each other, eyes locked in concentration. Each one waited and watched for the other to strike. An instant later, Mina found herself wondering what had happened. In a mere flash, the man had used his free hand to cuff Rabil in the jaw, knocking him off balance. Then the man plunged his knife at Rabil's exposed neck as his chin went up while the other hand slammed into Rabil's wrist, causing him to drop the knife. The next thing she knew, Rabil was on the ground, the man's knife to his throat.

"Go ahead, kill me," Rabil grunted out. "And the location of the gold dies with me."

"I won't kill you, Rabil, but you are going to wish I had."

A tall young man burst through the alley onto the scene. "Enough!" he cried. Mina stared. She knew him.

"Shammina, I told you to stay away from me after what happened." Rabil's voice was husky as he strained to lift the other man off him.

"Now I can see why. You never told me you worked for someone."

"I don't. Your kind general hired me without asking my permission."

"General Dorar hired you? To find me? But I trusted you."

The man released Rabil and clapped his hands hard. A group of men appeared, blocking each alleyway. He relaxed his stance, like a cat that knows its prey is caught and observed the conversation.

Rabil cursed under his breath, but in the end, he simply continued explaining. "Shammina, your father and uncle knew you were training under my command. General Dorar wanted you back, since it is illegal for you not to fight and also because of the gold."

"Gold?" Shammina widened his eyes, but glanced down seeming uneasy. Layth narrowed a suspicious gaze upon the boy, but Rabil hurried on with his reply.

"You know that your father is extremely wealthy, right?"

"No."

"You know what he used to do for a living?"

"No."

"He was a bounty hunter before the plague."

"You're joking."

"No, Shammina, your father made a fortune doing that, but he wanted to conceal it after the epidemic so he wouldn't attract too much attention. He wants Assyria to rise up in power and he desires for the Emperor to attack Egypt. He's saving the gold for when that time comes."

"But General Dorar—"

"Knew you'd come to me."

"How?"

"He knew that he could not train you in Egyptian warfare himself, because then he would attract too much attention. But he saw your longing and knew where you would go. You're an incredible soldier, Shammina. So is your father and uncle. You have nearly exhausted my capacity to teach you. Your father also had big dreams. He wanted a band of men who could get into Egypt, murder the current Pharaoh, and completely tear the government to bits. He already has thirty men."

"He wants to completely demolish Egypt?"

"Once the Pharaoh is gone, the empire will be a mess. Emperor Ashur-Dan will be much easier to convince that Egypt is weak enough to attack."

"So, my father is a conspiracy generator?"

"Essentially, he is. But in the end, he needs your support, and he needed me to bring you in. He paid another retired general to train a select few men in private after you left. But when he died, your uncle took over. He never paid me to train you, I did that of my own accord; but now he has leverage on both of us and intends to use it to bring you over to his side."

"I will never join my uncle."

"He knows that. But like I said, he has leverage."

"What could he possibly have, General Rabil?"

"He has Marbita."

* * *

The grass crunched irritably against the hot ground as Jonah tried to settle himself into a comfortable position. Nineveh stood above him, the river flowing from it like a fountain. It was a pity that it was not possible for the great city to fall into Israelite hands—or even Judean hands for that matter.

Now that he was rid of the girl, he felt his tense muscles beginning to relax. She could not pester him about Assyrians being people; she could not prod his conscience. Instead, she was in the bottom of a filthy well. He had shown her the truth of her city. With his mind at ease, he could sit and watch, waiting for the final destruction that was soon to come. Jonah watched the tiny trickle of people emerging from the gate to his left. Though they wore sackcloth as ordered, it was clear they had no intention of sticking around in a doomed city. Jonah wiped the sweat off his forehead, glaring up at the sun with contempt. What business of it was the sun's to make him miserable on such a joyous day?

He stumbled down to the river's edge and stepped in. As he bent down to splash water over himself, he saw a dark hulk move past him. He practically leapt from the water as the creature came up to the edge of the bank, jaw agape. It stilled, a six-foot long menace with a corresponding row of razor-sharp teeth. Jonah had heard of imported devil catfish patrolling the Khosr River, but he had thought them a myth. Quite clearly, he was wrong. And it was certain to deter anyone from trying to enter the city by way of the river, even if the bars were not enough. Apparently, the catfish survived the change from lurking in the waters of southern Asia to terrorizing the audacious in Nineveh.

For a moment, Jonah placed himself in the perspective of an invading army. First, they would have to contend with the Assyrian soldiers. And though the empire was weak, her soldiers, few as they might be, were some of the best fighters to be found. Then there was the river, which acted somewhat like a moat around the city, and the fact that Nineveh was on a rise surrounded by walls thick enough to live inside. Jonah rubbed the nape of his neck. Any general who even considered the prospect of conquering Nineveh would have to receive infinite miracles to accomplish it. Again, he wondered if Israel could ever posses such a fortress.

Retreating a safe distance from the water, Jonah resumed a seat in the scorching sun. What had ever possessed him to think that being a prophet of Yahweh was a good thing? Then he remembered the visions. Surely such an experience would convince most people that their calling was an incredible opportunity. But Jonah knew that the thrill that had accompanied the visions was not enough to carry his task through to completion. He had ended up in the middle of the sea, fleeing from God in the end. Indeed, that had worked out wonderfully. Jonah considered all that he had seen in Nineveh: the shrines to false gods, the bodies lying in the streets, the man who had offered his niece as a sacrifice. It was no wonder God saw Nineveh as a people steeped in wickedness.

"Oh Yahweh, when will their destruction come?" Jonah moaned. The agony of not knowing what would happen lay heavily on him. The city had to be destroyed. The people of Nineveh had to perish. It would take a thousand deaths before Jonah was satisfied that Zillah's murder had been compensated for.

"Will even a thousand be enough? When will your need for revenge be complete?" Jonah pushed at the voice that prodded his conscience. It fought back. "It will never be enough, will it? You will never be satisfied." The world around Jonah began to tremble, and he felt the sun intensifying. But it wasn't the sun.

"Jonah." The voice spoke his name.

"I am here, Lord."

"Jonah, *I have seen what the Ninevites did, and how they turned from their evil ways. I will relent and I will not bring on them the destruction I had threatened.*"

Jonah felt his blood heating at the Lord's declaration. Relent and not destroy Nineveh? Yahweh, the God of Israel, was relenting on such a wicked city! Jonah felt his hopes crashing down around him. All his anticipations, all his aspirations, were for nothing.

"*Isn't this what I said, Lord, when I was still at home? That is what I tried to forestall by fleeing to Tarshish. I knew that You are a gracious and compassionate God, slow to anger and abounding in love, a God who relents from sending calamity. Now, Lord, take away my life, for it is better for me to die than to live.*" Jonah knelt in the scorching heat and blinding light. He had not avenged Zillah's death after all. He had not gotten revenge for the loss of his home, for those who had died on the caravan's journey, for those who had been recaptured. He had failed to recompense all the decimated villages, all the broken hearts, and all the dashed hopes of a new beginning. He had been fortunate, but how many had not been able to start anew? How many had returned home to find nothing and no one? How many had lost even more than he?

"*Is it right for you to be angry?*"

Jonah stood and shook his fists in the air, his blood boiling. "The God of Israel, the God of my fathers is asking me if I have a right to be angry for my losses, for the losses of countless others? You are implying that I am sinning by hating the Assyrians for all the damage they have caused. You ask me why I am angry that thousands of wicked people are being spared. The Assyrians are the very essence of evil in this world, Yahweh. And You are asking me why I'm angry that You forgave them?" He collapsed to his knees. Exhausted from his rant, to which there was no response. God remained silent. He made no explanation for why He had so absurdly forgiven the Assyrians. "They don't deserve to be forgiven!" Jonah shouted. He felt as if his entire purpose in life was crumbling around him.

"If they don't deserve forgiveness, then neither do you."

"That's a lie!" Jonah opened his mouth again to protest the words, but he realized that he was talking aloud to the voices inside of him. And worse, he knew the words were true. Jonah turned to the water and stepped toward it. Images of returning home flitted in his mind, stepping through the door and seeing his family, his friends. What was he supposed to tell them? That God forgave the Ninevites and he had argued with Him? That he, a lowly worm of the earth had dared to argue with his Creator and God? The catfish watched Jonah curiously as he stepped off the bank and into the shallows. Zillah would forever haunt him, forever remind him that he had failed. Jonah remembered his vow. The one he had made all those years ago. He was a failure.

"That's the prophet of Yahweh!" a young voice shouted.

Jonah reeled at the voice. A young boy was jumping up and down and pointing at him. His mother, part of the group fleeing the city, held tightly to his hand.

A man in their group shouted at him, "You there, prophet. Get out of that water. There's devil fish in there for a reason."

Jonah felt he had no true way of reasoning with the man, so he stepped out of the water, pretending shock at the revelation of there being devil fish. Suddenly, the group of three stopped along with a few others that were accompanying them. Jonah watched them as they turned their attention to the city. Out of the blue, he heard a chorus of cheers and shouts of merriment. Curious, he meandered over to the gate.

"What's going on?" he asked the sentry on duty.

The man bowed before answering. "Sir, the Great Emperor Ashur-Dan, High Priest of Assur has announced that the God of Israel has relented upon us."

"Yes, I know, but how did he find out?"

"Sir, I hear he had a vision. Yahweh of Israel spoke to him and told him that He would not destroy Nineveh because the people repented."

"No!"

The sentry jerked as Jonah rushed away from the gate, from the city. There was no denying it now. God had made His mind up, and it was official.

Chapter Seventeen

The funeral was held the following week as they had no reason to wait. Jonathan's other three sons were asked to come, and Zedekiah was also welcomed. To their surprise, they managed to locate Amos and requested that he also attend Jonah's funeral. There was no body to bury and no family tomb in which to bury him even if they had. So, they hired workers and had one dug for all of them. For though neither Benjamin, Jonah, Anan or Jonathan were related by blood, they were still family. As a show of her sweet nature, Atarah completely set aside her joy of looking forward to a daughter and grieved beside her husband. Amittai was inconsolable.

The morning of the funeral was appropriately dull. And the sun seemed to shy away from the wailing mourners who arrived that afternoon. Caleb did what he could, but Amittai was too broken to take part. He stayed locked away in the house, refusing to eat or speak to anyone. Benjamin too was nowhere to be found. Anan informed them that he had likely gone off to revisit his past, for Benjamin was much like Jonah. He would likely never return to the present, in order to forget.

Anan welcomed his brothers with tears of joy and sorrow. It had been many years since all of Jonathan's sons had been reunited. It was clear the brothers considered Anan no different than themselves. He was their brother, even if not by blood. Haggith had prepared the food beforehand, and it was just as well, for she mourned deeply along with all the others. This was much to their surprise, for none had expected her to show any great amount of emotion. Zedekiah, not being as close to Jonah, was composed enough to help console Amittai and Caleb. Atarah wailed louder than any of the hired mourners, and her son watched her in bewilderment. Bithiah also came to grieve and soothe her sister. Since there was no body to bury in the tomb, they had a large clay model made. It was carefully wrapped in cloth and perfumed, just like any body would be before burial. When the day came to a slow close, Zedekiah bid farewell with a final word of sympathy to the family. Amos was asked to stay, and he accepted. Haggith laid out the food and they gathered around a solemn table as the sun lowered beneath the horizon.

"Benjamin should be here," Atarah said when they had settled.

"It is best that he is alone," Anan countered softly.

"No." Caleb stood. "I thought the same with Jonah, but it only became worse. It is not better for Jonah's son and twin to be alone either. Being by himself will only encourage him to stew on this matter, and it will do nothing but multiply his grief. Benjamin, I believe, was closer to Jonah than we ever thought. They fit together like a hand in a glove. I will go and find him."

He hurried from the house and Haggith dragged another seat to the table just in case he returned successful. They waited in silence a moment before footsteps alerted them that Amittai was coming down. Another seat was brought as he joined them. The streaks of gray in his hair seemed to have multiplied, and his movements were slow and weary.

"Of three children," he muttered softly, "one is left. One."

"Perhaps this is not the best time to mention this," Amos said, shifting uncomfortably. "But it is not impossible for Jonah to still be alive."

In an instant, Atarah was on her feet. "We will all thank you, sir, to not bring such matters up on the day of a funeral."

"I am very sorry." Amos hung his head. "You know, Jonah had such promise as a boy. He was unmistakably called to be a prophet."

"Then why did God take him before he had a chance to prophesy?" Amittai cut in. His voice was thin from disuse. "And why didn't you tell

us where he was going? If you had told us, he might never have been
killed!"

"I..."

"If God truly is a God of love, then why is my son gone?"

"Amittai..."

"It's all right, Amos, I understand." Amittai stood. "You have never
prophesied anything but doom all your life. How could you explain to
me the love of God?" With that, he left, taking his food upstairs with
him. No one said a word as they continued to eat. There was a tiny
knock on the door before Caleb entered, Benjamin behind him. Jonah's
son had adopted the stance of a dog about to be beaten, and he kept his
head down as he entered.

"Come join us, Ben," Atarah called to him sweetly. Benjamin
lowered himself down uncomfortably on the cushion beside her.

"I don't believe he is dead," he murmured.

"Oh, sweet child. Atarah, do you think he can cope properly?"
Bithiah leaned forward and placed a hand on Benjamin's arm.

"He's fine, Bithiah," Caleb intervened, relieving Benjamin of
having to keep Bithiah's pity at bay.

"You should apologize for your father," Atarah told her husband.

"Oh, no, no offense was taken." Amos put his hands up to ward
off the apology.

"Nonsense, some empathy is needed here." Atarah told Caleb what
had happened and he was quick to speak.

"I am so sorry, Amos. My father is taking this extremely hard,
perhaps harder than any of us."

Amos replied again that there was no need for an apology.

The conversation was stifled and uncomfortable for the rest of the
night, and before long, all parties gave up on it. Anan caught up with
his brothers as they were to leave the following morning due to work,
and Amos spoke with Caleb and Atarah. Bithiah assisted Haggith in
clearing away the dishes and preparing rooms for the guests. Benjamin,
well, he vanished into the past.

*"I'm so hungry, Benjamin." Ruth, the only bearer of Abba's
blue eyes, tugged on her brother's sleeve. "Can't I have some food?"*

"Don't bother your brother. He needs to pay attention to where

we're going." Abigail lifted her sister and carried her as they continued to walk.

"We are almost to Hebron, Abigail."

"Thank goodness."

Benjamin knew he would never forget the sight of the landscape of his first trip to Hebron—the city where he had been apprenticed...so far from home. He felt Oded bobbing sleepily on his shoulders.

"I'm hungry," Nathan whined. Abigail let out an exasperated sigh. What had she been thinking?

"We will stop and eat when we reach Hebron," Benjamin said. He too felt and heard his stomach protesting about being empty. He pulled the goatskin of water from his bag and passed it around.

"Benjamin, what are you doing?" Abigail's voice quivered slightly as if she feared he had lost his sanity. "I thought we agreed we should ration the water very carefully." She watched Jonah chug down the water with dread.

"It will help satisfy their hunger," Benjamin explained, taking a sip himself. "When we reach Hebron in about an hour, we will refill it."

"Only an hour?"

"Yes."

Abigail smiled for the first time in days it seemed. There was a small squeal from Ruth, and she leapt from Abigail's arms.

"Abiram!" The boy lay sprawled on the ground where he had tripped. "Benjamin, he isn't moving." Abigail rushed forward as Benjamin set Oded down.

"Come on, Abiram. It's okay; we're almost there." Abigail knelt beside her brother.

"When we reach Hebron, we will take some time to recover." Benjamin knelt as well. "Though it isn't the safest place."

"Why not?" Abigail glanced at her brother.

"Because it is one of the Cities of Refuge."

"Where people accused of manslaughter await trial?" Abigail's eyes widened.

"Manslaughter is different from intentional killing, Abigail. It is considered..."

"*I know, unintentional, but still.*" *She sighed heavily.* "*I appreciate that you took the time to mention that before we entered the city.*"

"*I'm sorry, Abigail. And honestly, it isn't that bad.*" *She glanced down at Abiram. Reaching down, she placed her hand above his mouth.*

"*He isn't breathing, Benjamin!*" *She turned to him, eyes filled with tears.* "*Will we lose him too?*" *Benjamin shook his head. He placed his hand on Abiram's chest, then, very slowly he nodded.* "*Benjamin talk to me! What's wrong with him?*"

"*We've lost him.*"

* * *

Jonah sat and stared at the city for ages it seemed. His mind spun in no apparent direction. He absently smiled at the makeshift tent he had created. It wasn't bad, though it did have some holes. It was growing dark, and he was grateful for the shelter and its appearance was starkly inviting compared to the backdrop of emptiness. Jonah closed his eyes and closed his mind to thoughts of the Assyrians, then he promptly fell asleep.

The following morning was sweltering. By the time the sun had crested the horizon, Jonah found himself soaked through with sweat. As if things weren't bad enough for him already! He rose and stumbled out of his shelter. Very cautiously he approached the water and cupped the liquid in his hands, drinking great gulps of it. When he saw one of the devil fish coming to pay him a visit, he returned to his shelter. It was then that he noticed the small stem of a plant emerging from just inside his shelter. Seeing no reason to bother it, he let himself relax and dozed the rest of the day. In early afternoon, he smiled to himself, noticing that his shelter was exceptionally comfortable. When he opened his eyes, he stared in shock. The little shoot was gone, replaced by a plant that had woven itself around his wood and cloth shelter and providing enough shade that the sun could not shine through. What luck! He felt his stomach growling and decided to eat.

He trotted over to the gate and was only mildly surprised when the sentries bowed and allowed him to enter without question. It was highly unlikely that there were many others that looked like him in Assyria. He also found it very easy to get something to eat. The merchants in the market practically fell over one another in their haste to feed him. It was clear that they all thought he had pleaded their case before Yahweh, which had resulted in their being spared. And because of the fine treatment he received, Jonah made no effort to correct them. Once satisfied, he left the city, unable to spend too much time around the Assyrians. He climbed back under his shelter as dusk fell, smiling again at his plant. It was pleasant to have things going his way for once.

Morning came a little earlier than he would have liked, but he awoke grudgingly to the sun blazing overhead. Why was it now so hot? He glanced up, and his eyes widened. His plant was slowly wilting. Gaps had appeared in the tent-like foliage, and the leaves were turning brown before his very eyes. By the time the sun was directly above him, it was as if there had never been a plant. Jonah found himself once again drenched with sweat.

What was the point in sitting out here and waiting for the destruction of Nineveh when it would never come? Somehow, in the very back of his mind, a tiny seed of hope still lived. Perhaps, maybe, in forty days the grand city before him would be in ruins. His mind became a fog as the heat hit him. It was almost as hot as it had been in that cursed whale. Jonah moaned and wiped the sweat from his eyes. There was no longer any point in struggling to endure the heat.

"*It would be better for me to die than to live.*" He said aloud. And it was true.

"*Is it right for you to be angry about the plant?*"

Jonah jumped at the voice. He had not expected any word from Yahweh since his last plea for death. "*It is, and I'm so angry I wish I were dead.*" Maybe God would kill him just for arguing.

"*You have been concerned about this plant, though you did not tend it or make it grow. It sprang up overnight and died overnight. And should I not have concern for the great city of Nineveh, in which there are more than a hundred and twenty thousand people who cannot tell their right hand from their left, and also many animals?*"

"No, Yahweh! Those one hundred twenty thousand people should be dead by now." Jonah stood and turned his face up toward the sky. "They don't have to know that they are evil to be evil, do they?" But God remained silent in the face of Jonah's anger as before. "I deserve an answer after all You've put me through," Jonah shouted. "You owe me!"

"Go home."

Jonah jumped in surprise. "Go home? That's all You have to say?" He was met with silence.

"Abba and Caleb have likely disowned me by now." He waited again, but there was no answer. Yahweh would not back down. Jonah sighed. "Fine. You don't have to get a really big bird to pick me up and drop me at Jonathan's house."

"Go home to Israel."

"But..."

"And prophesy to Jeroboam the words which I will give you."

"Prophesy to the king of Israel?"

The Lord made no reply. There was no need for Him to repeat Himself. Jonah stood and ambled down the road. Truly fearful that God would send some creature to take him home if he didn't go himself. If he was fortunate, perhaps he would die on the way and be done with his frustrations regarding the Assyrians.

"Remember David's words, Jonah? How far have I removed your transgressions from you? as far as the east is from the west." Yahweh's voice said. "As a father has compassion on his children. Recite it, Jonah." The words spoken a request, nothing more. And Jonah knew that Yahweh would not force him to recite the Psalm. It was his choice to make.

Jonah knew the words well, and though he had no real desire to, he recited some of it aloud, "*Praise the Lord, my soul; all my inmost being, praise His holy name. Praise the Lord, my soul, and forget not all His benefits: who forgives all your sins and heals all your diseases, who redeems your life from the pit and crowns you with love and compassion. The Lord is compassionate and gracious, slow to anger, and abounding in love. He will not always accuse, nor will He harbor His anger forever...*" Jonah sighed. Pardons all, heals all, redeems all, will not be angry forever. The little voice inside of him whispered into the ear of his heart. Keep going. "*He does not treat us as our sins deserve, or repay us according to our iniquities. For as high as the heavens are above the earth, so great is His love for those who fear Him. As far as the east is from the west, so far has He removed our transgressions from us. As a father has compassion on his children, so the Lord...*"

Benjamin. Jonah shook his head. Surely God did not look upon the Assyrians just as he looked upon Benjamin. Yahweh's words echoed through his mind:

"Should I not have concern for the great city of Nineveh, in which there are more than a hundred and twenty thousand people who cannot tell their right hand from their left?"
Jonah felt the anger and hatred, pent up for so many years, slowly draining away. He had no reason to hate every Assyrian. He had no right to. If he dared to judge them and contradicted God in the process, it meant he considered himself wiser than the God of Israel. He remembered Caleb saying that there would be no certainty for anyone if God's love only extended to some, and his brother was right. If Jonah assumed that God didn't love the Assyrians, then he could not know for a fact that he was loved? Who could ever earn the love of their very own Creator?

Jonah placed a hand over his heart. The only reason it was beating was because Yahweh willed it to. The only reason he breathed was because Yahweh had created the air for him and had given him lungs. What right did he have to question such love? The Assyrians might be wicked, but so was he. At least they had not thought themselves wiser than God. Most of them, as Mina had said in his dream, were victims of the crimes of their own people. Mina. Jonah turned and ran back toward the city, back into the heart of Nineveh.

* * *

Rabil watched an expression of surprise play across Shammina's features. "He has her?" the boy asked.

"Yes."

The boy sank slowly to his knees.

"Now son, keep in mind that she is the only leverage he has on us."

"It is enough." Shammina looked up at the man. "I will join you."

Rabil stepped forward, his dark eyes wide with a myriad of emotions. "Now wait—"

"We will be glad to have you join us, Shammina son of Nineel," Layth cut in. His was voice like a purr. "Seeing as the good general here failed to bring you in himself, I am pleased to see that you came to us."

Shammina's eyes darkened a shade, but he remained silent. Rabil watched him solemnly.

"Now, Shammina." Layth crouched beside him. "Where is your father's gold? Do you know?"

"It's—"

"Be quiet, Shammina!" General Rabil raged. "Please, Shammina, come to your senses. These men work for your uncle. Remember who your uncle is."

"So you do know!" Layth exclaimed, ignoring Rabil's words and focusing all of his attention on Shammina. "Well played, my boy. Unfortunately, you're acting is still in its nascent stage." Each word hissed from his mouth as if he were a viper, waiting to strike. "Where is it?"

Shammina stared at the ground, his jaw tightly clenched with what appeared to be rage. He opened his mouth a moment, as if to speak.

"Shammina." Rabil warned, his voice like ice.

"He doesn't have to tell me," Layth stated as he stood and backed off. Rabil and Shammina watched him in surprise. "But he'll want to." He snapped his fingers at one of the men blocking an alley. "Bring me the girl's tongue. I've heard from Ador that it wags too much."

Panic surged through Shammina, and before he could think to do otherwise, he blurted out, "It's in the house! In the closet in the house!"

"Shammina!" Rabil grabbed the boy's shoulders, but Shammina wasn't listening.

"Take however much you need." His words tumbled out desperately, incoherent in his own ears.

Layth smiled. "Thank you very much, Shammina." Turning toward his men, he barked out orders, "Take the boy to General Dorar. Kill our good friend Rabil."

Suddenly, from seemingly nowhere, Shammina's sister appeared. Fire burned in her eyes as she started toward them.

"Marbita! No!" Shammina yelled, grabbing her and, without thinking, pulling her behind him toward one of the alleys. It was blocked. "You lied to me!" he seethed to Layth.

The man's eyes widened and he shook his head. "I thought your uncle had her. Apparently, she escaped." He pointed to another man. "You, take care of the girl and the man. We will take Shammina with us."

"No! That's against the bargain," Rabil shouted. "You have the gold, leave her alone!" He snatched his dagger from the ground and moved to throw it. In an instant, the air was alive with whizzing blades. Shammina knew the target of each weapon. And he also knew that Assyrian soldiers were trained to use their weapons with unrivaled accuracy. Rabil didn't stand a chance. Fortunately for him, neither did he suffer. Rabil gasped once, his eyes wide, and then he fell to the ground, unmoving.

Shammina gathered his sister close to him. "If you hurt her, I won't join you."

"We don't need you to agree to join us," the man sneered. "In fact, we don't truly need you at all. Kill them both. The boy's nothing but trouble."

The men closed in, but a voice in Aramaic cut through the air, startling them all. "Wait!"

"It's the prophet!" one soldier shouted. "He's come to announce destruction on us all."

Layth laughed contemptuously. "Superstition is not an issue I expected to run into. We have the ear of Assur and his approval. We need fear no other god." But he spoke as if to himself, and none seemed to hear him.

A man, white as a ghost, entered their midst. "He's right. I have a message of destruction for you all. For Yahweh, the God of Israel, did not forgive your city to have you continue in your violence. And I have faith that, if I pray to Him, He will curse you all with leprosy."

The leader took a step back. His other men vanished. With less men to contend with, Shammina seized his chance. He grabbed the leader and lifted the small man off the ground. The man delivered him a crushing blow, but Shammina was ready, and with the advantage of height, bashed the leader in the face. The man gargled once, then went limp, unconscious. Shammina walked over to the well and pushed the man down inside, adding an additional shove to send him down toward the bottom. "That should give us time to escape." He took his sister's hand, and soon all three of them were away from the dark alleys.

"Why did you save us?" his sister asked the man.

Shammina glanced at her in surprise. The tone was one of familiarity. "Do you know him?"

"Yes, he shoved me into the well."

Shammina drew his dagger.

"No! Wait, Shammina. It's fine. He saved us."

"You have some explaining to do," he said to the white man. Shammina did not put his blade away. He locked eyes with his rescuer.

"I believe I do," the prophet said. They found an empty booth and the prophet told them quickly about who he was and his past. When he was finished, they were silent a moment. The prophet asked about Shammina's reasons for being in such a situation, and he explained his time with Rabil and his father's plan.

His sister watched him, her eyes wide. "Shammina?"

"Yes?"

"I'm your sister?"

Shammina jerked slightly. Surely, she hadn't put that as a question. "Marbita..."

"She can't remember anything," the prophet told him. "My guess is she is still in shock from receiving that wound on her neck."

"That makes sense." Shammina recounted his and Rabil's fight with his father and uncle and his sister's involvement. "Your name is Marbita," he told his sister when he was finished. The look of slow recognition that crossed her face pained him. "I am your brother Shammina. Do you remember helping me while I trained with Rabil?"

She thought a moment, then nodded. "Mother found you in the closet because you kept sneezing." She laughed slightly, then stopped. "Did you kill her?"

"Mother? No. I checked the house. It was empty. She's gone."

"Did Uncle Ador..."

"No. I went straight there. I'm certain I got there first."

"So she's alright?"

"I...I don't know, Marbita."

"Oh." She glanced at the area where they had just come from. "You were the light of General Rabil's world, Shammina. You completely changed him. He went from a madman to a noble soldier overnight."

"Speaking of madmen," Shammina said, quickly as if he didn't wish to dwell on his mentor's death, "We still have the problem of Uncle Ador." He took his sister's hand. His tone turned urgent. "You have to leave. Perhaps with the prophet. He isn't so bad."

"Leave? Now? But I just got my memory back. You and I could—"

"No, Marbita, it isn't safe here in Nineveh anymore."

"Then you're coming too?"

"No."

"Why not?"

"Because I want to continue to fight."

"Judah has an army," the prophet interrupted. "If fighting is what you really want to do. You could become Judean."

Shammina snorted. "That is almost the same as you becoming a prophet of Assur. Changing armies is changing sides."

"I do not wish to see you among the ranks if Assyria ever invades Judah or Israel."

Shammina lowered his head. "I cannot assure you that you will not see me."

"Very well."

"Hold on a moment," Marbita interrupted. "I don't want to leave you, Shammina. You are the only family I have left that isn't crazy." He laughed and kissed her cheek.

"I will miss your spirit, sister." He turned to leave the booth.

"Wait! Please don't go, Shammina."

"I'm just going to get Rabil's body for proper burial. It isn't safe for you to come. Wait here with the prophet." He trotted down the alley toward the clearing.

Marbita sighed. He would be back soon enough. The prophet spent the time apologizing, to her gratification. After a while, he began to repeat himself though, and she told him once again that it was fine and that she understood the anger he had felt.

A thought struck her, and she asked, "Was that true? What you said to the men about leprosy?"

The prophet chuckled. "I have no doubt that Yahweh is capable of anything. But that announcement was a little drastic."

She smiled, closing the topic with a nod. Returning to their conversation about anger, she began to tell him about her father, when suddenly, she realized how much time had passed. "My brother isn't back yet."

"No. And he won't be coming."

"Why not?" She glanced around, searching for the face she had grown to love so much.

"It completely slipped by you, didn't it?"

"What?"

"He didn't go to get Rabil's body, Marbita. He told you that so you wouldn't follow him. He left you, because he knew you would not leave without him. And now you have to leave."

"I don't have to go anywhere."

"Think about it. He knows you are a target since you escaped your uncle's men. He did what he did because he wants you to leave. He risked a lot going back there. He could have gone elsewhere, but he did not. He chose those back alleys so you would neither find him nor follow him."

"I can go where I like."

"And get killed?"

"That doesn't matter."

"Then what of your brother's sacrifice? What of Rabil's sacrifice? Come with me, Marbita. Come home with me, and I promise to treat you as a daughter. I have a wonderful family, an adopted son, a brother who has a loquacious wife and son, a loving father, and a good friend who is very kind and whose father is also a wonderful mentor."

Marbita felt hot tears running down her cheeks as she watched the darkening alley that her brother had gone down. "But why did he go?"

"Because he loves you, Marbita." The prophet gently took her hand and led her out of the booth. "He entrusted you to me when he suggested you leave Nineveh with me. I don't intend to betray that trust." Marbita glanced up at Jonah, truly seeing him for the first time. He meant to take her away from her home and everything she knew. But he was also taking her away from certain death and she attempted to find solace in the thought. She wiped her eyes and looked back over her shoulder at the alley one last time. In her mind, she pictured Shammina, standing there and waving goodbye to her. That image she would carry with her for the rest of her life.

Chapter Eighteen

As much as Jonah desired to return home to Tekoa first, he knew his first action had to be going to Samaria. Yahweh wanted him to prophesy to King Jeroboam, though he didn't even know what he was to say yet. Marbita spoke very little on the journey. He could tell she thought about her brother often, and her dark eyes were full of sorrow. Jonah remembered fearing losing Caleb and did not find it too difficult to place himself in her position. So, he allowed her to keep her silence and remain remote, knowing that a spirit as lively as hers would shine through in time.

As expected, it had been easy to request food, water, and money for their journey from the Ninevites, though Marbita had had to remain hidden for both her safety and his own. Jonah had been unable to satisfy his desire to avoid travel, seeing as he sat atop a great muscular stallion, black as the night, ready to make the journey back to his home, Israel. The stallion was a predictable choice by the Ninevites who had tried to honor him as much as possible on his departure. He had easily obtained a second packhorse that Marbita would use. He was no longer surprised when people gaped at his pale skin and bald head, and he had even used it to his advantage from time to time. Many people were more than willing to help a traveler who had been swallowed by a whale, if they indeed believed the story.

The great black stallion snorted, and Jonah glanced up, coming to full awareness of his surroundings. The wind whipped around his face and stung his skin.

Marbita too held tightly to her mount with one hand and shielded her face with the other. "Is this wind common?" she asked.

"No. We should stop so the horses don't spook." He pulled on the reins and she did likewise.

"Look!" Marbita pointed to a small, squat, square structure over to their right.

"Good eye." He urged the stallion into a canter and they covered the distance quickly. Jonah dismounted, groaning as sore and weary muscles were used and stretched. Handing the stallion's reins to Marbita, he left them and knocked on the door. There was no answer.

"No one's about. Do you think they will mind a couple of travelers staying the night while they are gone?" Jonah asked.

"I don't exactly care what they think as long as they are gone."

He laughed and returned to take his horse. Marbita dismounted and they led their mounts to the little makeshift barn in the back.

"Do you think it will hold?" Marbita glanced warily at the tattered wood.

"The walls have some stone, likely whatever the builder could find. It will do." Jonah entered and verified that the stalls were suitable for the horses, and soon their mounts were bedded down and watered. Jonah and Marbita returned to the house and made themselves at home, though they tried not to take too much food or move anything around. In the end, it proved a pleasant experience. Jonah distracted Marbita from thoughts of her brother by telling her stories of his times in Tekoa. He described long days of work, the antics of Jonathan and Anan, the days when Haggith was in rare form, and anything he could think of that could cheer her. They held a mostly one-sided conversation long into the night, holding worry at bay as the winds howled around the house.

"How close are we to Samaria?" she asked as they rolled out two sleeping mats.

"Another week I'd say."

She sighed and collapsed onto her mat in a dramatic show of weariness. "It seems to me that if Yahweh intends to send you all over the world, the least He could do is transport you Himself." They laughed and the wind laughed with them.

"Some journeys are meant to be traveled," Jonah replied. And he knew it was true. His life had been a journey up until then. If it hadn't been for his background with the Assyrians, the outcome of his life would have been incredibly different. If Benjamin had never been injured, Jonah would not have adopted him. And if he had never fled from Yahweh, he would not have the testimony of God calling him back. If he had never prophesied to the Assyrians, Marbita would have likely died and perhaps her brother with her. He smiled to himself. Every life fit together like a puzzle, if you looked at it from the right angle.

Marbita lay still, her breathing was even and he knew that she slept. He made his way to her side and knelt by her mat. She lay on her back, one arm slightly away from her body, her fingers were curled in the gentle way that all fingers are in rest. Jonah thought of her story. Of her wicked father and uncle and of her courage in helping Shammina, for she had told him everything, though in pieces, on their journey. Jonah recalled his dream and the conversation he had held with her, and he remembered her saying that there could be fighters as well as victims and that she herself was not a fighter. A gentle smile touched his lips and he reached out and touched her hand with the touch of a father.

"You are wrong, Marbita." He whispered, in a voice he could not recall using before. He spoke his next words without bitterness or anger, but only kindness. "You *are* a fighter."

By the time a week had passed, they were both thoroughly exhausted and bone weary. Jonah's great stallion seemed to care little about how much farther he had to go, but Marbita's horse showed the wear of weeks of traveling. Fortunately, they had encountered very few problems since the mild sandstorm and had high hopes for an uneventful entrance into the city.

Jonah took his time finding a good stable for their mounts. It needed to be close to the city, just in case. After seeing their horses settled in, Jonah and Marbita approached the city.

The sentry at the gate glared at them from beneath oversized eyebrows. "Who is requesting entrance? What is your business?"

"My name is Jonah ben Amittai and this is my daughter, Marbita."

The sentry looked from one to the other, his eyes scrutinizing. "Ya don't look much alike."

"Ya needn't pry so," Jonah grumbled.

The sentry chose to ignore his comment. "Is this bleached man here your father?" he asked Marbita. She nodded and smiled. She had already assured Jonah that she would be more than happy to be considered his daughter. The sentry leaned back on his heels, apparently satisfied. "Right then, what is your business here?"

"I am a prophet of Yahweh. I have come to prophesy to King Jeroboam."

The man threw back his head and laughed. "King Jeroboam could care less about Yahweh. No king of Israel has even bothered with that God since Jehu, and even Jehu was not completely devout. What makes you think King Jeroboam wants to hear you?"

"Nothing."

"Then you are wiser than I thought. Come in." The sentry opened the gate with a smirk. "And I expect I shall soon see you and your daughter rushing out of the city within a day's time, perhaps with half the palace guard on your heels."

Despite the sentry's prediction, Jonah felt confident as he strode up to the palace. Yahweh would provide a way for him to enter and speak his message. All he had to do was open his mouth.

When they reached the entrance, Marbita peered around in bewilderment. "Where are the guards?"

"There aren't any." Jonah should have been surprised, but a strange peace had settled over him—one he was certain was not his own. They walked unchallenged down the palace corridor and managed to meander their way to the throne room.

"Stay here in the shadows," Jonah told Marbita. Should anything go wrong, and a million things could, he did not want her endangered. He pressed his ear to the door. There was no sound coming from inside that he could hear. He pushed it open, and as soon as he entered, he felt the power of God surging through him. King Jeroboam lounged on his throne, swirling wine round and round in a silver chalice with one hand and signing documents with the other. He stopped both actions upon seeing Jonah.

"What is this creature doing here?" he bellowed. Soldiers poured out from every corner of the room. Jonah was prodded with spear points down onto his knees. "Who are you? What are you?"

"My name is Jonah ben Amittai. I am a prophet of Yahweh, the God of Israel."

"Yahweh?" Jeroboam glanced over at his chief advisor and laughed. "Is that old menace still being talked about?"

Jonah felt his blood heating at the blatant disrespect. "I bring a message from the God of Israel who speaks through me, His servant."

Jeroboam sighed and waved his hand lazily to dismiss the guards. "Let's hear what the God of Israel has to say then."

Jonah stood, his eyes met the king's with sharp intensity. "*You will be the one who restores the boundaries of Israel from Lebo Hamath to the Dead Sea, in accordance with the word of the Lord, the God of Israel, spoken through His servant Jonah son of Amittai, the prophet from Gath Hepher. The Lord has seen how bitterly everyone in Israel, whether slave or free, is suffering; there is no one to help them. And since the Lord has not said He will blot out the name of Israel from under heaven, He will save them by the hand of Jeroboam son of Jehoash.*" The power, there one moment and gone the next, left Jonah feeling weary and empty. He stood, shaking a little on unsteady legs in the silence that followed.

Jeroboam drained his wine in one long swallow and snapped his fingers. His cupbearer rushed forward to refill it as the king turned back to Jonah. "You know, that message is considerably optimistic compared to the previous one I received from a prophet of Yahweh."

"Previous?"

"Yes, it was a man named...Amos. He told me that Yahweh would rise up against my house with the sword."

"And this does not concern you?"

"No, Amos is a conspirator. I cannot say what it is he is trying to do, though I suspect he wants me dumped off my throne. How strange it is that you bring prophesies of a clear future full of success and victory."

"I believe that you have misunderstood."

"Continue."

"Yahweh has declared that Israel is suffering afflictions which are very bitter. Surely that is not a thing to be celebrated."

Jeroboam leaned back against his throne. "Do you have anything else to say, Jonah ben Amittai?"

"I do not."

"Then kindly leave my country and don't ever return. I don't trust you prophets, and the next one that dares to preach doom or otherwise to me will sorely regret it." Jeroboam leaned forward, his mouth tipping in a mocking frown. "Take your little words from your worthless God and go babble to a king that will close your mouth forever."

Jonah bit his lip until he tasted blood. He fought the urge to charge Jeroboam, a proud mocking creature on the beautiful throne of Jonah's birth country. He took a step closer, and then another. His gaze boring into the king's until at last Jeroboam shifted uncomfortably. Lifting his hand, Jonah pointed his index finger and clenched his fist, saying each word through teeth so tightly clenched that they throbbed in his jaw. "Understand this; in a matter of years, the very words I spoke to you as a testament to both your victories and God's fulfilled prophesy will be recorded for all to see. It will be a great victory as you have said, but not a victory for you. It will be God's victory, and a victory for His people living in Israel. And you as well must understand that even a king sitting high upon a throne with an army in his palm and a country to call his own has nowhere to run from the God of Israel." Jonah turned and left the throne room, slamming the door on a stunned group of guards and an outraged king.

Marbita jumped back from the throne room door where she had been listening as Jonah burst through.

"I think that went well." She smiled as he glared at her and pulled her down the hall.

"I will agree with you if we make it out of Israel."

"Do you really think you upset him that much?"

"Kings are unpredictable creatures, Marbita."

The guards at the palace exit had returned. One held up a hand to halt him, but Jonah paid no attention. He and Marbita continued past the guards and toward the gate.

"Stop, in the name of the king!" The guards drew their swords and sprinted after the pair.

"Why exactly didn't we stop, Jonah?" Marbita asked as they broke into a run.

"I didn't feel like it."

"Ah."

"And because Jeroboam will likely have us executed as soon as he convinces himself that I'm a conspirator, as he likely will."

They rushed across the market square, their pursuers hot on their heels.

"This way." He pulled her down an alley that branched off from the main street. They navigated through a series of twists and turns until they were certain they had lost the soldiers.

"Now that's all fine and dandy, Jonah, but now that the palace guard and probably all of the sentries are watching for us, how do we get out?" He didn't respond. The wall was a few blocks away, and they headed toward it. The homes were mere shacks, though still not bad compared to Nineveh's.

"Find some rope," he said.

They searched the homes, one after the other until they found a man that mended fishing nets. He was there, busy at work when they entered. They bought some rope from him and returned to the wall. After locating the stairs, they sat on the bottom step and watched the guards march past. Dusk fell as they sat and waited.

Then, just as the sun touched the horizon, there was a change of shift. Jonah and Marbita wasted no time mounting the stairs. They reached the top and tied the rope off to a niche in the stone meant for viewing an attack below without being seen. Jonah tied a loop in the other end and slipped it over Marbita. She carefully climbed over the edge, all too aware of the drop beneath her. Jonah let out the line, and before long, she was close enough to the ground to jump. The line ran out and she dangled a moment. By grabbing hold of the line above her, she hoisted herself up until she could slip out of the rope. Then she dropped the remaining eight feet. She allowed herself to roll from her feet to her knees and summersault to lessen the impact.

Above her, she could hear shouting. The rope was quickly hauled up and disappeared from sight. A moment later, Jonah could be seen at the top of the wall. Having no one to lower him, he had to work his way down the rope, allowing the slack to dangle beneath him. If he were to slip, he would die from the impact of hitting the end of the rope. Marbita held her breath as she saw soldiers running to and fro on the wall top.

Hugging close to the stones, she prayed that they would not see the small piece of rope attached to their wall. Jonah was halfway down when he glanced up in alarm. Marbita followed his gaze to where a hand reached down and took hold of the rope. Fortunately, Jonah had all the slack still below him, but the other end was beginning to disappear over the top of the wall. He hurried down until the line was taught, but in the end, he had mere seconds to drop the remaining dozen or so feet when he ran out of rope. Marbita forced herself to inhale and then exhale as he slipped from the rope and dropped. The fall wasn't all that far, but it was far enough. He came down hard in a blur of white and brown. When she rushed to his side, he tried to get up onto his hands and knees. One arm would not hold his weight.

"It's broken," he grunted, trying to stand.

"Your legs?"

"Are fine." They started off at a run, trying to put as much distance between themselves and the guards as possible.

"Which direction is the stable?"

"That way, only about a half mile." Jonah pointed in the direction, and they turned their course respectively. As the squat outline of the stable came into view, they were both sucking wind, and Marbita turned for just a moment to see the gate opening.

"They're coming." They hurried their pace, feet stumbling over the dry rocky ground. The thundering of hooves made Marbita's heart sink with dread. How could they possibly outrun horses? She glanced over to see Jonah's eyes close for a moment, then they opened. She felt power in her legs, and her breathing eased. They raced on faster than before and reached the barn well ahead of the soldiers.

"What...what happened?" she asked as they prepared to leave.

"I prayed." He shrugged a shoulder. "It must be Yahweh's will that we escape." In a moment, they were at the door to the barn, horses' reins in hand. The men were close enough to see the foam dripping from their horses' hides and out of their mouths. Locating a stump of wood, Marbita clambered onto her horse and watched Jonah struggling to do the same. His broken arm lay limp, as if it were a chain meant to hold him down.

"Hurry," Marbita hissed. With a groan, Jonah hoisted himself onto his horse and balanced himself, smiling. But his jaw was clenched tightly with pain. They urged their mounts into a canter and took off south, heading for the border.

* * *

Anan practically dropped his club at the sound of the shofar that announced that their work was done. Even though summer was past and fall was setting in, he was positively drenched with sweat. He glared up at the olive tree with distaste. The limbs were practically drooping with fruit. Why couldn't they just fall off themselves? He brushed a scattering of leaves off his tunic and sighed, a job was a job, and he should be content as long as he was paid. He longed to be off to some foreign country, buying and selling goods. It always brought a smile to his face when he thought of all the training he had undergone before being able to bargain and trade. His thoughts drifted to Anapa the Egyptian merchant. He should pray for him, and he did. In fact, he had done more praying over the last few days than he had in years. Abba needed it, so did Amittai, Caleb, and Benjamin, the list went on and on.

Haggith was busy working when he returned home, sweeping floors, sorting grain, and feeding the animals. "You still here then, Master Anan?"

"Yes Haggith."

"Still resisting the urge to be off then?"

"I am needed here."

Her eyes flickered down a moment, then met his. "It is appreciated, Master." She quickly returned to her sweeping as he settled down for the evening.

"Have you seen Benjamin?"

"Not since the morning meal, sir."

"Well I suppose the boy will have to be back for food."

"Likely so. How did the olive gathering go?"

"Fine, I suppose. I felt quite foolish beating a tree with a club. But I suppose it's as good as any method of getting the olives to come off." He opened the door and stared out at the yard a moment. "Even though Benjamin is in mourning for his father, he will have to work again soon, hard as it may be." He stepped out into the still evening air. "If I am not back by the evening meal, eat without me."

Haggith turned, frowning slightly. "Of course, Master Anan."

Benjamin was nowhere in a good mile radius of the house, and Anan worried that he might have wandered too far and gotten lost. The endless stretches of fields and scattered houses looked the same, especially to one who had not grown up in the area. He decided to check with Zedekiah, but when he reached the house, he found that there was no one on the premises. Pushing hard at rising panic, he worked to clear his mind. Benjamin was a grown man. He was capable of finding his way home himself. But in his current condition, Anan realized that he was more than capable of becoming lost as well. He lowered himself to his knees and took a deep calming breath.

"Lord, help me." He spoke the words aloud, and they almost covered up the soft footsteps that approached from behind. He turned to see Amos watching him, concern in his eyes. Anan stood and embraced the prophet wordlessly. It was very generous for Amos to donate his time to help the family recover from their loss.

"He is grieving, Anan. Those that grieve should be given privacy, but not be left on their own."

"But for so long?"

"I realize that it isn't necessary for him to be officially mourning, Anan, and I don't think he is. He's just broken."

"I know; I have searched our house, and Zedekiah's." Anan stopped, clearing the emotion from his throat. "I checked the surrounding area too. It is like he has evaporated into thin air."

"I will help you search for him."

"Thank you." They fell into step, walking toward the setting sun.

"Rather than just searching, perhaps we should think about where he might go."

"He is walking the paths of his past, Amos. How are we to know where he is?"

"What do you know of his past?"

"I know that he lost two sisters and four brothers."

"Six siblings? How?"

"Fever and on a long journey."

"That's terrible."

"I know. When he told me about it, he was very vague. Didn't mention any details."

"Perhaps he is not processing his grief properly."

"If you know the proper way, all of the Levant should know your name." They shared a brief smile.

"That is a valid point."

"Nonetheless, I agree. But back to where he might have gone. How does this discussion help?"

"Well, they are likely traveling, right?"

"Yes."

"And he starts his journeys from a select location." Anan nodded, wondering where the conversation was headed. "So, I am guessing he would likely start from a city."

"A city?"

"A resting place where he and his brothers and sisters would stop for the night."

"And?"

"And where is the nearest city?" Anan's eyes widened. They broke into a run, heading for Tekoa. Ten minutes later, they were in sight of the walls.

"Would he be in the city?"

"It depends if he has left yet or not."

They questioned the guard at the gate. Yes, they had seen a young man with blond hair enter the city, and no, he had not left.

* * *

Benjamin held the bread toward his sister, begging her to take a bite. "It isn't your fault, Abigail, it isn't."

"But none of them made it, Benjamin. You were right; the trip was too far."

Benjamin sighed and sagged against the wall, staring at his sister a moment, seeing for the first time how much older she appeared. She was no longer his older sister, but a woman. He had seen enough women in his lifetime to know that she was stunning. His mother had also been so with blond hair the color of ripe grain and amber eyes that held the attention and fascination of others. Would some man, like Abba, fall in love with Abigail some day and marry her? Would someone take his beloved sister from him? Still, he knew that she would need to find happiness someday, and perhaps he would have to lose her in order for that to happen. Beyond her, a lamp flickered, casting shadows over the home's dull interior. The kind widow that had taken them under her wing was out in the market and was not there to assist him. Abigail had to eat something; she had to try.

"Think of Abba...he would want you to eat it."

"Abba is dead."

"Please, Abigail."

"No."

Benjamin was tempted to grab her shoulders and shake her, to jolt her out of the daze she had fallen into. "We did all we could, Abigail. You can't blame yourself."

"But I do." She stood and moved about the room, touching the widow's sparse possessions as if they could take her back in time. When she had walked the home's circumference, she sat down again, pulled her knees up and wrapped her arms around her legs.

Benjamin shook his head in frustration. He was running out of ideas, ways to cajole her, convince her. He could think of only one remaining maneuver. If this one did not work, then nothing would. "Abigail, listen to me." She met his gaze, her amber eyes filled with tears. "If you don't eat, then I won't either."

"But you have to eat, Benjamin."

"And so do you." He held his breath, watching as more tears welled up in her eyes. Her lips quivered and her head drooped in defeat. Very slowly, she took the bread and bit into it. He cautiously let himself relax. Everything would be alright; they would pull through. He heard the door swing open, then close. The widow was home again.

"Has she eaten yet, child?"

"Yes ma'am, a little bit."

The widow smiled, her crooked teeth appearing in the midst of a once beautiful face. "That's good, that's good." She knew very little about them, but it was enough for her to understand. She too had lost loved ones. Benjamin rose and helped her put things away—a sack of flour, a few vegetables, and some dried fish. The shelves, built into the crumbling stone walls, appeared bare even after the food had been put away. "You know, child, things have gotten worse since my mother's mother was a young girl."

Benjamin glanced at her curiously. "What do you mean, ma'am?"

"Way back when Jehu was king, we were a prosperous nation. Yahweh blessed Jehu with the promise that his sons down to the fourth generation would sit on the throne of Israel. But he did not determine to walk with the Lord, and so he strayed from Yahweh. So, the Lord began to cut off portions of Israel. We began to see more warfare, and the land was taken from us. No king since Jehu has walked in the ways of the Lord. And so, Yahweh has pronounced judgment upon us. He has sent prophets to declare destruction and exile." She eased herself down onto a cushion and folded her hands in her lap. "It is a sad thing, child, that the sins of our king have become the sins of our people. And Yahweh knows these sins will destroy us. So, because of His great love, He must punish His children to save them from themselves. He has not stopped us from following the evil desires of our hearts, and so we are facing the results of our sins. The people, your people and my people, have faced much loss in the past years. And we will continue to until we see the connection."

"The connection?"

"Between following Yahweh and prosperity, child. He has promised that they will be paired together. If we follow Him faithfully, He will bless us."

"Then how come some of the most devout followers of Yahweh are not prosperous?"

"When bad things happen, child, humans curse God and say He must not be in control if we are suffering. But everyone must have their trials in order to come out on the other side stronger."

"So, we face hard times to build our character?"

"And our faith."

Benjamin sat on the cushion facing her. "But how can I understand what my losses and trails are meant to teach me?"

"Ask Yahweh." She patted his shoulder and stood.

Benjamin wiped the grime from his eyes and opened them. He still sat on the same cushion of the night before. He remembered pouring his heart out to Yahweh; had it made a difference? The widow was away, and he saw the jug was absent from beside the door. She would be waiting in line to draw water. And where was Abigail? Perhaps she had gone with the widow. Benjamin shook his head and blinked. Abigail hadn't left the house since they had arrived a week earlier. There was nothing to suggest she would leave now.

"Abigail?" His voice rang through the house. There was no reply. Standing, he found himself in momentary blackness as the blood rushed from his head. He stumbled out the front door and into the street full of people. Jerusalem was alive and laughter rang off her walls. Benjamin realized that it was spring, the time of grain harvest and festivity. How was he to ever find his sister in such a crowd?

Pray.

He turned to see who had spoken.

Pray.

The word came again. Benjamin glanced around. The little voice inside nudged his mind.

Pray, Benjamin.

He hurried back into the house. Kneeling on the cushion, he bowed his head.

"Yahweh, help me to find her. She needs to comprehend Your love, Lord. She needs to understand."

The wall.

Benjamin jumped at the voice. When he opened his eyes, there was no one around. What did the wall have to do with anything? A thought, deep in the recesses of his mind came forward. The idea made him feel like a hole had been cut through his heart. It couldn't be. He sprinted out the door and raced toward the nearest set of steps leading up to the wall, ignoring the booths full of delights meant to catch his eye and not seeing endless waves of people. Animals ran squealing or squawking past, adding an unpleasant odor to the air, but he paid no heed. The sun, directly in his eyes, had no effect on his fogged mind. He didn't even bother to apologize to those he bumped into. Time was too precious.

He took the steps two at a time, his breath coming faster as he neared the top. Stopping where the steps opened onto the wall, he glanced left and right. The only people in immediate sight were soldiers. Had he imagined the voice? He raced along the wall top, hardly noticing the view. The guards occupied each wall, but only sporadically. There were plenty of gaps for a person to.... He spotted her, partially hidden by a tall watchtower. Her red headscarf was *unmistakable even from this distance. His heart hammered into his ribs as he ran.*

"Easy boy, you'll give yourself a heart attack running like that," one of the guards called to him.

He paid no attention. His eyes were locked on the spot of red. When he drew close, he forced himself to slow down. His heart sank in his chest. Abigail sat on the parapet, her legs dangling over the edge. She turned her head and spotted him. Her eyes widened, then she relaxed when she recognized him.

"Come back with me to the widow's house, Abigail." Benjamin framed the words carefully as if he were speaking to a small child. He extended a hand toward her as he took a careful step forward. "Abigail, you are all I have left in this world. What happened on the road isn't your fault. I need you. Everyone else is gone, come back with me."

She smiled very slowly. Her amber eyes alight with emotion. "I love you, Benjamin." He lunged forward, but he was not quick enough. He slammed into the parapet in the place where she had been just a moment before. He wanted to scream when he glimpsed the tiny speck of red far below. But no words came out. He wanted to run, he wanted to curse and yell, but his body would not obey. Very slowly he turned, forcing himself to look away.

He felt as if he were walking through water as he descended the stairs. He didn't care that he was traveling against the flow of the crowd as he moved down the street toward the widow's home. The smell of baking bread registered in the back of his mind as he opened the door.

"Good morning to you, child," she called as he stepped into the room. The widow glanced at him. "Is she not with you then?" When he didn't reply, she stopped her work and looked into his eyes. "What is it?"

He opened his mouth, then closed it again. A look of consternation crossed the widow's features and she beckoned for him to sit down. "What happened, Benjamin?"

"She..."

"She what, Benjamin?" The widow sat beside him, her gray eyes flickering from his face to the dim room around them.

"She jumped."

"Jumped?" The woman stared at him.

"Off. She jumped off..."

The widow's eyes widened with comprehension. "Dear child!" She wiped at the tears that slipped down Benjamin's cheeks.

"I must leave," Benjamin said suddenly.

"Leave?"

"I will not have her name tainted."

"But Benjamin..."

"If I go elsewhere, I can say she died of a fever. Her name will be stained if I stay here."

"If you leave, people might think you did it."

"That is another reason to leave. There will be no one to question if I am gone. No one to suspect. I am the only one anyone saw on that wall."

"Benjamin, that is unnecessary. You've had a hard year; I can see it in your eyes. Think it over; take some time."

"I cannot stay within these walls either," he declared as if she had never spoken. "These walls are meant to protect, to save lives." He stood. "I cannot thank you enough for your hospitality."

The widow placed a hand on his head. "Benjamin, I can see that you are determined to go. May God bless you."

He nodded mutely. The widow turned and lifted a bag from her meager belongings. Inside she put a goatskin of water and some food. Then she lifted a small item that glinted when light struck it. Handing Benjamin the bag, she handed him the object as well.

"Strap this on."

"What is it?"

She did not answer at first, so he took it and examined the keen blade. "That was my husband's. He wore it for protection."

"I could not take a thing that you hold so dear."

"Of course you can." She showed him how to strap it on and then smiled down at him. "May the peace of God go with you, Benjamin."

"And with you." He turned and walked slowly out the door and then down the street toward the gate that led out of the city. Every step brought him closer to an uncertain future, and he never looked back.

Benjamin leaned on the wall that stood tall over the fields below him. Tears streamed down his face as he examined the widow's dagger. His fingers trailed over the leather encased hilt and down toward the glinting tip. It's shining metal reflected the soft blue sky above. It had been carefully cleaned after the incident, and he still wore it each day, not for protection as much as to remember her by.

"Benjamin!" He turned to see Anan jogging toward him. "Benjamin, we were so worried."

"I'm sorry."

Amos appeared behind Anan.

"I apologize, to both of you that I caused you anxiety."

"Well, we found you now, and I've worked up an appetite." Anan led the way down off the wall and out of the city. Amos watched Benjamin as they walked, an unspoken question in his quiet golden eyes.

"I know you told me to stop visiting the past."

Anan turned. "Yes, I did."

"And I will." They all stopped and Anan and Amos stared at Benjamin in surprise. "My past has come to a close," he explained. "It has met the present."

"May I ask why?" Amos asked.

"Why, what?"

"Why you journeyed to the past."

"I needed to remember and to understand."

"And do you understand?"

"Yes."

"And what do you now understand?"

"That my trials teach me and that I can and have come out on the other side a stronger person."

"And how did you discover that?"

"I prayed."

By the time they reached the house, Benjamin had told them both the entire story of his past and of the journey he had just taken.

"Each time I would close a scene of my past, I would pray and ask Yahweh to show me the meaning behind my trials."

"And what did He reveal?"

"Nothing at first. But then, just today I prayed that He would give me understanding regarding all of my past. He showed me that I was broken and that I could help to heal others in their own pain. He wants to turn my trials into something beautiful, and He told me it would be soon. I learned that I never have to be afraid of anything."

"Never? What do you mean?" Amos asked, surprised.

"I mean that there is nothing out of God's control. And that anything that happens has a purpose. So, I never have to fear the darkest moments of my life, because I know there is light on the other side. If I had not left Jerusalem to escape the memories of Abigail, I would not find myself here. And this is where God wants me. He used my trails to bring me here, to help the broken."

"Well, there are plenty of people to be helped," Anan broke in. He swung the door of the house open wide and nearly fainted as he stepped over the threshold upon seeing the man within.

"Who is this man?" Benjamin demanded as soon as he saw the person standing in the house. There was hardly a single strand of hair on his body, and his skin looked like old parchment. Behind him stood a plain girl with black hair and the boldest eyes any of them had seen. She looked startlingly Assyrian.

"Benjamin." The man spoke the word and Benjamin gasped. "Abba?"

"It's a ghost!" Anan took a step back.

The man smiled. "I am not a ghost, Anan. Just an ordinary man with a rather extraordinary tale to tell."

Epilogue

"More like an unordinary man with an extraordinary tale."
Jonathan murmured, his wide eyes panning over Jonah. "Who is your
friend?"

"This here is Marbita." Jonah beckoned to her and she stepped up
beside him. "She was my traveling companion from Nineveh, and much
more."

Caleb swallowed hard, displaying a weak smile. "Well, don't keep
us waiting, little brother, tell us what happened."

"Oh, no, Master Caleb! Master Jonah appears exhausted, and so
does his traveling companion." Haggith shook her head, clucking with
disapproval. "It will have to wait. I'll make the beds and have the
evening meal ready before you know it." She patted Jonah cautiously on
the arm as she passed him, heading into the kitchen.

Elon, huddled beside Caleb in a nervous flurry of energy, appeared
to find his peace and stopped fidgeting. His round face was pale as he
stared at the newcomers. Suddenly, he blurted, "Uncle Jonah! Before
you go to bed I want to show you your tomb!"

Jonah awoke to find the door cracked and a myriad of eyes
watching him. To his detriment, he was unable to hold back a smirk
and they bustled into the room, the energy and excitement practically
causing the air to vibrate.

"Jonah, I tried so hard to sleep last night, but you kept us waiting all that time," Anan complained.

Amittai agreed. "Son, we nearly went mad after the first hour. Patience does not run in the family as you know."

"And even Amos couldn't sleep," Benjamin added.

"Caleb gave up and paced back and forth," Atarah said. "He kept little Elon up."

"I apologize that everyone had a sleepless night, but I myself slept just fine." Jonah stood and rubbed his eyes. "Though another few weeks of rest could have done me no harm."

"It's going to take a while to become accustomed to your appearance, little brother," Caleb chuckled.

"Jonathan, could you spare some writing materials?" Jonah asked, choosing to ignore the comment. Jonathan's eyes twinkled in reply. "I'm a merchant with numbers to work, Jonah. How am I supposed to spare you some writing materials after returning from the dead?"

Downstairs, Jonah saw to it that the entire assembly was seated, Marbita among them, and Amos prepared to take the highlights down on parchment.

"Yahweh has taught me many lessons," Jonah began. "He has taken me many places, and shown me many things." He sat on the bottom step as he spoke, leaning wearily against the wall. "But before I understood all of this, He took me on a journey, and I will share my journey with you." He took his time and made sure to leave nothing out. He started with his lie about Benjamin's desire for a box of ivory, then on to the ship, the whale, and his journey to Nineveh. He told them about having Marbita thrust upon him and about his argument with Yahweh. All throughout the narrative, the group gave constant feedback as their imaginations took in his story.

Benjamin laughed about the first little lie that Jonah had used. Amos was disgusted by the behavior of the innkeeper in Joppa. Everyone gasped and moaned as Jonah described the terrible storm out at sea, and Amittai had to be placated when he told of being thrown overboard by the sailors, and for his father's benefit, Jonah refrained from being too detailed about residing inside the whale. They waited in apprehension as he described being vomited up by the whale and the eccentric hospitality of On.

Jonah skimmed over his trip to Nineveh, but did his best to describe the city. Explaining to the best of his abilities the size, the grandeur, and the wicked parts, such as the evil bloodthirsty thugs in the streets. Atarah was aghast at his treatment of Marbita, and then she wept when he described saving her and Shammina. Jonah sensed them leaning forward as they listened intently to his description of conversing with God. He told them about his anger, wishing to die, the plant that came up overnight, and how God had transformed him with a single passage of King David's writings. They were all touched by Rabil's sacrifice. And even Jonathan and Anan swiped at their eyes when Jonah described Shammina's departure from his sister. Jonah's voice built with excitement when he told of prophesying to King Jeroboam and their miraculous escape.

When Jonah finished his account, there was a long moment of silence, broken only by the soft scratching of ink on parchment as Amos completed his work. Then he presented Jonah with what he had written down. "You and I are prophets, Jonah," he said. "What we have said must carry through the generations for all time."

Jonah scanned the parchment. His eyes glanced off the words that told of his unwillingness to go to Nineveh and ended with his conversation with God. At the bottom, was a small section regarding his prophecy to Jeroboam. "Thank you, Amos."

The prophet shrugged, displaying his usual humble acceptance. "I will make several copies and keep one to put with my own writings. Yahweh has impressed upon me that your work is complete. You have served Him well. Your tasks to follow will be sharing your testimony that it may impact the lives of others." The older man smiled warmly. "You know, if you were to ask me, I would say you are the best prophet of all time."

Jonah coughed to hide his smile. "I suppose you have forgotten my reluctance to go to Nineveh."

"Yes, but there is something more I do not think you have understood." Jonah could feel the gathering's attention shift to Amos. "A prophet is an intermediary between man and God. They represent the people whom God is communicating with. You are a very accurate representation of Israel."

"How so?"

189

"You were lost and running from God. But in His omnipotence, He knew that your running from Him was hurting you more than anything else. So, He saved you from yourself. Israel is the same. They are lost and running from God, and yet they are ever loved and ever forgiven. That is the miracle of grace, Jonah. It is love and forgiveness. Something that we do not deserve, yet something that He freely gives."

The remainder of the day was spent with more accounts and stories from the others. Marbita, poor girl, was questioned and forced to communicate at great length with a large group of strangers, but she didn't seem to mind. She opened up, at last, since leaving her brother, and told them her entire story. Benjamin too was encouraged to tell of what he had been doing inside of his mind for so many days. Atarah practically drowned herself in tears at hearing of Benjamin's losses, especially regarding Abigail. Long kept secrets were opened, and the sun set as they continued to converse.

That night, each lay down on their mat with a sense of closure and peace. Each of them had lost much, yet each of them had gained a testimony by it. Jonah closed his eyes and listened to Marbita and Benjamin's quiet breathing. Life no longer seemed demure, but full of hope and light. Yahweh's presence filled his heart and settled like a loving cloak over their home. He felt peace resting gently on his soul and let his mind drift, preparing himself to live out the rest of his years with Amos's words in his heart and on his lips. There were so many out there lost and running from God, and yet they were ever loved and ever forgiven—never able to leave the reaches of God's unfathomable grace.

Author's Note

To find the biblical account of Jonah and all that he did, please read the Book of Jonah, chapters 1-4.

Biblical passages that are italicized were quoted directly from the New International Version of the Bible with the exception of times when the author changed the tense from past to present. This accounting of Jonah ben Amittai is fictional, though some of the characters and events can be found in the Biblical account. To learn more about the non-fictional aspects of this book, please view the Books of Jonah, Amos, and 2 Kings.

About the author

Jensina Wilson is thirteen years old and lives with her family in North America. In addition to historical fiction, she enjoys writing poetry and morality tales for the glory of the Lord.

Made in the USA
Lexington, KY
02 November 2019